## VIRAGO
## MODERN CLASSICS
### 536

**Barbara Pym** (1913–1980) was born in Oswestry, Shropshire. She was educated at Huyton College, Liverpool, and St Hilda's College, Oxford, where she gained an Honours Degree in English Language and Literature. During the war she served in the WRNS in Britain and Naples. From 1958–1974 she worked as an editorial secretary at the International African Institute. Her first novel, *Some Tame Gazelle*, was published in 1950, and was followed by *Excellent Women* (1952), *Jane and Prudence* (1953), *Less than Angels* (1955), *A Glass of Blessings* (1958) and *No Fond Return of Love* (1961).

During the sixties and early seventies her writing suffered a partial eclipse and, discouraged, she concentrated on her work for the International African Institute, from which she retired in 1974 to live in Oxfordshire. A renaissance in her fortunes came in 1977, when both Philip Larkin and Lord David Cecil chose her as one of the most underrated novelists of the century. With astonishing speed, she emerged, after sixteen years of obscurity, to almost instant fame and recog            in *Autumn* was published in 1977 and was                                    *The Sweet Dove                                             wes was publi                                            y 1980.

*Also by Barbara Pym*

Some Tame Gazelle
Excellent Women
Less than Angels
A Glass of Blessings
Quartet in Autumn
The Sweet Dove Died
A Few Green Leaves
Crampton Hodnet
An Unsuitable Attachment
An Academic Question
Jane and Prudence

# NO FOND
# RETURN OF LOVE

---

## Barbara Pym

## Introduced by Paul Binding

*To Hazel Holt*

VIRAGO

First published in Great Britain in 1961 by Jonathan Cape Ltd
First published in 2009 by Virago Press

9 11 13 15 17 19 20 18 16 14 12 10 8

A CIP catalogue record for this book
is available from the British Library.

ISBN 978-1-84408-450-0

Typeset in Goudy by M Rules
Printed and bound in Great Britain by
Clays Ltd, St Ives plc

Papers used by Virago are from well-managed forests
and other responsible sources.

MIX
Paper from
responsible sources
FSC® C104740

Virago Press
An imprint of
Little, Brown Book Group
Carmelite House
50 Victoria Embankment
London EC4Y 0DZ

An Hachette UK Company
www.hachette.co.uk

www.virago.co.uk

# INTRODUCTION

*No Fond Return of Love* (1961) was the sixth novel by Barbara
Pym to be published and for many years it was the last.
However, it was the first I read, twelve years after its appearance
on the enthusiastic recommendation of Lord David Cecil.
David had not only been Goldsmiths' Professor of English
Literature at my old Oxford college, he was the father of my
closest university friend. After his retirement I often went to
stay with the Cecils at their house in Dorset, and David, who
delighted in finding books for his guests, urged on me one
evening what was then Barbara Pym's most recent novel.
A critic who valued writers for their intrinsic merits rather
than their standing in current fashion, he said Barbara Pym
was a writer of remarkable insight and artistry. It was a disgrace
that none of her books was in print, and a great pity that no
new novel had come out for so long. He pointed out the novel's
arresting Jane Austen-like opening sentence, observant, amused,
ironic and sympathetic: 'There are various ways of mending a
broken heart, but perhaps going to a learned conference is one
of the more unusual'.

So impressed was I by *No Fond Return of Love* that I went on to Pym's other novels, hunting out copies. I discovered that Cedric Chivers Ltd had issued editions for members of the Library Association, and I acquired these, PVC wrappers over unstylish jackets (*Some Tame Gazelle*, a wry study of two middle-aged sisters in an English village, showed an antelope in the bush, the design department presumably not having read beyond the title-page). I connected Pym with certain other writers whose creative life began in the immediate post-war years, and who had illuminated the fifties as they evolved: Elizabeth Taylor, Angus Wilson in *Anglo-Saxon Attitudes* (1956) and *The Middle Age of Mrs Eliot* (1958), and also Philip Larkin in those two poignant, poetic novels, *Jill* (1946) and *A Girl in Winter* (1947).

At that time I was working for Oxford University Press after two years at a Swedish university, and I delighted in the accuracy with which Barbara Pym delineated the English circles I myself had now joined. I was living in London for the first time, and she struck me, as she still does, as one of our capital's greatest celebrants. Her books convey the diversity of lives the city not merely offers but bestows – its ability to put unexpectedly in your path persons who either mysteriously chime in with your own current preoccupations, or else confound them by their sheer unlikeness. Barbara Pym may specialise in quiet, obscure lives, but she is a highly sophisticated writer, urban and urbane. For all the keen descriptions of church bazaars and tea shops, of the ways of her 'excellent women', I found, as I read and reread her work, a happy congruity between her writing and the seventies feminism and gay liberation movements to which I was committed.

Within a seemingly secure world, the Pym protagonist

initially appears secure enough, bounded, and to some extent defined, by central institutions of English life: the Anglican Church, university departments, libraries and learned organisations. Though reflective by temperament she seems largely to share this world's underpinning assumptions, but as the novel develops she comes up against some stubborn individuality – in her own character or in persons to whom she is, often involuntarily, drawn – that defies the orthodoxy around her, religious, political or social. She may not herself understand the implications of what is happening to her, but the reader does. Without exception, the heroine emerges from this challenge the stronger. Pym, broadly speaking, takes her central characters and the greater number of her dramatis personae from the comfortable middle class, but the period being the 1950s, which continued the social loosening-up brought about by the Second World War, they feel free to range far more widely in their associates, and sample more milieus, than would have been possible for their pre-war counterparts.

Curiosity about other lives is a feature of all Pym protagonists, and *No Fond Return of Love* provides a splendid introduction to her work, for Dulcie Mainwaring has this quality par excellence. Pym sees it as essential to any good life. To serve it requires imaginative courage, even daring, but it will prove the best possible remedy for inevitable disappointments and sorrows, and the most effective weapon against that corrosive self-absorption to which the gentle and introverted (like Dulcie) are especially prone. From this conviction comes the unmistakable Pym tone: a controlled but highly personal blend of the interested (the engaged, the sympathetic) and the disinterested (the objective, the analytical). Wilmet Forsyth in *A Glass of Blessings*, looking back over a day with a man with whom she is half in love, thinks of it as 'a confusion of pleasure, sadness, uneasiness and expectation'. The phrase is wonderfully apt for any of the novels Barbara Pym produced between 1950 and 1961, except, of course, for the word 'confusion'. Each book is distinguished by the authorial imposition of order on a tangled variety of emotional responses to existence.

Why then had year after year gone by since *No Fond Return of Love* – so characteristic, so assured in its art, and so satisfying an entity – with no addition to the Pym oeuvre? And this from a writer who up to then had been reliable in her output (one novel every two years). Her books had mostly been favourably reviewed, her sales respectable if unspectacular. Had she suffered a severe writer's block or given up writing for some other more mysterious reason? Who indeed was she?

It was inevitable that I should mention my pleasure in her books to colleagues at OUP, and when I did so, some time in 1974, to Audrey Bayley, she exclaimed: '*I* know Barbara Pym! – I went to her retirement party not so long ago.' Audrey coordinated the Press' dealings with *Africa: Journal of the International African Institute*, of which Barbara had been Assistant Editor. 'At the lunch,' Audrey told me, 'they were saying "We've all been in her novels".' This was good to hear, since one of the Pym novels I liked best, *Less Than Angels* (1955) has Africanists at its centre. Nobody could have written it, I now saw, without intimate knowledge of them. She promptly ceased to be a disembodied literary intelligence. But where was she now? Gone to the Oxfordshire village of Finstock, said Audrey, to live with her sister, Hilary Walton; she could give me the address.

This information interested me greatly, because by then I knew that I would soon be relocated to Oxford, to the Press' headquarters. I had already decided not to live in Oxford itself, and a few months after this conversation, I bought an old cottage in Wroxton, near Banbury. Long and low, it dated from the seventeenth century, was built, like most of the village, of the local honey-coloured stone, and situated on a rough-surfaced lane leading to a farm. Moving took a while, and it wasn't until summer 1975 that I looked on the map and saw that Finstock lay about twelve miles to the south of my new home. Acting on the kind of whim that has never failed to serve me well, I wrote Barbara Pym a full, probably fulsome letter, thanking her for the intense pleasure her work had given me, and suggesting we meet some time. In fact, why didn't she come over to Wroxton one evening for dinner? I am stupefied, looking back, by my audacity; today I wouldn't dream of issuing such an invitation. My social life was then, as now, informal. I really must have liked her books *very* much!

Two evenings later my telephone rang. 'Hullo? This is Barbara Pym,' said a gentle, lilting voice at the other end. I hadn't expected this to happen at all, even less her saying yes, she would greatly like to visit Wroxton, but would I mind if her sister who was, unlike herself, a driver, came too? Of course not, I said, and we fixed time and date. On the evening itself, ten minutes after the agreed arrival hour, I began to feel anxious. Perhaps my directions hadn't been clear enough; perhaps the sisters had forgotten all about their engagement. I opened my front door and saw, to my consternation, at the end of my always muddy lane, two middle-aged women in full, long-skirted, beaded evening dress, looking perplexedly about them. Surely they could only be my invitees – and so they were.

What they made of entering my cottage to find themselves the only guests for a meal consisting of shepherd's pie with peas, followed by junket (I hadn't become the strict ethical vegetarian I am now), it's maybe just as well I don't know. But in no time we were talking very easily. In her thank-you letter, enclosed in a signed, first edition of *Some Tame Gazelle*, Barbara praised my 'delicious food' – something few others have done.

I learned that evening what is now one of literary history's saddest facts: her writing life had *not* ended with *No Fond Return of Love*. Her publisher, Jonathan Cape, had rejected the next novel, and she hadn't succeeded in finding another one for it. Since then she had finished several other books – 'I've written so *many* novels!' she remarked wistfully, one of which she thought was probably the best thing she'd done (*The Sweet Dove Died*), and all were still homeless. Barbara spoke without bitterness, but later I was to appreciate that she had minded these many refusals acutely. They had damaged her confidence. She had rightly considered herself a novelist, fulfilling very early aspirations, and felt this identity had been taken from her. But Philip Larkin, Pamela Hansford Johnson, David and Rachel Cecil, and her old friend Robert (Jock) Liddell had been supportive.

She was diffident but not awkward, responsive, humorous and friendly, yet with a dignified reserve. Her face showed the effect of the slight stroke she had suffered in 1973. Her relationship with her sister was clearly deep and loving; she was fond of cats (that thank-you letter ends, 'Greetings to Hodge!', my ginger tom); and knowledgeable about the historical associations of the area. I liked her a lot, and that evening was the first of many meetings – I myself visited Finstock, mostly with neighbourhood friends. She had a gift for lightly intimate conversation; all my visitors took to her, from my favourite former

Swedish colleague, to John Bayley, my old Oxford tutor and his wife, Iris Murdoch, who lived nearby. Barbara appeared equally entertained by my former London landlady, who had composed a song-cycle to her cat, Monty Python, and Iris who told her how she had to write things 'many times over'.

Cutting through these years of Oxfordshire friendship is the watershed date of 21st January 1977. The *Times Literary Supplement* had invited distinguished literary figures to nominate the most underrated writers of the century: David Cecil, true as ever to his convictions, and Philip Larkin chose Barbara Pym, making her the only writer to be nominated twice. Reading this at work, I wondered if Barbara would see this feature; she probably didn't take the *TLS*. So when I got home, I rang her up. She knew nothing about it. I read out the laudatory sentences; she was all incredulity and gratitude. By the next morning her life had changed for ever. Thenceforward publishers competed to issue or re-issue her work; the country appeared to swarm with old admirers. Her novels were made available again, and two extraordinarily fine new ones appeared, *Quartet in Autumn* (1977) and *The Sweet Dove Died* (1978), both critical and commercial successes. They are more pared down in their art and more sombre in theme and tone than the earlier books: the first is a study of retirement and aging, and the second is an unflinching portrait of selfishness and emotional delusion.

I have before me now a card from Barbara, with a charming pen-and-ink drawing of Barn Cottage, dated 25th June 1977:

Things go well with me. Macmillan have taken another novel which will come out in the spring – I had written it some time ago, but hadn't got a publisher . . . I'm so very grateful to all the people who encouraged me when I was 'in the wilderness' – of which you are certainly one.

Sadly she didn't have long to enjoy this reversal of fortune. Two years after its advent, malignant cancer, treated some years before, returned. In her last letter to me she wrote that she was, 'as they strangely say now, "under the doctor"'. She died on 11th January 1980, aged sixty-seven.

*No Fond Return of Love* belongs to, indeed nicely rounds off, the first sextet of novels (the one she wrote immediately afterwards, subtle, bittersweet *An Unsuitable Attachment*, published 1982, heralds in the darker later productions). Certainly its story of Dulcie Mainwaring's test-and-quest is quintessential Pym. It is the novel most bound up with the heterogeneity of London, and with ways of discerning unifying strands behind it. It is the novel most concerned too with the 'thankless task' (its original title) that most of us (its author included) must cope with, both for our bread-and-butter and to keep occupied. Dulcie's curiosity serves her well, from her attendance at the richly presented learned conference onwards. But we should never forget that she has a 'broken heart' and that its breaking gave her hard instruction in the selfishness that governs too many lives, and that social convention offers no palatable rites or modes for expressing wounded feelings or concomitant fears of being alone. Its comedy is among Pym's most hilarious – the Beltane household with Felix the blue-rinsed dog and the kilt-wearing Brazilian lodger; the visit to Mrs Forbes' Eagle House Hotel in Devon where the eponymous eagle has to be vacuumed – but Dulcie's journey is also an astringent demonstration of effective stoicism, the more potent as, explicitly, unlike most of Pym's protagonists, she lacks attachment to the church.

As well as humour, readers will find here the wealth of detail about clothes, furniture and food which delights so many Pym admirers. Yet the longer I read her, the surer I am that what makes her contribution to literature important is something quite else. Speaking to me of her favourite writers she said: 'Jock Liddell and I feel we *discovered* Ivy Compton-Burnett.' Compton-Burnett isolates her people from the hurly-burly of contemporary living to concentrate on those essentials of human nature that they manifest. So too do Barbara Pym's characters transcend their richly worked contexts to stand as universals, reminding us not merely how they all lived in the fifties, but of what complex material we ourselves, like those we encounter daily, are made.

*Paul Binding, 2008*

# CHAPTER ONE

There are various ways of mending a broken heart, but perhaps going to a learned conference is one of the more unusual.

When Dulcie Mainwaring realised that her fiancé did not want to marry her after all – or that he was not worthy of her love, as he put it – she endured several months of quiet misery before she felt able to rouse herself from this state. When the notice of the conference came, it seemed to be just the kind of thing that was recommended for women in her position – an opportunity to meet new people and to amuse herself by observing the lives of others, even if only for a weekend and under somewhat unusual circumstances.

For what could be more peculiar than a crowd of grown-up people, most of them middle-aged or even elderly, collected together in a girls' boarding school in Derbyshire for the purpose of discussing scholarly niceties that meant nothing to most of the world? Even the rooms – fortunately they were not to be crowded into dormitories – seemed unnatural, with their twin iron bedsteads and the prospect of strange companions at such close quarters.

Dulcie began to speculate on who hers would be, and looked forward to her entry – for surely the room-mate would be female? – with some apprehension. But at least it would be interesting, she told herself bravely, to share a room with a stranger, and when she heard footsteps coming along the corridor, she braced herself and wondered what they would say to each other when the door opened. But the footsteps went past and stopped a little further on. Then, looking again at the second bed, she noticed that it seemed suspiciously flat, and when she lifted the cover she saw that it was not made up. She was at once relieved and disappointed. When she had plucked up enough courage, she would go and see who was in the room next door.

It had been a mistake to come. Viola Dace realized that now, as she looked round the little cell-like room in dismay which approached panic when she saw that there was a second bed, covered like her own with a white honeycomb quilt. So she might have to share this miserable room with an unknown person – the idea was insupportable! Cautiously she lifted a corner of the quilt to see if the bed was made up; to her relief it was not, for underneath were only a pillow in a striped ticking cover and a pile of grey blankets. At least, then, she was to have the room to herself, and it might just be possible to endure it for three nights.

She lit a cigarette and leaned out of the window. There was a fine display of dahlias in a border below her, apples and pears hung heavily on the trees, and in the distance moors stretched away to hills and what was apparently the world outside and freedom.

There was a light tap on the door and Viola turned round,

startled, saying 'Come in' rather sharply. She saw a rather tall woman in her early thirties, with a pleasant-face and fair hair, standing on the threshold. She wore a tweed suit and brogued shoes which looked too heavy for her thin legs.

Already halfway to being a dim English spinster, Viola thought, conscious of herself 'making a contrast' in her black dress, with her pale, rather haggard face and untidy dark hair.

'I'm Dulcie Mainwaring,' said the fair-haired woman. 'My room seems to be next to yours. I wondered if we might go down to dinner together?'

'If you like,' said Viola rather ungraciously. 'My name's Viola Dace, by the way. What does one do and wear?'

'I suppose nobody really knows,' said Dulcie. 'It might be like the first night on board ship when nobody changes for dinner. I believe it's the first time a conference of this sort has been held here. I know they have "religious bodies", and writers, too, I believe. I suppose *we're* writers, in a way.'

'Yes, we might call ourselves that.' Viola had taken out her lipstick and was applying it almost savagely, as if she were determined to make herself look as unlike somebody who worked on the dustier fringes of the academic world as possible.

Dulcie gazed fascinated at the result, but the brilliant coral-coloured mouth in the sallow face certainly looked bizarre and striking, and made her slightly dissatisfied with her own careful 'natural' make-up.

'It's an unusual idea having a conference of people like us,' said Dulcie. 'Do we all correct proofs, make bibliographies and indexes, and do all the rather humdrum thankless tasks for people more brilliant than ourselves?'

She seemed to dwell on the words almost with relish, Viola

3

thought, as if she were determined to create an impression of the utmost dreariness.

'Oh, my life isn't at all like that,' she said quickly. 'I've been doing research of my own and I've already started a novel. I've really come here because I know one of the lecturers and . . .'

She hesitated, the feeling of dismay rising up in her again, for surely it *had* been a mistake to come. This worthy Miss Mainwaring, whom one could just imagine doing all the dreary things she had described, was not, however, the kind of person in whom she would dream of confiding.

'I just do odd jobs and make indexes,' said Dulcie cheerfully. 'I found it better to work at home when my mother was ill, and I haven't really thought of taking a full-time job since she died.'

A bell began to toll, which seemed to Viola to add to the gloomy feeling Dulcie had given her.

'That must be dinner,' she said. 'Shall we go down?' It would surely be possible to shake her off some time during the evening.

Aylwin Forbes lifted a flat half-bottle of gin out of his suitcase from among the folds of his pyjamas, where it had travelled safely from London to this remote Derbyshire village. He placed it first of all on the dressing-table, but it did not look right with his yeast tablets and stomach powder and hair tonic, so, as there was no other cupboard, it had to go in the wardrobe after all – that traditional, if rather shameful, hiding place for bottles.

The other important item in his luggage – the notes for the lecture he was to give on 'Some problems of an editor' – he placed on the chair by his bed.

Then he noticed that there was, in fact, a small cupboard

above the washbasin, presumably intended for medicines, so he took the bottle of gin out of the wardrobe and put it in the cupboard. A thought occurred to him, and he wondered if the servants were honest, imagining one of them lifting the gin bottle to her lips and taking a quick swig as she did his room in the morning. Well, he would have to risk that, he decided, and put the gin with the yeast tablets and the stomach powder in the little cupboard; but he could not decide where he was likely to be when he was using the hair lotion, so he left that on the dressing-table. He next took up the lecture notes from the chair by the bed and placed them on the dressing-table by his brushes and Florentine leather stud box.

All that now remained in his suitcase were the latest number of the literary journal of which he was editor and the large photograph frame – also of Florentine leather – containing the photograph of his wife, Marjorie. He took out the journal and laid it on the chair by the bed, with a slight feeling of distaste, as if picturing himself lying in bed reading it, but there was no convenient place for Marjorie so he put the frame back into the suitcase, shut it and pushed it under the bed. After all, there was really no point in having it out now.

He opened the door cautiously and looked down the long corridor, wondering where the lavatory might be. He had even taken a few hesitant steps in one direction, when he saw an elderly woman in pince-nez, hair-net, and quilted dressing-gown patterned with large red flowers, carrying a towel and sponge bag, walking purposefully towards him. Wherever he had been making for, she would surely get there first. He withdrew rapidly into the shelter of his room, deeply disturbed. Was there not even to be segregation of the sexes?

The woman's footsteps went padding past and seemed to

stop at the room next to his. And then he realized that it was Miss Faith Randall, a fellow lecturer. In his mind's eye he saw the title of the lecture she was to give – 'Some problems of indexing'. Was every lecture to be on 'Some problems of something?' he wondered, going out into the corridor more boldly this time.

When he got back to his room he poured some gin into a toothglass, added water from the tap, and drank it off rather quickly, as if it were medicine – which, in a sense, it was. I must go down to dinner, he thought, comforted by the remembrance that the lecturers sat at a table apart from the other members of the conference. He remembered Miss Randall with her hair-net and pince-nez, and wondered if he would find himself sitting next to her and what they could talk about. Indexes I have known? Abortion, adultery, administration . . . pottery, prawns, pregnancy – good-oh! Perhaps he had drunk the gin a little too quickly.

'Who is that good-looking man?' Dulcie whispered to Viola, as they stood in the ante-room waiting for the final gong to sound for dinner.

'Good-looking man – where?' Viola had been lost in contemplation of their fellow conference members, who were not, on the whole, good-looking. Indeed, she had been wondering what conference could possibly consist of good-looking people, unless it were one of actors or film stars. But as soon as Dulcie spoke she knew who it must be, and was annoyed and almost disappointed that she should not have felt his presence in some mysterious way.

She looked up and saw the blond leonine head, the well-shaped nose, and the dark eyes, so unusual with fair hair.

'That's Aylwin Forbes,' she said.

'Ah, yes. "Some problems of an editor",' Dulcie quoted. 'He looks as if he might have other problems too – being so hand-some, I mean. What is he editor of? – I've forgotten for the moment. Does he really know about *our* problems?'

Viola named the journal which Aylwin Forbes edited. 'I happen to know him rather well,' she added.

'Oh?'

'He and I were once . . .' Viola hesitated, teasing out the fringe of her black and silver stole.

'I see,' Dulcie said, but of course she did not see. What was it they were once, or had been once to each other? Lovers? Colleagues? Editor and assistant editor? Or had he merely seized her in his arms in some dusty library in a convenient corner by the card index catalogues one afternoon in spring? Impossible to tell, from Viola's guarded hint. How irritating it sometimes was, the delicacy of women!

'Is he married?' asked Dulcie stoutly.

'Oh, of course – in a sense, that is,' said Viola impatiently.

Dulcie nodded. People usually were married, and how often it was 'in a sense'.

Aylwin Forbes now came over to where they were standing.

'Why, hullo, Vi! I wondered if you might be here,' he said in a jolly tone, which seemed as if it might have been assumed specially for the conference.

'Hullo, Aylwin,' said Viola, inhibited by Dulcie's presence and annoyed that he had called her 'Vi'. She did not like to be reminded that she had been christened Violet, from some con-fused Wordsworthian fancy of her father's – 'a violet by a mossy stone, half hidden from the eye' – such a charming idea, he had thought, not realizing that the name Violet did not

7

really suggest this. When she was seventeen she had called herself Viola.

'I see you are to lecture to us,' Viola went on. 'No doubt we shall be meeting later on.'

'Yes, we must have a good gossip together,' said Aylwin, but at that moment a gong boomed, and the crowd moved forward into the dining-room, an old man with a white beard leading the way.

The dining-room was large and capable of seating many more than were assembled at the two long tables. There was a smaller table set aside for the organizers and lecturers and Aylwin moved over to it quickly, relieved to have an excuse to leave the two women. He made a rather feeble joke about sheep and goats, feeling that he could hardly have done less, and took his place between two harmless-looking middle-aged men, one of whom he recognized as a fellow expert who was to lecture on the terrors and triumphs of setting out a bibliography correctly.

Dulcie and Viola, meanwhile, found themselves at the end of one of the long tables at which a tall comfortable-looking woman was beginning to ladle out soup from a large tureen. She seemed to be enjoying herself, plunging the ladle into the steaming savoury-smelling broth as if she were a medieval nun or friar feeding the assembled poor.

'It seems that whoever's at this end has to cope with the grub,' she said in a loud, jolly voice. 'Would you mind shoving the plates along?'

Dulcie and Viola did as they were told and the meal began. After the soup a plate of sliced meat and some dishes of vegetables were brought, which they helped to serve.

'What do you *do* exactly?' said Dulcie to Viola rather

8

bluntly. 'Do you make indexes or sub-edit a journal or what?'

Viola hesitated, then said, 'I've done some research of my own. I was working for a Ph. D. at London University but my health broke down. As a matter of fact,' she added casually, 'I once did some work for Aylwin Forbes.'

'That must have been fun.'

'Well, it was a stimulating experience, of course,' she said, a little reproachfully. 'He's very brilliant, you know.'

'Yes, and so good-looking,' said the woman who had served out the soup. 'I always think that helps.'

Dulcie looked at her curiously. The participants in the conference had been asked to wear their names and she now noticed beside a large finely carved cameo brooch of Leda and the Swan a small circle of cardboard, bearing the name JESSICA FOY in block capitals. She recognized it as that of the librarian of quite a well-known learned institution and instinctively drew back a little, unable to reconcile such eminence with this jolly woman serving out the soup.

'Research, with a good-looking man,' Miss Foy went on. 'That's an enviable lot. What was the subject of your research?'

'Oh, just an obscure eighteenth-century poet,' said Viola quickly.

'You were lucky to find one so obscure that not even the Americans had "done" him,' commented Miss Foy dryly. 'It's quite serious, this shortage of obscure poets.'

'Perhaps the time will come when one may be permitted to do research into the lives of ordinary people, ' said Dulcie, 'people who have no claim to fame whatsoever.'

'Ah, that'll be the day!' said Miss Foy jovially.

'I love finding out about people,' said Dulcie. 'I suppose

9

it's a sort of compensation for the dreariness of everyday life.'

Viola stared at her, astonished that any woman could admit to such a weakness as the need for compensation.

'You might get married,' she said doubtfully, remembering the heavy shoes on the thin legs.

'Yes,' Dulcie agreed, 'I might, but even if I did marry I don't suppose my character would alter much.'

'You would not allow yourself to be moulded by any man,' said Miss Foy in a satisfied tone, 'and neither should I.'

Dulcie turned away to hide a smile.

Viola looked a little annoyed, as if, Dulcie thought, she wouldn't have minded being moulded. But of course the question didn't always arise. Sometimes it was the other way round. Maurice, Dulcie's ex-fiancé, would be quite incapable of moulding anybody, for he was rather a weak character – could she really admit that now? – and also three years younger than herself.

'Perhaps other people's lives are a kind of refuge,' she suggested. 'One can enjoy the cosiness of them.'

'But they aren't always cosy,' said Miss Foy.

'No, and then one finds oneself looking at the horror or misery in them with detachment, and that in itself is horrifying.'

Miss Foy laughed uncertainly. 'I wonder if you'll find a subject here.'

'Probably not. It seems too obvious a hunting-ground, if you see what I mean.'

'Yes – too many eccentrics,' said Miss Foy, realizing that her own greatest pleasure in life was a tricky item of classification or bibliographical entry. 'Look, here's the pud. Shall I serve it or would you like to?'

'Oh, you do it,' said Dulcie. 'I'm not very good at measuring things out.' She felt that the performance of this simple task might be satisfying a deeply felt need in Miss Foy, which was something more than mere bossiness.

At the end of the meal the tables were cleared; it seemed that nobody could leave without carrying something, even if it was only a jug of custard or an unused fork. They then moved over to the conference hall to hear about the programme for the weekend. It was announced that on this, the first evening, there would be no lecture or discussion, but a kind of 'social gathering' so that members could get to know each other better. Coffee would be served.

Viola heard this with dismay, for she was not of a gregarious nature. If she could not talk to Aylwin Forbes she would go to bed and read, but the thought of the little cell-like room was not inviting and she found herself moving with the others into a sort of common-room, crowded with little armchairs and pervaded by the smell of coffee and the clatter of teaspoons.

'It will be nice to have a cup of coffee,' said Dulcie.

Viola thought with irritation that Dulcie was just the kind of person who would say it was 'nice' to have a cup of indifferent coffee with a lot of odd-looking people. She had already classified her as a 'do-gooder', the kind of person who would interfere in the lives of others with what are known as 'the best motives'. She determined to shake her off as soon as she could. It was unfortunate that their rooms were next to each other. Viola even considered asking that her room might be changed, but it seemed hardly worth while for a weekend. Besides, she did not know whom to ask.

The common-room had glass doors at one end, beyond

which there seemed to be a kind of conservatory. Viola contrived to get separated from Dulcie in the coffee queue and to slip through the doors – unnoticed, she hoped.

It was indeed a conservatory, with potted palms and the gnarled stem of a vine breaking out into a profusion of leaves overhead. Viola sat down in a basket chair and looked up at the leafy ceiling from which bunches of black grapes were hanging. It was wonderful to get away from all those dreadful people. What ever had possessed her to come to this conference? She closed her eyes self-consciously, imagining that somebody might come in and find her. But Aylwin Forbes, looking through from the common-room, withdrew hastily at the sight of her, and began an animated conversation with Miss Foy and Miss Randall about mutual acquaintances in the academic world. Eventually, it was Dulcie's voice, with those of two other women, that broke into Viola's solitude, saying, 'Look, here's a charming conservatory, with a real vine. And grapes too, how lovely! Do you mind if we join you?'

'Of course not,' said Viola coldly. 'Anyone can come in here, I imagine.'

So the evening came to an end, Dulcie and Viola and two women in flowered rayon dresses sitting on the basket chairs, offering each other cigarettes and speculating about the hardness of their beds. It was not long before conversation petered out and Dulcie and Viola retired to their adjacent rooms.

Before she slept, Dulcie thought of the big suburban house where she had lived with her sister and her parents and which was now hers, her parents being dead and her sister married. Outside her bedroom window was a pear tree on which the pears were now ripe; she could almost see them in a Pre-Raphaelite perfection of colour and detail, leaves and fruit.

September was her favourite month – the garden full of dahlias and zinnias, Victoria plums to be bottled, pears and apples to be 'dealt with', windfalls to be collected and sorted. It had been a good year for fruit and there would be a lot to do. The house was big, almost 'rambling', but very soon her niece Laurel – her sister's child – was coming to London to take a secretarial course and would be living there. Dulcie looked forward to planning her room. She would have liked the house to be full of people; it might even be possible to let rooms. There were so many lonely people in the world. Here Dulcie's thoughts took another turn and she began to think about the things that worried her in life – beggars, distressed gentlefolk, lonely African students having doors shut in their faces, people being wrongfully detained in mental homes . . .

It must have been much later – for she was conscious of having been woken – that there was a tap on her door.

'Who is it?' she called out, curious rather than alarmed.

A figure appeared in the doorway – like Lady Macbeth, Dulcie thought incongruously. It was Viola, her dark hair hanging loose on her shoulders, wearing a dressing-gown of some material that gleamed palely in the dim light. Dulcie saw that it was lilac satin.

'I'm so sorry, I must have woken you up,' Viola said. 'But I couldn't sleep. The dreadful thing is that I seem to have forgotten my sleeping pills. I can't think how it can have happened. I never go *anywhere* without them . . .' She sounded desperate, on the edge of tears.

'I've got some Rennies,' said Dulcie, sitting up in bed.

'Oh, I haven't got indigestion,' said Viola impatiently, irritated at Dulcie's assumption that it was a stomach upset that had prevented her from sleeping.

'I always find that if I read a nice soothing book it sends me off to sleep,' said Dulcie, meaning to be helpful. 'But is there something worrying you? I think there must be. Is it Aylwin Forbes?' she asked kindly.

'Yes, I suppose so.' Viola sat down on the bed.

'You love him or something like that?' Dulcie was not perhaps choosing her words very skilfully, but it was, after all, the middle of the night.

'I don't know, really. You see, his wife has left him, gone back to her mother, and I should have thought – all things considered – that he'd have – well, *turned* to me.'

'Turned to you? For comfort, yes, I see.'

'We did this work together – we were such friends, so of course I thought . . .'

'Perhaps he thinks it's rather soon – I mean, to turn to anybody.'

'But comfort – surely one could do so much. I should be so glad to do what I could.'

'Yes, of course one does like to, perhaps women enjoy that most of all – to feel that they're needed and doing good.'

'It isn't a question of *my* enjoying anything,' said Viola sharply. 'I want to do what I can for *him*.'

Dulcie wanted to ask more about the wife's leaving – had she been driven to it by something he had done? – but she did not feel she could do so yet. From the way Viola was talking it seemed that Aylwin Forbes was the injured one.

'Perhaps his grief has gone too deep,' she suggested.

'But he has come to this conference.'

'Yes, to take his mind off things. It might well do that.'

'But I feel he's avoiding me,' Viola went on. 'He was very awkward when we met before dinner, didn't you notice?'

'Well, the gong rang almost immediately and everybody started to push forward – it would have been awkward for anybody.'

'Then afterwards, when I was sitting by myself in the conservatory' – Viola seemed to be speaking her thoughts aloud – 'I *think* he looked in through the glass doors and didn't come in because he saw me there.'

'He may have thought it would be draughty, or that you didn't want to be disturbed,' said Dulcie, becoming increasingly feeble in her reassurances as sleep threatened to overtake her. 'I'm sure things will be better in the morning,' she went on, feeling that this was really the coward's way out. 'Do you think you will be able to sleep now?'

What a pity we can't make a cup of Ovaltine, was her last conscious thought. Life's problems are often eased by hot milky drinks.

# CHAPTER TWO

Next morning Dulcie was conscious of a tramping of footsteps past her door, almost as if the place were on fire and people were hurrying to safety. It was some time before she realised that it was nothing more alarming than enthusiasm for early morning tea. All these people, whose thoughts were normally on learned matters, had shown themselves to be human. Dulcie got out of bed, put on her dressing-gown and combed her hair. She decided to get a cup of tea for Viola, who had probably slept badly after her disturbed night.

Aylwin Forbes lay in his bed listening to the clink of spoons in saucers. In his capacity as a lecturer at the conference he had imagined that a servant – perhaps even in cap and apron – would bring him a tray of tea at a suitable time. He was unprepared for the appearance of Miss Randall, in hair-net and pince-nez and the flowered quilted dressing-gown he already knew, standing in the doorway with a cup and saucer in her hand.

'You lucky men, lying in bed while we women wait on you,' she said, in an uncharacteristically arch tone, perhaps to cover her embarrassment at seeing him all tousled and in his pyjamas. 'Sugar's in the saucer – I didn't know if you took it.'

She put the cup down on the bedside table and tiptoed heavily from the room.

'Thank you so much!' he called after her. 'I didn't realise we had to . . .' but she was gone, and anyway he felt at a disadvantage, lying in his bed.

He raised himself on one elbow, pushed aside with the spoon the two brownish sodden lumps of sugar in the saucer, and took a sip of tea. It tasted strong and bitter. Like life? he wondered. Perhaps like the lives of women – his wife Marjorie, and Viola Dace, reclining in a basket chair in that conservatory with her eyes closed. 'Some problems of an editor', he thought, recalling the title of his lecture, did not, or were not generally reckoned to, include women. Marjorie – going back to her mother in that prim house overlooking the common: what was he supposed to do about that? Viola was perhaps a little easier to deal with: he could try to speak kindly to her in the presence of others – not at breakfast, of course, but before or after some other meal, when people strolled round the gardens admiring the herbaceous borders.

Breakfast was a rather uneasy meal. It seemed as if the strain of being with a crowd of strange people was felt more at this early hour. Conversation flowed less easily, and the absence of Sunday papers seemed to be deeply felt. Even Miss Foy, serving out porridge and then sausages, was rather subdued.

'Bangers,' she murmured in a low tone, but her observation was received without comment.

When the meal was nearly over, two men and a little group of women, wearing hats, came in with the self-conscious air of people who have risen early from their beds to go to church, and now hope – though very humbly – for a breakfast they feel they have earned.

Dulcie noticed that Viola had not yet appeared, though she had seemed to wake up when Dulcie had taken her a cup of tea. As she walked along the corridor to her room Dulcie saw her coming out of a bathroom, wearing the lilac satin dressing-gown, her hair hidden in a flower-printed bath cap to match.

'You've missed breakfast, I'm afraid,' said Dulcie.

'Breakfast?' Viola repeated the word as if it were unfamiliar to her. 'I couldn't face it. I never do eat breakfast anyway. That cup of tea was quite enough.'

'We had sausages,' said Dulcie, in what she felt was a solid tone.

Viola shuddered. 'Then I'm *certainly* glad I didn't come down. What's the programme for this morning?'

'First we are to have the lecture by Aylwin Forbes' – Dulcie hurried over the name, remembering the painful revelations of the night before – 'and then' – her tone brightened – 'there's to be a short service in the chapel, undenominational, taken by somebody who's a lay reader and allowed to take services, I suppose, saying "we" and "us" instead of "you".'

Viola looked puzzled, so Dulcie hastened to explain, 'I mean in the blessing and that sort of thing – a lay reader can't say the Lord bless you, he has to say us, because he isn't in Holy Orders.'

'Oh, of course,' said Viola in a bored tone.

'I must go and tidy my room,' said Dulcie. 'I expect I'll see you at the lecture?'

'I expect so,' said Viola, drifting into her room. It was surprising, she felt, that Dulcie had not offered to 'bag' her a seat.

Presumably, Dulcie thought, as she contemplated her hollowed mattress, it wouldn't be particularly upsetting to hear a lecture on a rather dry topic on a Sunday morning from a man one loved or had once loved. But in this she may well have been wrong, not having experienced the power of the tie that shared academic work can forge between two people. Whatever there had been between her and Maurice, it had certainly not been that. 'You and your "work",' he would say, in a fond, mocking tone that Dulcie found painful to recall at this moment.

The lecture was not to be held in the large hall, but in a kind of lounge, with comfortable chairs and a grand piano shrouded in a holland cover. Soon the air was thick with cigarette smoke, the women seeming to smoke more than the men.

Because of the emptiness of their lives, no doubt, most of them being unmarried, Aylwin Forbes thought, as he shuffled through his notes before beginning his lecture.

But before very long he began to wish that smoking had been forbidden – surely it ought to have been? – for it seemed to be making the room uncomfortably stuffy.

He looks even paler than usual, Viola thought. I could never love a man with a ruddy complexion. Marjorie's leaving him has affected him in some way, undoubtedly – it must have been a shock to his pride, if nothing else. But now he must begin to rearrange his life. It wasn't natural for a man to be alone. But *was* he alone? Did one know even that?

Of course, thought Miss Foy, the journal he edits is fortunate in having an exceptionally able assistant editor. What does A. F. *really* know of the problems of an editor; he didn't have problems as *she* knew them. Still, it was always interesting to hear one's own particular kind of shop talked, though she had heard him lecture better than he was doing this morning. She took another crushed-looking filter-tipped cigarette from a squashed packet and lit it from the stump of the old one. Coffee after this, she hoped. She wouldn't be attending the church service. A brisk walk round the grounds would be more her idea of worshipping God, if, indeed, He existed.

People always look on indexers as unintelligent drudges, thought Dulcie a little indignantly, as she smiled faintly at an old joke he had just trotted out; but a book can be made or marred by its index. And love and devotion are not necessarily the best qualifications, she thought, remembering the wives and others who undertook what was often acknowledged to be a thankless task. He looks very pale. When you have the opportunity to study him like this you can see that he must be very attractive to women.

Perhaps he could ask for a window to be opened, Aylwin thought, for the room really was extraordinarily hot. Although he was not reading from his notes, he was disconcerted to find that he had lost his place and for a moment he stopped speaking, unable to remember what he had been going to say next. He found himself looking into the audience. Viola Dace was gazing at him – that was the only word for it; embarrassed, he turned his glance elsewhere. Miss Foy's cigarette holder seemed to be jutting right into his face, then it receded, the room became very dark and from a long way off he heard a woman's voice, rather a pleasing voice, saying, 'Something's the matter – he's ill!'

Dulcie had hurried up to the platform when she saw him

clutch the stand on which his notes were arranged and then stumble, but the chairman had taken him by the shoulders and sat him down in a chair.

'Brandy!' called Miss Foy in a loud voice, looking hopefully around her. But it seemed unlikely that any would be forthcoming in such circumstances and company.

'There is water here,' said the chairman, pouring some from a carafe which stood on the table.

'I have some smelling salts,' said Dulcie calmly. 'They should revive him, and perhaps a window could be opened?'

Fancy carrying smelling salts about with her, thought Viola scornfully, but wishing that she could have supplied them.

Aylwin opened his eyes. 'Where am I?' he asked, really knowing perfectly well where he was, but feeling that some such remark might excuse his weakness.

'You were in the middle of giving a lecture and you – er – had a nasty turn,' said the chairman solemnly.

Aylwin smiled. 'Ah, yes, "a nasty turn",' he repeated, his lips quivering with amusement.

Why, he's beautiful, thought Dulcie suddenly. Like a Greek marble, or something dug up in the garden of an Italian villa, the features a little blunted, with the charm of being not quite perfect.

'So stupid of me,' he murmured. 'I felt rather odd for a moment. But I've just had flu.'

'Well, it's nothing to be ashamed of,' said Dulcie, rather in a brisk nurse's manner. 'The room was so frightfully hot. I think I should go and lie down in your room if I were you,' she added sensibly.

'Yes.' He looked up at her gratefully. 'Perhaps I shall.' The lecture had been nearly finished and he always disliked the quarter of an hour or so of pointless questions at the end. Nobody could expect him to go on with it now.

'Oh, dear,' lamented Miss Foy, 'I *had* wanted to ask . . . but perhaps later, when he's feeling better.'

The chairman was still standing on the platform, wondering whether it was necessary to bring the proceedings formally to an end. He decided that nothing of the kind was needed, for anything he could say would be an anticlimax after the dramatic scene that had just taken place. He stepped down from the platform and looked rather ostentatiously at his watch.

'Half an hour to go before the service in the chapel,' he said to nobody in particular, but as he was the lay reader who was to conduct it he felt that some reminder was necessary. Most of the women seemed to have gathered round Forbes, he noticed, and were all prescribing different remedies and courses to be followed – strong sweet tea, a good rest, a *darkened* room, a brisk walk in the fresh air, were some that he heard.

His thoughts turned to the service and he hoped that the unfortunate occurrence would not have an adverse effect on the numbers attending it. He also hoped that the harmonium was in good working order and that the lady who had offered to play it was reasonably competent.

'Of course I'm really an Anglo-Catholic,' said Viola rather crossly as she and Dulcie walked in the garden, not mentioning Aylwin Forbes, who was sitting on a seat being talked to by Miss Foy. 'I had hoped to be able to get to Mass somewhere.'

'Some people went to a Communion service in the village,' said Dulcie vaguely. 'Would that count?'

'Yes, but I couldn't get up for it after that wretched night. I don't think I closed my eyes till dawn and then I slept until you came in with the tea.'

'I hope I didn't wake you,' said Dulcie anxiously. 'I thought you might like to have a cup.' That was the worst of trying to be helpful, she reflected; so often one did the wrong thing.

'I should have had to wake up some time,' said Viola, not really answering the question. 'And it was kind of you to bring the tea, even though it was Indian.'

Dulcie bowed her head and they walked in silence into the little chapel, which seemed to be filled with a greenish light from the leaves of rhododendrons and other shrubs pressing against the windows. A youngish woman, looking grimly determined, sat pedalling at the harmonium.

It seemed hardly suitable that the first hymn should be 'All things bright and beautiful'. Dulcie sang in a loud indignant voice, waiting for the lines

*The rich man in his castle, the poor man at his gate,*
*God made them high or lowly and ordered their estate,*

but they never came. Then she saw that the verse had been left out. She sat down, feeling cheated of her indignation.

The lay reader then gave a short address. He tried to show how all work can be done to the Glory of God, even making an index, correcting a proof, or compiling an accurate bibliography. His small congregation heard him say, almost with disappointment, that those who do such work have perhaps less opportunity of actually doing evil than those who write novels and plays or work for films or television.

But there is more satisfaction in scrubbing a floor or digging a garden, Dulcie thought. One seems nearer to the heart of things doing menial tasks than in making the most perfect index. Again her thoughts wandered to her home and all that needed to be done there, and she began to wonder why she had come to the conference when she had so many better ways of occupying her time. It was not until the lay reader, in his extempore prayers, made a vague reference to 'one of our number who has been taken ill' that she remembered Aylwin Forbes and his beauty, the way his eyes had opened when she bent over him, the hollows of his temples. The sight of him had made her forget Maurice for a moment. Then there was Viola who, in spite of her rather hostile manner, seemed to be an 'interesting' person, somebody who might even become a friend.

Before lunch she saw the two of them standing in the vinery together, and it occurred to her that she might easily see them again – if not by chance, then by asking them to her house for a meal one evening. She almost began to plan the menu and the other guests.

Aylwin lifted his glass to drink the cold dark wine which might almost have been made from the wizened grapes hanging above their heads. Only in a Mediterranean climate can one experience a shock of pleasure from the roughness of such a wine, he thought. Certainly not in Derbyshire.

'Evenings are really better than lunchtimes for me,' Viola was saying, 'and there's more time to talk.'

# CHAPTER THREE

Dulcie lived in a pleasant part of London which, while it was undoubtedly a suburb, was 'highly desirable' and, to continue in the estate agent's words, 'took the overflow from Kensington'. 'And Harrods *do* deliver', as her next door neighbour Mrs Beltane so often repeated.

Dulcie did most of her work at home – an arrangement which dated from the time when her mother had been alive and in need of attention during the day. Now she was free, but she still preferred not to be bound by routine and had built up a useful reputation as a competent indexer and proof-corrector, the sort of person who could even do a little mild 'research' in the British Museum or the libraries of learned societies.

The day after she got back from the conference was a brilliant September morning. She did a little work on an index, washed some clothes and had lunch in the garden. The woman who came to help her in the house was due in the afternoon, and she prepared herself to listen to her varied conversation.

Miss Lord was a tall grey-haired spinster who had formerly worked in the haberdashery department of one of the big Kensington stores. But she had found the long mornings, standing about with nothing much to do, boring and exhausting, and had turned to housework, for which she had a natural talent and which nowadays did not seem to be regarded as in any way degrading. Probably because of her connection with haberdashery she had a passion for small gadgets and 'daintiness', as she put it, which was encouraged by the advertisements on commercial television with their emphasis on this aspect of life. She did not care for men, with their roughness and lack of daintiness, though the clergy were excepted, unless they smoked pipes. She herself liked a filter-tipped cigarette with a cup of tea or coffee, and she sat smoking one now, while Dulcie made Nescafé at the stove.

'I tried a new place for lunch today,' she said.

'Oh? What did you have?' Miss Lord always told Dulcie exactly what she had eaten for lunch on the days when she came in the afternoon.

'Egg on welsh and a Russian cream,' said Miss Lord. 'Quite nice, really.'

'It sounds . . .' Dulcie hesitated for a word – '*delicious*,' she pronounced with rather more emphasis than she had intended. 'What exactly is Russian cream?'

'It's a kind of mousse with a sponge base and jelly on the top,' said Miss Lord. 'The jelly can be red, yellow or orange.' She finished her coffee. 'Were you going to throw these flowers away? Unsightly, aren't they?' She bundled up some slimy-stalked zinnias and dahlias in *The Times Literary Supplement* and went out to the dustbin with them.

'The garden's looking lovely,' she said as she came back. 'Will you be cutting some fresh flowers for these vases?'

'Yes, later,' said Dulcie, 'but I must do something about the plums. I've been worrying about them all the weekend.'

'Oh, a garden's a responsibility,' sighed Miss Lord. 'The fruits of the earth . . . Harvest festival soon. Will you be sending something along to the church?' she asked deliberately.

The same question was asked every autumn and the same answer given, for Dulcie was not a regular church-goer and Miss Lord was.

'I don't think so,' Dulcie said, 'but if you'd like to take anything, please do. Plums or apples, and flowers, of course.'

'So kind of you, Miss Mainwaring. Of course we have no garden and one does like to do one's bit. I suppose I could bake a loaf, but anything to do with *yeast* is so troublesome, isn't it. One never knows . . . A year or two ago we did have a loaf in church, quite a beautiful thing, a fancy shape, plaited. But do you know,' she lowered her voice, 'it was made of *plaster*. I thought that very wrong. You couldn't send a plaster loaf to the hospital, could you.'

'I suppose not – it would indeed be a case of asking for bread and being given a stone.'

'Well, Miss Mainwaring, it would be being given plaster, wouldn't it. It was when we had the new vicar, the one who wanted us to call him Father – that, on top of the plaster loaf! Well, we complained to the Bishop and could you blame us?'

'No, change is a bad thing on the whole,' said Dulcie. 'You know that my niece Laurel is coming to live here soon, don't you?'

'Your sister's eldest child? Yes, Miss Mainwaring, you did mention it. Which room is she to have?'

'I thought the big back room would be best.'

'The room Mrs Mainwaring had?' asked Miss Lord in a hushed tone.

'Yes, I think it's better that it should be used again now. I thought we might do something about it the next time you come. We could put the big bed in the spare room and move in one of the divans; and then she will want a bookcase.'

'All this reading,' said Miss Lord. 'I used to like a book occasionally, but I don't get time for it now.'

'I took my degree in English Literature,' said Dulcie, almost to herself.

'But what does it lead to, Miss Mainwaring?'

'I don't know exactly. Of course learning is an end in itself, and a subject like English Literature can give one a good deal of pleasure.'

'Yes, I suppose it's nice,' said Miss Lord doubtfully.

'One can always teach,' Dulcie went on, 'or get some other kind of job.'

'Like you do, Miss Mainwaring, with all those cards and bits of paper spread out on the floor.' Miss Lord laughed, a light derisive laugh.

Dulcie felt humbled and went on in silence picking out the overripe plums from the not-so-ripe.

'I think I'll stew these for this evening,' she said. 'I'll put them on now.'

As she worked, Dulcie planned Laurel's room. The old blue velvet curtains were rather drab and faded, though they kept out the draughts in winter and the room seemed cosy when they were drawn. Perhaps a modern print would be gayer and more suitable for a young girl . . . What dreary thoughts to have on a fine afternoon, she told herself, ashamed even of the language in which they had framed themselves. It must be the contact with poor Miss Lord or the thought of herself as an aunt responsible for a niece. Laurel's mother, Dulcie's sister Charlotte, lived in Dorset, where her husband Robin was headmaster of a grammar school and curator of the local museum in his spare time. Laurel was the eldest of their three children and had just left school. Dulcie imagined herself trying to cope with the mysterious moods of adolescence, lying awake worrying when Laurel was out late. She was not looking forward to it very much, but it seemed inevitable that the girl should come to live with her. She could hardly have stayed in digs or a hostel when she had an aunt in London, or so Charlotte thought.

Through the trees and the fence at the end of the garden Dulcie could see her neighbour, Mrs Beltane, sitting in a flowery dress in a flowery canvas chair from Harrods, watching her hose watering the lawn with its special spray attachment. She was an elegant blue-haired, stiffly-moving woman of about sixty, who imagined herself to have seen better days. At least, this was the implication, for she had let the top floor of her house as a flat to a Brazilian gentleman, a diplomat admittedly, and she never tired of reminding people that of course she would never have done such a thing in 'the old days'.

Senhor MacBride-Pereira – for he was, like many Brazilians, of mixed nationality – was a nice person, Dulcie thought. He was in his late fifties, rather fat, with soft brown eyes and a delightful smile. He spoke English well and was steeped in English ways and conventions. 'To be a foreigner is bad enough,' he would lament, 'and perhaps to be an American, too, but to be a *Latin*-American – that is really terrible!'

This afternoon he sat by Mrs Beltane, playing with Felix, the little grey poodle, and talking in his musical voice. Dulcie could not hear what he was saying, but occasionally Mrs Beltane's silvery laugh was heard tinkling out. In spite of the come-down of having to take a lodger, she enjoyed his company: but there was no risk of scandal, for her two children Paul and Monica lived at home.

Dulcie crept to the fence with a dish of plums in her hand. She did not like to interrupt her neighbours too suddenly, but preferred to stand for a while pretending to tie up the dahlias, then, if they did not notice her, she would creep away with her dish.

'Why, Miss Mainwaring,' called out Mrs Beltane in a gracious tone, 'how splendid your dahlias are!'

'I was wondering if you'd like a few plums,' said Dulcie.

'Plums?' Mrs Beltane sounded as puzzled as if she had been offered some rare tropical fruit. 'But how kind. One can always do with *plums.*'

'Are they Elvas plums?' asked Senhor MacBride-Pereira.

'Well, no, plums off this tree,' said Dulcie, gesticulating vaguely. 'I think they're Victoria plums.'

'Ah, *Victoria* plums,' echoed Senhor MacBride-Pereira with deep satisfaction. 'My grandfather was at Balmoral once. That was before he came to São Paulo, of course.'

Mrs Beltane had advanced towards the fence to receive the dish, which was an ordinary glass casserole.

'They will look delightful on my Rockingham fruit plates,' she said. 'What beautiful ones they are! And how did you enjoy your conference?'

'Oh, it was great fun!' said Dulcie enthusiastically, and then began to wonder if it had been exactly that. 'A lot of people doing the same kind of thing always find plenty to talk about,' she explained, conscious that this was a dreary description.

'I never remember what it is that you do, exactly,' said Mrs Beltane graciously. 'Some kind of secretarial work, isn't it?'

'Yes, you might call it that, really. I do odd jobs for people.'

'And did you meet anyone nice at this conference?' asked Mrs Beltane, her tone rising a little with expectancy.

'There were some nice people there, and interesting people too,' said Dulcie, wondering if the two qualifications could go together. 'Aylwin Forbes,' she said, pronouncing his name with conscious pleasure. 'He's very well known in certain circles,' she added quickly, sensing Mrs Beltane's boredom. 'And a very attractive young woman called Viola Dace.'

'Oh, I see. Dace. Isn't that a kind of fish?'

'I don't know, perhaps it is. I haven't ever had it.'

'Not to eat, but I think it *is* a fish. Senhor MacBride-Pereira, isn't dace a kind of fish?'

He smiled and spread out his hands in a helpless gesture. 'Perhaps it is eaten by Roman Catholics here?' he suggested.

Dulcie felt a sense of unreality coming over her, as she often did when in conversation with her neighbours. It was one of their chief charms, their being so out of touch with everyday life and reminding her of England in the 'twenties or São Paulo in the 'nineties.

Later that evening Dulcie looked up Viola Dace in the telephone directory, but could not find her name. Then she looked up Aylwin Forbes. He lived in the Holland Park or Notting Hill area to judge by the address – 5 Quince Square, W.11. I might see him one day, Dulcie thought. She imagined herself in various places but could not exactly visualize the meeting. Perhaps, she told herself with a quickening of excitement, it would have to be contrived. Women were often able to arrange things that men would have thought impossible.

# CHAPTER FOUR

One isn't safe anywhere, thought Aylwin Forbes, turning his head away quickly. He had just spent a fruitless morning discussing his matrimonial affairs with his solicitor, and now this had happened.

And yet it had been a small harmless incident with no danger apparent in it. He had been walking through the Temple, and, attracted by the fine weather, had made a slight diversion into the gardens in front of Temple station which were now full of office workers enjoying their lunch hour in the sunshine. They sat crowded together on seats among the dahlias, reading books and newspapers, holding hands, talking, or doing nothing. Those who had found no seat lay sprawled on the grass, some prudently on newspapers or macintoshes, others not caring or asking themselves if the grass might be damp after yesterday's rain. And among these last he had suddenly noticed Viola Dace, sitting upright, her hands clasped around her knees, her face raised to the sun. He had looked at her with curiosity before he recognized her, for his attention had been drawn to her feet in red canvas laced-up shoes, which he thought distinctly odd. That was why he had not realised at first who she was, for such a lapse of taste was not to be expected of the Viola he knew, though Vi or Violet might well have been capable of it.

He hurried past her and into the station. As he sighed with relief and bought his ticket to South Kensington, he wondered what she had been doing there in such unlikely surroundings. Had she become a little eccentric, even unhinged, sitting on the grass in red canvas shoes with office workers, apparently worshipping the sun? Could it be for love of him that she did this strange thing? He looked around him, as if the faces of the people surging up the stairs from a train which had just come in might give him the answer. And among the faces, he saw one that was vaguely familiar. It was a fair pleasant face and the sight of it reminded him of that unfortunate lecture where he had made such an exhibition of himself. But he could not put a name to the face, and in a moment he had forgotten all about it and his thoughts had gone forward to the Victoria and Albert Museum where he planned to spend the afternoon.

Dulcie was half annoyed and half amused to find that the sight of him gave her a fluttery disturbed feeling in the pit of her stomach — what people called 'butterflies', she believed. He had looked preoccupied and a little worried, but then people usually did when they were caught unawares. She noticed that he had been carrying an *Evening Standard*, and it gave her an insight into his character to see that he was the kind of person who bought an evening paper at lunchtime, thus spoiling his evening's pleasure, or so she thought. She might almost have spoken, but the encounter had been over so quickly. And what would she have said?

She had had a busy morning, shopping for curtain material

for Laurel's room and ordering a bookcase and desk to make the room more useful and attractive. But somehow it made her feel old and depressed to be doing this for a nearly grown-up niece. Then, at Oxford Circus, she had seen a new and particularly upsetting beggar selling matches; both legs were in irons and he was sitting on a little stool, hugging himself as if in pain. She had given him sixpence and walked quickly on, telling herself firmly that there was no need for this sort of thing now, with the Welfare State. But she still felt disturbed, even at the idea that he might be sitting by his television set later that evening, no longer hugging himself as if in pain. Such a way of earning one's living seemed even more degrading than making indexes for other people's books or doing bits of hack research in the British Museum and the Public Record Office. It was for the latter that she was bound this afternoon, and the chance sight of Aylwin Forbes made her feel, in an obscure and illogical way, that there was perhaps something in research after all. She decided to walk through the gardens in front of Temple station where there were always such lovely flowers.

Viola was still sitting in the sun. Just as Dulcie had felt that there was something in research after all, so Viola felt that there was something to be said for the unintellectual, even pagan, way of life – sun worship, nudism, even something really cranky. She opened her eyes and fixed them on her red canvas shoes, so ugly, really, but comfortable for walking about and looking at City churches, which was what she intended to do that afternoon. It was not the kind of occupation in which she was likely to meet anyone that she knew, so it didn't matter what shoes she wore, or that her cotton dress would be crushed from sitting on the grass.

'Why, hullo – surely it's Viola Dace, isn't it?'

Viola looked up suspiciously, not realising who had spoken to her. Then she saw Dulcie standing over her, smiling, carrying a shopping-bag full of books and a brown-paper parcel.

'What a good idea to sit here,' she said, flopping down on the grass beside Viola, the books spilling out of her bag. 'I think I'll join you for a minute, if you don't mind. '

Viola could hardly say that she did mind, but she was not particularly anxious to see Dulcie again. I am unlovable, she thought, and unfriendly. When some nice well-meaning woman comes up to me my instinct is to shrink away.

'I was just going,' she said ungraciously. 'There's no good place to lunch round here so I brought sandwiches and ate them in the open air with all the office workers.' She laughed self-consciously, dissociating herself from them.

'Poor things, I suppose they'll have to hurry back soon,' said Dulcie. 'Now tell me what you've been doing since we last met.'

Viola shrank even further into her shell at this disconcerting question. What, indeed, *had* she been doing?

'I've written a couple of articles,' she lied, 'and I'm thinking of writing a novel. It seems more worthwhile than doing research,' she added provocatively.

'Yes, perhaps it may be,' Dulcie agreed. 'It's creating something of one's own, certainly, even if it isn't any good. I'm sure,' she added hastily, 'that yours will be awfully good. I should think you have the gift for observing people and getting them down on paper.'

'Oh, it won't be *that* kind of a novel,' said Viola distastefully.

'How far have you got?' asked Dulcie bluntly.

'It's only in my head at the moment, but I've made a few notes. And what have *you* been doing?' Viola counterattacked.

'Bottling fruit and making jam and chutney,' said Dulcie briskly. 'And I've also been getting a room ready for my niece who's coming to live with me soon.'

'Have you got a big house? I can't remember.'

'Yes, too big for me, anyway. It was my parents' house. It has four bedrooms.'

'But it's in the suburbs. Yes, I do remember now,' said Viola thoughtfully. 'I've got a little flat near Notting Hill Gate, but I've been having trouble with the Rent Act and various other things and I don't suppose I shall be able to afford it much longer.'

'I looked you up in the telephone book,' said Dulcie, 'but couldn't find you. I was thinking it would be pleasant to meet again.'

Viola did not answer, so Dulcie went on, 'And wasn't it a strange coincidence, just before I saw you I met Aylwin Forbes.'

'You *met* him?' asked Viola sharply. 'You mean you spoke to him?'

'No, he was going down to a train and I was coming up. I don't think he even saw me, but of course I recognized him at once. Have you seen much of him lately?' Dulcie asked, hardly meaning to be catty.

'No,' said Viola stiffly. 'Where are you going this afternoon?'

'The Public Record Office.'

'We might walk along together,' Viola suggested. 'I was

going to look at City churches. That's why I'm wearing these shoes.'

So at last it was out, the reason why she was wearing those uncharacteristic red canvas shoes. Dulcie imagined them padding brightly about the dim aisles of ruined or restored churches and wondered if the vicars would notice them. But probably there wouldn't be any vicars, only elderly vergers or caretakers, who might even be women.

'Perhaps we shall meet again,' she said rather more timidly than usual, when they reached Fleet Street.

'Yes. You must come and have a meal with me one evening,' said Viola casually, as if she might be saying it because it was expected of her, with no intention that the meal should ever really take place.

That would be nice,' said Dulcie.

'Perhaps we could fix a date now?'

'Why, certainly.'

'What about Monday, then?' said Viola flatly.

She wants to get it over as soon as possible, thought Dulcie, agreeing to Monday. 'I shall look forward to that.'

'It's 91 Carew Gardens – you ring the top bell and just walk up. Come about half past seven, will you?'

'That *will* be nice.'

'Oh, it won't be much of a meal, I can assure you. Goodbye.'

Dulcie went on her way encouraged, even by the thought of a not very good meal on Monday. One did not go out to see people for the sake of a meal, she told herself stoutly, thinking of all the things she disliked most – tripe, liver, brains, figs and semolina. She was certain that Viola needed her friendship, and was gratified that she had made this move. Work at the

Public Record Office seemed less attractive now, even though the things she had intended to look up had once concerned living people.

She turned off Fleet Street and into the doors of a learned institution which offered her library and cloakroom facilities. She decided to wash her hands, but when she went into the cloakroom she found that the washbasin was filled with flowers. It would be impossible to wash without removing the flowers, and there was nowhere to put them.

'What a nuisance,' she said, as a tall woman came into the cloakroom, 'somebody's cluttered up the basin with flowers and I wanted to wash my hands.'

'I'm very sorry,' said the woman rather stiffly. 'I'm afraid the flowers are mine. There wasn't anywhere else to put them.'

'Oh, I didn't realise,' said Dulcie apologetically. 'Of course one must put flowers in water to keep them fresh.'

'I'm taking them to an *invalid*,' said the woman, her voice rising on what sounded to Dulcie like a note of triumph.

'An *invalid*,' Dulcie repeated. 'I *am* sorry. If only I'd realised . . .' Another distressing picture was added to her day but somehow it was less disturbing than the beggar in the street, Aylwin Forbes's face in the crowd, or Viola lying on the grass in her red canvas shoes. She saw the invalid as a brave, tight-lipped person, without pathos, sitting up tidily in bed, doing good to others by her example. The kind of person to make a visiting clergyman feel small – really *he* was the one to benefit from the visit, not she . . . Dulcie could hear the voice flowing out from the pulpit. She prepared to creep away from the cloakroom, her hands unwashed, but the woman went on in a more friendly voice, 'Weren't you at the conference last month? I'm sure I remember your face.'

Dulcie said that she had been there.

'Jolly, wasn't it,' said the woman. 'And that lecture when the man fainted . . .' she broke into nervous laughter. '*That* was unexpected, if you like!'

'It certainly was,' Dulcie agreed. 'Such a pity that we heard so little of it.'

'Some problems of an editor,' repeated the woman, faintly sarcastic. 'Do you think many people *really wanted* to know about them?'

'I don't know. Does one ever really want to hear any lecture, if it comes to that? One just submits, as it were.'

'Ah, now you're going very deep,' said the woman. 'But I was curious to see Aylwin Forbes because he happens to be our vicar's brother.'

'Your vicar's *brother?*' Somehow it was an astonishing statement.

'Yes. Even an unmarried vicar may have nearest and dearest, and ours has a brother – Aylwin Forbes.'

'Well, what a coincidence,' said Dulcie.

It was only afterwards, sitting in the Public Record Office, that she realised that she had not asked the woman the name of the parish where Aylwin Forbes's brother was vicar. But a short visit to the public library would give her the information she wanted, and she decided to save it up as a kind of treat for herself.

For this was really the kind of research Dulcie enjoyed most of all, investigation – some might have said prying – into the lives of other people, the kind of work that involved poring over reference books, and street and telephone directories. It was most satisfactory if the objects of her research were not too well known, either to herself or to the world in general, for it was rather dull just to be able to look up somebody in *Who's Who*, which gave so many relevant details. *Crockford* was better because it left more to the imagination, not stooping to such personal trivia as marriages or children or recreations.

Love was a powerful incentive to this kind of research, and, ridiculous and impossible though it obviously was, Dulcie did feel that she had fallen a little in love with Aylwin Forbes. It might be that the absurd conference had served some useful purpose after all.

# CHAPTER FIVE

Laurel leaned forward anxiously in the taxi, wondering if the driver was taking her the right way. Then she saw a building that she recognized as the Albert Memorial, and sat back in her seat, relaxed. Now she would be able to take more interest in her surroundings. She wished she were going to live in one of the tall cream-coloured houses facing the park rather than with Aunt Dulcie, but perhaps that would be better than a hostel where you had to be in by half past ten. As far as she could remember, her aunt was a reasonable sort of person and quite young for an aunt, but there was nothing elegant or interesting about her. She wore tweedy clothes and sensible shoes and didn't 'make the most of herself'. Laurel's mother had told her that Dulcie hadn't bothered since a love affair had 'gone wrong'.

Now, standing in the doorway as if she had been watching out for the taxi, which indeed she had, Dulcie seemed to Laurel just like anybody's fussing aunt. It was a wonder she had been allowed to come from Paddington by herself, a young girl of eighteen who might let herself be spoken to by some strange person who would entice her away to South America, Laurel thought scornfully; only now it would probably be as near home as Bayswater.

'There you are, dear, so punctual!'

Dulcie ran out and began to help the taxi-man to unstrap the trunk. Laurel got out of the taxi with her small case and a cardboard box containing a roasting fowl and a dozen new-laid eggs which her mother had made her bring. She put them down in the doorway and looked around her.

The road was full of substantial-looking houses and bushy pollarded trees, now beginning to shed their leaves. An elderly man paused and said good-afternoon to Dulcie with exaggerated, almost foreign, deference. In a garden opposite a woman was tying up chrysanthemum plants, while from the upper window of another house a face peered out from behind net curtains. Really, it was not London at all, thought Laurel, a wave of depression overwhelming her. Of course she had known what it was like from visits to her grandparents when they had been living here, but she had been a child then and the surroundings had had the attraction of novelty. Now she was grown up and had her own idea of living in London – brightly lit streets, Soho restaurants, coffee bars, and walks and talks with people of her own age. Still, that would come later. It might not be a bad thing to stay with her aunt for a little while before she found a place of her own.

Looking at her niece, Dulcie thought nervously, why, she's a stranger now, no longer a schoolgirl but a self-contained young woman who must be treated as an equal. She began to wonder what they would find to talk about – their work and the domestic trivia that bound all women, whatever their ages, together?

'I expect you'd like to see your room,' she said, leading the way upstairs. 'I've given you the one at the back looking over the garden. I thought it would be easier for you to study there. Of course it's been redecorated.'

'Since Granny died?' Laurel prompted.

'Well, yes, it was her room. You don't mind? I thought it was the nicest.'

Laurel remembered it vividly as a child would remember – the figure in the bed (what exactly was the matter with Granny?), the faint scent of lavender water, the fire burning in the grate even in summer, the family photographs in silver frames, and the Victorian watercolour of Mount Vesuvius. But when Dulcie opened the door, of course it was all changed. The walls were pale turquoise and the paint white; there was a divan bed, an armchair, a desk, and an empty bookcase. There were no pictures on the walls now.

'I thought you'd rather choose your own things,' Dulcie explained, apologising for the room's bareness.

'Yes, of course. But I did love that picture of Vesuvius. What have you done with it?'

Dulcie wanted to explain that she too had once been a child who had loved that picture. 'It's in my room now,' she said, 'I always loved it.'

Laurel went to the window and looked out. The garden was like the garden at home on a smaller scale. There was the same early autumn richness and untidiness – windfalls lying in the grass, eaten by birds and wasps, zinnias and dahlias and early chrysanthemums.

'There's a gas ring here,' said Dulcie rather brightly, pointing to the hearth, 'and a kettle and saucepan.' It had been convenient when her mother was ill to be able to fill a hot-water bottle or heat up milk, and she had imagined that Laurel might like to make tea or coffee here. Her imaginings had not extended beyond hot drinks but, now that she came to think of it, there was no reason why she shouldn't boil an egg or heat up a tin of soup. The possibilities were endless, only the circumstances under which all this might take place remained a little vague.

'You can bring your friends up here,' she said. 'I want you to feel that you can be quite independent. I shall be independent too,' she added firmly. 'But let's go and have tea now, shall we? It's all ready in the drawing-room. I've only got to put the kettle on. I'll leave you to tidy up.'

Laurel washed her hands and then returned to her room. As she stood by the window she saw the figure of a young man moving in the garden which lay beyond. He was slight and delicate-looking with fair hair which he wore rather long. He looked interesting, the kind of person one might meet in a coffee bar. And he seemed to live here. She went downstairs feeling encouraged. Perhaps Dulcie would know him.

'I've asked some people in for coffee tonight,' said Dulcie when they were washing up. 'Mrs Beltane and Monica and Paul and Senhor MacBride-Pereira – he's a Brazilian who has a flat in Mrs Beltane's house,' she added. 'They're neighbours.'

'How nice,' said Laurel, a little overwhelmed. 'Who are Monica and Paul?'

'They're Mrs Beltane's children – at least they're grown up now. Monica is a lecturer at London University and Paul works in a flower shop his mother bought for him. He's a very nice young man. I think you'll like him.'

Laurel was sure that she wouldn't, but she made some effort with her appearance, mainly for the benefit of the unknown

44

Brazilian, of whom she had formed a rather theatrical picture. But when the guests came she saw that she had miscalculated, for Senhor MacBride-Pereira was the elderly man who had said good-afternoon to Dulcie in the road, and Paul was the young man she had seen from her window. Monica was pale and fair like her brother, but rather gauche and unfeminine, so that it hardly seemed possible that she could be the daughter of Mrs Beltane, so scented and jingling with bracelets, carrying her little poodle, blue-rinsed to match her hair.

'Felix will be *very* good,' she announced. 'I've brought his own little cushion.' She placed a small rose-coloured brocade cushion edged with fringe down on the hearthrug.

Laurel, feeling that the presence of an animal was a good opening to conversation, put down her hand to stroke the small square muzzle thrusting itself up towards her.

'Hullo, Felix!' she said.

The little black beady eyes glared malevolently. Suddenly he snapped up at her bracelet and tweaked it from her wrist.

'His little teeth are so strong,' said Mrs Beltane fondly. 'Has he broken one of the links, the naughty little person?'

'It's all right,' said Laurel, rather confused. 'The clasp wasn't very good, anyway.'

'I hope it isn't damaged,' said Paul, who seemed to be as embarrassed as Laurel. He had a very quiet voice and beautiful brown eyes. 'May I see?'

Laurel handed him the bracelet.

'Yes, it is the clasp,' he said. 'I can get it mended for you very quickly.'

'It seems to be the least we can do,' said Monica brusquely.

'In Brazil –' Senhor MacBride-Pereira began.

'Now we know what you're going to say,' said Mrs Beltane

teasingly. 'We all know how you Latins treat animals, you nasty brutes! But Felix has been very naughty and I don't think Miss Mainwaring is going to let him have one of his favourite petit-fours, are you, Miss Mainwaring?'

Dulcie, busy pouring out the coffee, made a polite answer. She had not really catered for Felix, and it would certainly not have occurred to her to offer a dog a petit-four. 'Would he like a plain biscuit?' she suggested.

'No, thank you, we wouldn't, would we, Felix,' said Mrs Beltane in a doting tone. 'We don't like plain biscuits, do we. We like petit-fours.'

Felix, perhaps feeling that after all he was going to get something to eat, rose from his cushion and bounced about the room, yapping with excitement.

'There's nothing like an animal for breaking the ice,' said Mrs Beltane complacently. 'I find that wherever I go with Felix.'

'He breaks more than ice,' said Monica, with an attempt at laughter. 'We really must apologise for him.'

'You have no animal, Miss Mainwaring? No *pet*, as the English say?' asked Senhor MacBride-Pereira.

'No, I somehow haven't felt the need for one,' said Dulcie, thinking that, with her broken love affair and family upheavals, it was rather surprising that she had not. It was also surprising that Mrs Beltane, with two children, should have done so. Monica was not, perhaps, the kind of child who would welcome any lavishing of affection, but Paul always seemed to Dulcie to be very lovable. 'Perhaps when my mother died,' she went on, 'I might have got a dog or cat for company, but somehow I didn't.'

'No?' said Senhor MacBride-Pereira. 'And yet it is only the

English who would think of replacing a loved one with an animal.'

'Oh, come now, Luiz!' said Mrs Beltane in mock indignation.

'I believe you've come to London to take a secretarial course?' said Monica to Laurel. 'What do you intend to do after that?'

Laurel felt a little like a schoolgirl being interviewed by a headmistress, but she realised that Monica was trying to take a kindly interest, so she tried to sound intelligent and purposeful. 'I'd like to be secretary to a publisher,' she said. 'I think that would be awfully interesting.' She hurried over the last words, ashamed of their naivety. 'I don't really want to go into commerce or anything like that.'

'What were your best subjects at school?' Monica continued.

'I liked English and History best,' said Laurel lamely.

Ah, thought Dulcie sardonically, how many a young girl must have given the same answer to that question! And really what did it mean? A sentimental penchant for King Charles the First or even Napoleon, or a liking for the poetry of Marvell, Keats, or Matthew Arnold? That was what it had been with her, but she had been fortunate in having an ambitious English teacher and parents who, rather bewildered by the whole thing, could afford to send her to Oxford. And now she was making indexes and doing little bits of research for people with more original minds than herself. What, as Miss Lord would ask, did it lead to? And what answer should a girl give now when asked what had been her favourite subjects at school? Russian and nuclear physics were perhaps too far advanced, as yet, but English and History would hardly do.

'I am a lecturer in botany,' said Monica.

'Oh, how – *interesting*,' Laurel breathed, for what answer could one make to the kind of statement designed to bring conversation to a full stop.

'Yes, it is interesting to see how the same thing has come out in our family,' said Mrs Beltane. 'My husband was a great gardener and had a gift for water divining – *not* very useful in the suburbs,' she added with a little laugh. 'Monica has this passion for botany – the scientific side, you see – while Paul is very artistic and loves flowers for their own sake. And Felix is very fond of nature too, aren't you, darling?' She looked down at the poodle, who had lapsed into silence on his little cushion.

'Where is your flower shop?' Laurel asked Paul politely.

'In Kensington, just off the High Street,' he said.

'I must come and see it some time,' said Laurel. But how, exactly? she wondered. To buy a plant or a bunch of chrysanthemums, presumably. But she could not quite see how their friendship was going to prosper on this purely commercial basis.

# CHAPTER SIX

Dulcie had not forgotten that she was going to look up Aylwin Forbes's brother in *Crockford*, but it was some days before she was near to a public library, and when she went into the reading room she found that the clerical directory was in use. A shabbily dressed man with a raffish air appeared to be taking down names and addresses, perhaps with a view to writing begging letters to unsuspecting clergymen. Dulcie always found a public library a little upsetting, for one saw so many odd people there, and it must be supposed that a certain proportion came in because they had nowhere else to go. Others were less easy to classify and less worrying. Why, for instance, was a reasonably prosperous-looking middle-aged woman – the smartness of her clothes detracted from the dowdy laced-up shoes that told of bad feet – so anxious to get hold of a pre-war *Kelly's Directory of Somerset?*

At last *Crockford* was free, and Dulcie set to work. There were several clergymen called Forbes, but she finally picked out one as being the most likely brother for Aylwin Forbes,

49

and vicar of the parish where the lady who had cluttered up the washbasin with the flowers lived, and perhaps even 'worshipped'.

'FORBES, Neville Arthur Brandreth. – Univ. of Lond. B.A. 1937. Kelham Th. Coll. 1938,' she read. He had been a curate in West Hampstead, then a chaplain with the Navy, and was now (since 1954) vicar of a parish in North-West London, 'Gross Inc. 626*l.* and Ho' – did that rather jolly-sounding phrase mean an income or stipend of £626 per annum and a house? she wondered. She was glad that his parish was in an accessible part of London. Indeed, when she looked on a street map, she found that it was almost within walking distance, if one were wearing comfortable shoes, of where her Uncle Bertram and Aunt Hermione lived. She must make a point of going to tea with them soon, perhaps on a Sunday. Then it might be possible to go to the evening service at the church.

She tried to picture the Reverend Neville Arthur Brandreth Forbes, but all she could see was Aylwin Forbes in a dog collar. It was difficult to tell from the entry in *Crockford* which was the elder of the two brothers. Somehow she imagined that Aylwin was the younger, for in these days it was often an elder son who went into the Church. Now was the time for the little piece of research she had been saving till last, the looking up of Aylwin in *Who's Who*. Her fingers fumbled nervously with the pages as she prayed that there might be at least a short entry for him. There was – and it gave quite a wealth of information. His date of birth was 3rd June 1912, but his parentage was not mentioned. He had married Marjorie, daughter of James Williton, no date or children given. His publications – a modest half-dozen on seventeenth- and eighteenth-century literary subjects – were listed, and his recreations given as 'conversation and wine'.

Dulcie closed the book with a slight feeling of distaste. 'Conversation and wine' – what an affectation! He had got little enough of either at the conference – she smiled to herself at the memory of his avoiding conversation with ladies and sipping the cold dark wine in Derbyshire. And for you, she thought, a wife will go back to her mother, an unhappy woman will lie on the grass, wearing red canvas shoes and not caring about anything. And perhaps another – usually so 'sensible' – will begin to think she is falling in love . . . It was not to be considered for a moment.

Dulcie turned out of the reading room and walked down the steps, her mind full of confused plans for the future. She did not remember until she was nearly home that Laurel would be there in the evening, and was conscious of a slight feeling of dismay that she would not have the house to herself, that she would have to make conversation with a girl of eighteen.

But hardly had she entered the house when the telephone rang. It was Laurel, asking if it would be all right if she stayed in town for the evening. Some of them were going to a coffee bar for a snack, but she wouldn't be late. Dulcie urged her not to miss the last bus, purposely putting its time a little earlier than it actually was. Ought I now to worry? she asked herself, trying to put herself into her sister Charlotte's place, imagining that Laurel was her own child. If I had married Maurice, she thought doubtfully, I might have had a child, but the picture of herself as a mother did not become real. It was Maurice who had been the child. Theirs would have been one of those rather dreadful marriages, with the wife a little older and a little taller and a great deal more intelligent than the husband. Yet, although she was laughing, there was a small ache in her heart as she remembered him. Perhaps it is sadder to have loved somebody 'unworthy', and the end of it is the death of such a very little thing, like a child's coffin, she thought confusedly.

The evenings are drawing in, she said to herself, going to the window. In the dusk, men were coming home from the City, striding briskly along the road, looking forward to a drink and a meal. And Paul Beltane was coming to the house, carrying a sheaf of roses: the long, pale, thornless kind – rather like himself, Dulcie thought, so gentle and lacking in manly toughness.

'Good evening,' she said, anticipating his ring by opening the front door.

'Oh – Miss Mainwaring. Good evening.'

Dulcie was not the sort of woman to make some immediate and rapturous comment when somebody appeared on the doorstep with a bunch of flowers. After all they might not necessarily – indeed, could hardly be for her.

'You wanted to see Laurel?' she asked sympathetically.

'Yes, I brought the bracelet back. I think it'll be all right now. And these flowers . . .' he flushed.

Poor boy, thought Dulcie, he had not expected an aunt.

'How kind of you,' she said. 'I'm sure she'll be very pleased. I'm afraid she isn't in yet, but I'll tell her you called.'

Paul walked away, his hands, now that he had nothing to carry, hanging rather sadly at his sides. They looked a little red – from being in and out of water all the time, Dulcie supposed. Of course it's really nothing for him to bring a bunch of hot-house roses, she thought, hardening her heart against him. They would just be left over from the shop and would probably be dead tomorrow.

She arranged the flowers in a vase and took them up to Laurel's room. Entering a little nervously into the girl's private territory, she was nevertheless curious to see what she would find there.

The first thing she saw was the unmade bed – a peculiarly shocking sight at six o'clock in the evening. No doubt Laurel had been in too much of a hurry to make it this morning. But who had she supposed was going to make it? If Dulcie put the flowers on the table, Laurel would realise that she had been in the room and must therefore have seen the bed and would make some comment on it. And clothes all over the room, too, stockings on the floor, and drawers half open! Why, the child hadn't even unpacked properly!

Dulcie stood in the middle of the room, the vase of roses still in her hand. She was just about to go downstairs again, when her eye was caught by the photograph of a young man on the little table by the bed. She had not realised that Laurel had a boyfriend. Certainly Charlotte had said nothing about it. Bending over to study the photograph more closely she saw that it was signed, and with a name vaguely familiar to her. Then she realised that it was a popular singer on the wireless and television of rock-and-roll, jive, skiffle, or whatever they called it. It was a young, brooding face with an elaborate hairstyle. The signature was in block capitals, as if he had no handwriting of his own.

Dulcie went downstairs, smiling to herself. She would give the flowers to Laurel when she came in, without revealing that she had been into her room. Then she need make no comment on the unmade bed if she did not feel inclined to. She set about preparing her supper. It would have to be one of those classically simple meals, the sort that French peasants are said to eat and that enlightened English people sometimes enjoy rather self-consciously – a crusty French loaf, cheese, and lettuce and tomatoes from the garden. Of course there should have been wine and a lovingly prepared dressing of oil and vinegar, but Dulcie drank orange squash and ate mayonnaise that came from a bottle. While she ate she read an old bound volume (*circa* 1911) of *Every Woman's Encyclopaedia*, thankful that it was not in these days necessary to join 'a working party for charity', making useful garments for 'the poor'. She wondered what kind of clergyman Aylwin Forbes's brother was – did he preside at working parties, where the ladies made things for the church bazaar and the appearance of the vicar and the tea were the high spots? She could almost imagine Aylwin himself in such a role. It was, perhaps, a pity that she so seldom went to church. She wondered if Laurel ought to go – if her mother would wish her to; that might be another worry.

Later, when the girl came in, her eyes shining from the impact of coffee bar and London on a fine early autumn evening, Dulcie wondered if the time was approaching when she would have to enjoy herself in the lives of younger people, as mothers were said to – waiting up eagerly to hear about the dance and what the young man had said, and often getting precious little out of it, for all the waiting up with knitting and a dying fire and the kettle or saucepan of milk ready to be boiled for the hot drink. She rejected the picture of herself doing this as quickly as it came into her mind. Laurel was not late – indeed, it was barely ten o'clock – but suddenly Dulcie felt the desire to be a little annoyed; she decided that she would mention the unmade bed after all.

'Paul Beltane brought back your bracelet and these roses for you,' she said. 'And when I took them up to your room I noticed that you hadn't made your bed.'

'Sorry, I thought your Miss What's-it came today,' said Laurel, her attention on the roses. 'How sweet of him! I must thank him some time.'

'Miss Lord doesn't make beds,' said Dulcie rather stiffly. 'At least, not our beds. So you must make your own. Yes, they're lovely roses, aren't they. Will you write him a little note or call in the shop, perhaps, on your way home tomorrow?' Dulcie saw Laurel doing this as it might have been herself. She imagined Paul emerging from behind vases of tall exotic flowers, or sitting patiently making a wreath or a cross.

'Yes, I could do that,' said Laurel, not revealing which alternative she had decided upon.

'Are you making some nice friends at the secretarial college?' Dulcie went on, feeling more like an aunt.

'Yes, the girl I was with this evening has a lovely bed-sitting-room in Quince Square.'

'Quince Square, did you say?'

'Yes, near Holland Park – very convenient.' Laurel saw again the dark trees – some of them really *were* quinces, Marian had said – and felt the nearness of London through them. She longed for the impersonality of the hall as one came into the house, the utter privacy of Marian's room, with its concealed washbasin and the little electric cooker in a cupboard where she really cooked meals.

Quince Square, thought Dulcie. Some of those big houses had no doubt been turned into nests of bed-sitting-rooms where young girls dreamed or lonely women remembered, or perhaps dreamed too. Did Aylwin Forbes have a whole house, or just a flat? She must investigate.

'I know somebody who lives in Quince Square,' she began, but at that moment the telephone rang.

It was a woman's voice, unfamiliar to Dulcie until she told her name.

'This is Viola Dace.'

'Oh, how nice!' Dulcie's instinctive reaction was one of pleasure, then she wondered why Viola should be telephoning her and hoped she wasn't going to put off the supper invitation.

'I wonder if I might ask a favour of you?'

'Yes, of course.' Help with a piece of research, or an index to be made at very short notice – these unlikely and rather dreary alternatives came into her mind. 'What is it?' she asked.

Viola lowered her voice. 'I can't go into details here and now, but I've had a row with the woman whose house I'm living in and I wondered if you could possibly put me up for a time – I'd pay, of course.'

'Why, certainly . . .' Dulcie was so overwhelmed that she could hardly think what to say.

'You did say you had room,' Viola went on, 'and of course it would only be for a week or two, until I found somewhere else. I know it seems rather a lot to ask . . .'

'Not at all – it would be nice to have you,' said Dulcie. 'When would you want to come?'

'Well, perhaps we could discuss that when you come to supper.'

'Yes – all right then. I'm looking forward to that very much.'

'Oh, it won't be anything, I can assure you,' said Viola, and rang off.

Dulcie came away from the telephone with mixed feelings. She realised dimly that Viola was making use of her, yet it was flattering to feel that she had been chosen, even to be made use of. Though perhaps she had been approached only as a very last resort – 'that big house, plenty of room, but in the *suburbs* . . . a woman I met at the conference in August – rather dreary but a good-natured soul . . .'

Going into the kitchen she saw Laurel and wondered for a moment who she was, for she had imagined Viola in Laurel's room. Suddenly it had been Viola boiling the little saucepan of milk, heating up the tin of spaghetti, waking with the dawn chorus and making the quiet cup of tea. And all Laurel did was to leave her bed unmade – which Viola might also do – and have a photograph of a skiffle musician by her bed, where Viola might have Aylwin Forbes. But where was Viola to sleep?

'That was a friend of mine,' Dulcie explained. 'She wants to come and stay here for a bit.'

'Oh, but which room will she have?'

'Well, there's the spare room, or the little room over the porch, but that's a bit small.'

'And the spare room's got the ironing board and the sewing machine in it, not to mention "Prosperity" and "Adversity", and "The Last Watch of Hero".'

'Yes, it has,' Dulcie admitted, for she had deposited these favourite pictures of her mother's there, not liking to send them to a jumble sale so soon after her death, though the Scouts had called hopefully and, it must be admitted, most respectfully, with their little hand-cart less than a week after the funeral. She had given them only the shabbiest of her mother's clothes, the best having gone to the Distressed Gentlewomen. 'I don't think Viola will mind the pictures,' she went on. 'After all, it'll only be for a week or two.'

'It will be nice company for you,' said Laurel rather patronisingly.

'Nice company?' echoed Dulcie dreamily. 'Oh, yes it will.'

# CHAPTER SEVEN

Viola had said 'about half past seven', but Dulcie, too early in her eagerness, found herself approaching Carew Gardens nearly a quarter of an hour before that time. She began to walk more slowly, looking over the railings into the 'gardens', which consisted of a long strip of dry-looking grass, bordered with flower-beds and paths, and shaded by top-heavy trees about to shed their leaves. A woman was walking along one of the paths with a dog on a lead. She wore a grey tweed coat and transparent pink nylon gloves, and carried two books from the public library in a contraption of rubber straps. What is the use of noticing such details? Dulcie asked herself. It isn't as if I were a novelist or a private detective. Presumably such a faculty might be said to add to one's enjoyment of life, but so often what one observed was neither amusing nor interesting, but just upsetting.

There was hardly enough to occupy her for ten minutes in the road; perhaps she would have to arrive too early after all. Then she noticed that there was a telephone box ahead. She could spend the time making a telephone call, though to whom she could not think, even when she had shut herself into the box. An anonymous call of a scurrilous nature? Were calls of this kind made by people who had an odd ten minutes to fill in before arriving somewhere? Dulcie could think of nobody to telephone at this moment, when most people would be preparing or eating the evening meal, but she might do a little research in the directories. Why, for instance, had she not thought of looking up Aylwin Forbes's mother-in-law? Williton was an unusual name: indeed, as she ran her finger down the columns, Dulcie saw that there were no more than half a dozen, and out of these it was not difficult to pick out 'Williton, Mrs Grace, 37 Deodar Grove, S.W.13' as being the right one. The discovery excited her, for the address was so near where she herself lived, and she left the box quickly, unable to fill in time any longer. A song was ringing in her head, something that began 'Under the deodar tree'. She wondered if Viola knew.

'I know I'm too early,' she said breathlessly, as Viola came to the door, 'but I thought I could probably help in some way.' She saw herself preparing vegetables (though they might be frozen) scraping potatoes, grinding coffee beans, beating egg whites, opening a difficult tin, laying the table . . . 'There must be something I can do.'

'Yes, there might be,' said Viola vaguely. 'I'm afraid we still have another flight of stairs to climb.'

'Oh, that's all right,' said Dulcie gallantly. 'I always think it's nice to be high up.'

Her first impression of the house, with its peeling paint and dingy stair carpet of a colour that could only be described as 'fawn', had not been particularly reassuring. The neighbourhood had obviously 'gone down' and she was surprised that Viola should be content to live in it.

The room was a little better than she had expected, because it was on a corner with two large windows and an impression of greenness from the paint of the woodwork and the glimpse of trees beyond. Inside, she was struck by two things: the room was indescribably untidy, and there was no sign whatever that any kind of meal was being prepared. It was difficult to imagine oneself eating among the confusion of books, clothes, papers and cosmetics that seemed to occupy every flat surface. On one wall hung a large ornate crucifix, of the kind that is put up for artistic effect rather than as a sign of devotion. Dulcie remembered Viola saying that she was an Anglo-Catholic, and now wondered if she were one of the non-practising kind, who had been driven to it by boredom with the more ordinary church services.

'I've been sorting out a few things,' said Viola. 'I can't bring all my junk to you, can I?'

'Well, I have an attic,' said Dulcie doubtfully.

'But I feel I must make a clean break with the past,' said Viola, taking up a fringed Spanish shawl and draping it untidily over one end of the divan bed.

The past? thought Dulcie, wondering about the Spanish shawl which did not seem to fit in with the kind of past that people had nowadays.

'My father got it in Seville for my mother,' Viola explained.

'Oh, yes, in Holy Week,' said Dulcie. 'That's a great thing about Seville, isn't it – all those processions.' Then, thinking of the pictures 'Prosperity' and 'Adversity', she went on, 'Family things are rather difficult to dispose of. One never knows . . .'

Were they not to have a meal of any kind? she wondered. That cupboard over by the door – was it possible that it contained food? There was a gas-ring in the hearth, and a kettle, but no sign of any other kind of cooking utensils. Perhaps it was not surprising that Viola had said ' It won't be much,' when it was apparently to be nothing.

'I suppose we ought to be thinking about supper,' Viola said unpromisingly. 'I got some things when I was out, and there's a tin of soup we could heat up.'

'Oh, let me open it,' said Dulcie eagerly.

Viola handed her a tin-opener and began to unpack a shopping basket which had been lying in a corner. Dulcie saw cartons of exotic salads, cold meats wrapped in greaseproof paper, and a bag of croissants. How extravagant, she thought warmly, feeling that it was typical of Viola.

When they were sitting down to eat, Dulcie said, 'Did you know that Aylwin Forbes's mother-in-law lives quite near me?'

'Really?' Viola seemed uninterested. 'I didn't know, but it seems so remote.'

'Oh, it's not far – Deodar Grove.'

'I meant the connection – his wife's mother. Not even a blood relation. There could be nothing of *him* in Deodar Grove.' She pronounced the last words distastefully.

'No, perhaps not. But you never know.' Dulcie was a little damped. It had seemed exciting, finding the right name in the telephone directory; now perhaps it was nothing after all.

Hoping to start a conversation that Viola might find more interesting, she asked, 'Did you have a quarrel with your landlady here? Is that why you want to leave?'

'Yes, in a way. She said the daily woman found it impossible to clean my room because it was so untidy.'

Dulcie imagined the untidiness transferred to her own house, and tried not to look around her.

'And I had friends here late at night – even a man, once.'

Was it Aylwin Forbes? Dulcie wondered, unable to see him in such surroundings. 'A man,' she repeated. 'Yes, some land-ladies do seem to object to men; on principle, I suppose – leaning their brilliantined heads against the backs of chairs, knocking out their pipes on the furniture, clumping heavily up and down the stairs – it's for things like that, isn't it, rather than for fear of a woman's reputation. Well, you can certainly have men to see you when you're living in my house – as many as you like,' she added in a jovial tone, thus somehow spoiling the whole picture of Viola as a *femme fatale*. 'My niece is staying with me now, so we shall be quite a houseful of women. Like some dreadful novel,' she said quickly, fearing that it really might be like that. 'Shall I help you to wash up?'

'No, thank you, I'll do it when you've gone. We might have some coffee now.'

The coffee was very good, and they sat talking for some time.

'It will be a relief to get away from here,' Viola said. 'I find it painful being so near him.'

Dulcie suddenly wished that she had brought her knitting. There was that look about Viola that presaged the outpour-ing of confidences. It would have added a cosiness to the occasion – hot coffee, purring gas-fire, women knitting and talking. Or, rather, one talking while the other knitted in a kind of wildness and desperation, yet with the satisfaction of seeing a sleeve grow. And now, when it came, there was really nothing to tell. Viola had seen no more of Aylwin Forbes than had Dulcie herself. It was the pain of his near-ness that she wanted to enlarge upon – only four or five minutes' brisk walk away in Quince Square, and yet so utterly remote.

'Perhaps I could walk past the house on my way back,' said Dulcie.

'I'll come with you to the bus stop,' said Viola eagerly, getting up from her chair.

'Yes, it's nearly ten o'clock,' said Dulcie, feeling that she was being pushed away rather early. 'Perhaps I should be going.'

'The buses may stop running,' said Viola, 'and you've a long journey.'

'You knew, of course, that his brother is a clergyman?' said Dulcie as they walked out of the house.

'Yes, I did. A rather dreary vicar somewhere in North London,' said Viola.

'He doesn't *sound* dreary – Neville Arthur Brandreth Forbes. I plan to take a look at him some time. It should be possible to go to a service at his church.'

'Hush – this is Quince Square. He might be . . .'

'You mean Aylwin might be taking the dog for a walk?'

'I don't think he has a dog.'

'Well, not literally, perhaps. But going for some sort of evening stroll – smoking a last pipe or something like that.'

'This is the house – this next one,' said Viola, almost in a whisper. It was solid and richly creamy, with new paint glistening in the lamplight. There was a brass dolphin knocker on the gleaming black door. A sound of braying laughter, somewhat out of keeping with the dignified appearance of the house, could be heard coming from the basement.

'The servants listening to a television programme,' said Viola distastefully.

'Servants?' echoed Dulcie incredulously. 'Do people have *servants* nowadays – I mean, ordinary people like Aylwin Forbes?'

'He seems to be quite well-off, but actually the "servants" go with the house, I think. He has a maisonnette on the two top floors,' Viola explained.

'His parentage isn't mentioned in *Who's Who*,' said Dulcie. 'I suppose there could be money in his family.'

The concentration of one's thoughts on a particular person can sometimes have the effect of making him appear in the flesh, and so it was on this occasion. The front door of the house opened, and Aylwin Forbes came out. He looked older than Dulcie had remembered, and was informally dressed in a blue cardigan, old grey trousers, and red slippers.

It would have been better, Dulcie thought, as so often on these occasions, if they had not seen him or he had not seen them – if they could have slipped quietly away without having to say anything. As it was, she felt herself cringing with embarrassment at Viola's false-sounding exclamations of surprise, and at Aylwin's response which seemed almost to be – and perhaps *was* – one of dismay.

'Why, Viola and Miss – er . . .'

'Mainwaring,' said Dulcie quickly.

'Of course! We met at the conference, didn't we? I had no idea you lived round here.'

'I don't, as a matter of fact,' said Dulcie unhelpfully.

'Oh, I see.'

The little party walked on in silence.

'Miss Mainwaring has been dining with me. I have a flat in Carew Gardens,' said Viola.

'Dining' was perhaps not quite the word, thought Dulcie,

and neither was 'flat'. And why did she have to say *Miss* Mainwaring, making her sound like a worthy elderly female?

'I was on my way to post a letter,' he said, though no letter was in his hand.

'Miss Mainwaring has to catch a bus,' said Viola.

'Yes, I live miles away beyond Hammersmith,' said Dulcie, making a joke of it, as suburban dwellers sometimes must.

'Ah, yes,' said Aylwin, with a thoughtful air, as if he might be remembering the house in Deodar Grove where his wife now was. 'Here is the pillar-box,' he said, for there was no getting away from it. He fumbled in his pockets. 'But I seem to have forgotten my letter. How stupid of me!'

The women made no comment, and after saying goodnight he left them and went back to his house, presumably to fetch, or even to write, the letter.

'Somehow he reminds me of Rupert Brooke,' said Dulcie enthusiastically, when he was out of earshot.

'Rupert Brooke, good heavens!' There was contempt in Viola's tone. That handsome *vieux-jeu* kind of face, and the slender volume of poems that so many schoolgirls bought in the nineteen-twenties. 'My mother's favourite poet. Do you really think so?'

'I thought he had a look of him. And yet,' said Dulcie thoughtfully, 'Aylwin just misses perfection – there's the Greek-statue look, something blunted or marred about the features . . . Look, here's my bus. I think I'd better get it.'

'Goodbye,' said Viola. 'I'll see you on Friday.'

She turned away from the bus stop and hurried back past the house in Quince Square. But the door was shut and now from the basement came an unknown man's voice, saying unctuously, 'The tea is *delicious* and the packet is val-u-able!'

Then there was a snatch of song, like a little Elizabethan catch adapted to television advertising.

He had been gravely lacking in hospitality, not to have asked them to come in, thought Aylwin, hurrying up to his study and picking up the letter from the table. But Miss Mainwaring had a bus to catch – she would not have wanted to be delayed. She lived far away, in the same direction as his wife's mother, in that depressing house facing the common. He had not always found it

*Thanked be fortune, it hath been otherwise*
*Twenty times better,*

he thought. Once it had seemed the height of romanticism, on a January day shortly after their first meeting, with the stone squirrel in the next door garden, and Marjorie's pretty little face peeping through the net curtains that her mother had put up at every window, waiting for him to come to tea on a Sunday afternoon. He would have done anything for her in those days, have snatched even the stone squirrel from its hard earthy bed and pressed it into her hands as a ridiculous romantic present, meeting unembarrassed the surprised stare of his future mother-in-law as he waited with it on the doorstep.

He wished now that he could have asked the two women – Viola and Miss Mainwaring (had she no Christian name?) – in for a drink. A whisky, perhaps, or tea out of the big blue dragon cups. That would have been safe and cosy. And there would have been no danger of an embarrassing scene with poor Vi if Miss Mainwaring had been there.

As it was, he put down the letter again and turned to the material which his assistant editor had sent him for the January issue of his journal. 'Some problems of an editor', he thought, as various difficulties presented themselves. Then, bringing his fist down on the table, he heard himself saying aloud words that normally one only sees written.

'The Editor's decision is final,' he declared. 'No review shall exceed a thousand words.'

# CHAPTER EIGHT

Laurel was not sure exactly where the flower shop was, but she had been reluctant to ask Dulcie as she did not want her to know that she was going to call there. She must thank Paul for having got her bracelet mended and for the roses, and it would be much more interesting to call and see him than to write a stiff little note, or to go to his house and perhaps have to meet his terrifying blue-haired mother with her spoilt little poodle.

She hoped it would not turn out to be one of those big smart shops with chic flower arrangements, where inquiries as to the price of bunches that looked within one's means would be met with contempt – for she would have to buy something and was rather short of money. But when she found the street she saw to her relief that the shops in it were small, almost mean, and the flower shop itself reassuringly modest. She approached it cautiously, noticing the name 'Mirabelle', and looked in through the window. There was nobody visible inside, so she went on looking, studying the rows of plants and cacti arranged in the front, the fancy potholders and hideous vases, and at the back the green tins of gladioli, dahlias and chrysanthemums. In one corner, with the sacks of compost and fertilizer, there were some garden objects, rabbits and gnomes and little animals of indeterminate species, looking peculiarly sad in the dusk. And Paul, who now emerged from somewhere behind the rabbits and gnomes, also looked sad.

His face brightened a little when he saw Laurel, but it was a moment before either of them spoke.

'Good evening,' said Laurel at last, a little stiffly.

Paul returned her greeting.

'I came to thank you for getting my bracelet mended so quickly, and for the lovely roses.'

'Oh, that's all right.'

'I suppose you'll be closing soon? I wasn't sure if you'd still be open.'

'Yes, I usually close at six or sometimes half past. People seem to buy flowers on their way home.'

'Guilty husbands, I suppose,' said Laurel frivolously, then, seeing his puzzled look, regretted her remark.

'It seems to be mostly women,' he said seriously.

Women like Aunt Dulcie, Laurel thought, going back to dull and lonely rooms which they hoped to brighten with a bunch of cheap zinnias.

'Well, I must buy something,' she said.

'You don't have to.' A faint smile came on to his face. 'I expect Miss Mainwaring has plenty of flowers in her garden still.'

'Yes, of course, but I might get a plant for my room. A cactus, perhaps.' She peered rather desperately at the rows of plants, with their harsh spiky leaves. 'Or something trailing,' she went on more hopefully, fingering a variegated ivy. 'That might be better.' She wished he would help her to choose instead of standing silently, almost deferentially, at her side. She wondered if it was going to be embarrassing to pay, slipping the money into his hand with a little joke if she could think of one. At last she decided on a tradescantia with striped mauve leaves, and he took it away to wrap it up for her. In the back of the shop she now noticed a half-finished wreath – white carnations were being stuck into a heart-shaped base.

'Are you making a wreath?' she asked in a bright social tone, thinking as she did so what a very odd remark it was to make to anyone.

'Yes, it's a bleeding heart,' he said solemnly. 'There will be a spray of red carnations coming out of the side here.'

'What a strange idea. Rather horrible, in a way.'

'They're very popular round here. You see, this isn't really the grandest part of Kensington.'

Laurel smiled. 'No, I suppose there the wreaths might be more conventional or they might say "cut flowers only", or even no flowers at all. I wonder why poorer people make more of death? Are the upper and middle classes afraid of showing their feelings in such an obvious way?'

Paul smiled a little nervously, but seemed unable to add anything to the discussion.

'I must be going,' said Laurel, wondering if she had frightened him with her brittle, party manner. 'Oh, and the plant – how much is it?'

'Three and six,' he said.

Laurel found a half-crown and two sixpences in her purse; she could hardly have borne to have received change from him.

'Goodbye,' she said, 'and thank you again.'

Paul would have liked to say something more, to ask her to go out with him one evening, but he was too shy to think of anything quickly enough.

A pity he's so dumb, Laurel thought, hurrying out into the dusk, but there would surely be other meetings. The encounter, as was only to be expected when it had taken place in anticipation so many times, had been disappointing. Paul seemed younger and more callow than she had remembered, though his brown eyes were even more beautiful. Perhaps, really, she liked older men better; even the slightly ridiculous gallantry of Senhor MacBride-Pereira, whom she met in the road, was not unpleasing to her.

'A young English girl with a pot plant – what could be more charming . . .'

It was difficult to know how to answer this. Perhaps a Brazilian girl would not be seen carrying a pot plant and the sight was therefore unusual?

'I've bought it for my room,' she said.

'Ah, your "bed-sitter".' He brought out the word triumphantly, for he prided himself on his command of English slang.

Laurel watched him walk slowly away towards the pillar-box, turning out his feet in their orange suede shoes.

When she reached her aunt's house, she saw a taxi outside the gate. The driver, grumbling under his breath, was unloading suitcases and carrying them into the house. In the hall she found her aunt and a tall, untidy-looking woman in a rather dirty red coat, anxiously counting out money. Then she remembered with a slight sinking feeling that this was the evening when Miss Dace – Viola – was coming to stay. Dulcie had warned her about it at breakfast.

Repressed spinster, thought Laurel dispassionately, for Dulcie had said that she might be 'in rather a nervous state'. Life had, apparently, been a bit difficult. Well, it usually was, thought Laurel with all the easy scorn of her eighteen years. Life might improve if Miss Dace – could one *possibly* call her Viola? – were to send that coat to the cleaner and get herself a new hair style.

'This is my niece Laurel,' said Dulcie rather nervously. She had put a macaroni cheese in the oven and was now worrying lest it should not be enough . 'I expect you're in the middle of cooking dinner,' Viola had said, which made Dulcie wonder whether she had not better open a tin of some kind of meat and have the macaroni cheese as a first course. Viola had always seemed to eat so little, and was it not, perhaps, better to begin as one meant to go on, with the bigger meal in the middle of the day and a rather small supper? Surely she would not expect meat twice a day?

Viola also had her thoughts. It had seemed such a *very* long way in the taxi, as she watched the fare mounting up on the clock and familiar landmarks were left behind. Olympia had seemed the last bulwark of civilization. And then, when they came to the suburban roads, with people doing things in gardens, she had wanted to tap on the glass and tell the driver to turn back. Now, standing in the hall, she saw that the house was quite spacious. There was a glimpse of a pleasant garden through French windows – just like a scene in a play. Through another open door she could see a table laid for a meal – and there were several decanters on the Edwardian oak sideboard, one of which had some brownish-looking liquid in the bottom. Could it be whisky or sherry or brandy, perhaps, kept for 'medicinal' purposes only?

'You'll want to see your room,' said Dulcie, fussing rather. 'I'm afraid it's got some old pictures in it – I mean just *old* not in the sense of Old Masters. My mother was fond of them – they had belonged to *her* mother – so you see . . .'

'Yes, the taste of another age,' said Viola in a detached tone, examining the pictures. 'How very prosperous "Prosperity" looks, with that elaborate *coiffure*, lace at the throat, and all those pearls. And beside her, on that well-polished mahogany table, a dish – or perhaps an epergne – filled with hot-house grapes and peaches.'

'Yes, but she has a nice expression,' said Dulcie. 'Like the wife of a Conservative Member of Parliament about to open a bazaar, don't you think?'

'"Adversity" seems more modern,' Viola continued. 'That lank hair and waif-like expression – one sees so many typists and girls in coffee bars looking like that.'

'This is your bed, of course,' said Dulcie, indicating the divan with its striped folk-weave cover. 'It's rather narrow, but quite comfortable, I think.'

Viola examined it, testing the mattress with her hand, as if Dulcie were an ordinary landlady and she were deciding whether to take the room or not. 'I'm sure it will be quite comfortable,' she said.

'The bathroom is at the end of the passage,' said Dulcie, 'and supper will be ready whenever you are. There's nothing to spoil.'

Then it couldn't be anything exquisite like a lobster soufflé, Viola thought. She would smoke a cigarette while unpacking, and take her time. After a while she ventured out to the bath-room. It was an old-fashioned comfortable room with a faded rose-patterned carpet on the floor and the bath encased in mahogany. A shelf on the wall held a selection of books, their covers now faded and buckled by steam. Viola noticed *The Brothers Karamazov*, *Poems of Gray and Collins*, *Enquire Within*, *The Angel in the House*, and a few old Boots Library books, *A Voice Through a Cloud*, *Some Tame Gazelle*, and *The Boys from Sharon*. By the bath there was a tin of Gumption and a rag. Does she expect me to clean the bath? thought Viola with a sudden uprising of indignation. Of course one gave it a token swill around after use, leaving it perhaps not *exactly* as one would wish to find it, but Gumption and all that was hardly what she had expected. She went down to supper still feeling slightly indignant, as if she had really been giving the bath a good clean instead of only imagining herself doing it.

'There is some sherry here,' said Dulcie in a surprised tone, going to the sideboard and lifting up the decanter Viola had seen through the open door. 'Would you like some?'

'Thank you, that would be nice . . .'

'Macaroni cheese is the first course. Then there will be cold meat and salad,' said Dulcie rather firmly. 'Is that sherry all right?'

'Actually it seems to be whisky, but that's even better.'

'How stupid of me! I don't drink much myself, and now that I come to think of it my father did keep his whisky in that decanter. Wouldn't you like some water or soda with it?'

Sometimes neat whisky is the only drink, thought Viola, declining Dulcie's offer and wondering if there were to be many such meals, with the two of them making polite conversation and the silent niece watching them with the critical eyes of youth.

Let them get on with it, thought Laurel. She would be off to her bed-sitting-room in Quince Square as soon as there was a vacancy in the house where Marian lived. She tried to cheer herself up by thinking of Paul, but all she could remember were his cold-looking hands and the wreaths of wax flowers not favoured by the better-class Kensington residents.

Fancy that whisky being here all this time! thought Dulcie. Nobody had touched it since Father's death three years ago. A house where there was drink that was not drunk – she had not imagined that her house would be such a one. She would go to the wine merchant tomorrow and order something suitable. But was this 'beginning as she meant to go on'? Wouldn't it be better to let Viola bring in her own secret bottles?

The meal finished. 'Shall we wash up *before* we have coffee?' Dulcie asked. 'I always think it's nice to get the things out of the way.'

'Just as you like,' said Viola, who had not imagined herself washing up. Her inclination would have been to leave everything till the morning.

Laurel seemed to have disappeared to her room and soon afterwards the house was filled with sound – voices singing, if it could be called that, about somebody or something called a Bird-Dog – at least, that was how Dulcie in her confusion heard it, though perhaps it could hardly have been that. What were they going to do all the time, she and Viola, she wondered, as Viola silently dried the silver. Was the companionship of this rather odd woman what she really wanted? Supposing she did not get on with her after all?

These thoughts, and others like them, went through Dulcie's head as she stood bowed over the sink, but all she said was, 'What about breakfast? What time would you like it?'

'Oh, I never eat it, thank you. If I could just make tea in my room – I see there's a gas-ring.'

'Yes, of course,' said Dulcie, relieved. 'I'll give you the things.'

'I shall be rather busy,' said Viola casually, 'so you may not see very much of me.'

'You have some special job, then?'

'Yes. Aylwin has asked me to do the index for his new book.'

'Oh?' Dulcie was conscious of a ridiculous pang of jealousy. It was really too silly.

'Yes – it's really best that I should do it because I did help him a lot with the book,' said Viola rather smugly.

'I suppose he's paying you for it?' Dulcie asked, her brusque tone concealing the twinge of unworthy envy she felt at the idea of it.

'Well, no . . .' Viola hesitated. She did not want to admit to Dulcie that she had offered to do Aylwin's index, unfairly way-laying him on the steps of the British Museum so that he could hardly have refused.

'Oh, then you'll get some kind of acknowledgment in the foreword,' said Dulcie, trying to make light of it. 'Something about your having undertaken the arduous or thankless – though I hope it won't be that – task of compiling the index. But why didn't you tell me before?'

'I didn't know till yesterday.'

'How – *splendid*!' Dulcie emptied the washing-up bowl with a violent movement. 'And are you still – er – fond of him?'

Viola did not answer.

'Well, I hope you are,' Dulcie went on. 'I can imagine few tasks more distasteful than making an index for someone for whom one no longer cares. Or for whom one has ceased to care,' she emended, as if perfecting her little aphorism.

'There are some people one could never cease to care for,' said Viola, 'and I suppose Aylwin is one of those.'

'Obviously every man must be that to some woman,' said Dulcie, 'even the most unworthy man.' She had been thinking of Maurice, but surely she had ceased to 'care' for him? 'Of course,' she went on, 'those are the people from whom one asks no return of love, if you see what I mean. Just to be allowed to love them is enough.'

'Oh, I'm sorry,' said Laurel stiffly, coming into the kitchen with a little saucepan. 'I thought I might make some coffee.'

'There's plenty of milk in the larder,' said Dulcie, reassuming, much to Laurel's relief, her normal aunt-like manner. 'Take it from the bottle that's already started. Would you like to have coffee with me this evening?' she said to Viola . 'I don't suppose you'll want to get started on the index tonight, will you?'

It was nice to think that Laurel was really using that gas-ring, making herself coffee. Soon the three of them would all be making their little separate drinks.

# CHAPTER NINE

It was November before Dulcie managed to find a convenient afternoon for her expedition to Mrs Williton's house in Deodar Grove, a sad autumn day with the leaves nearly all fallen from the trees and the sky colourless, with no promise of brightness in it. She wished she had a dog to run ahead of her over the rough grass of the common, and envied two young men with a small mongrel which ran backwards and forwards ecstatically from one to the other. Then she saw that they were not as young as she had at first supposed, and the discovery added to the general melancholy of the scene – those two and their little dog against a hostile world. They talked to each other in low voices and regarded her suspiciously, though she could hardly imagine why. She plodded on in her sensible shoes, glad that she had put on a raincoat, for a few spots were beginning to fall.

On the other side of the common she could now see a row of houses. According to the map this should be Deodar Grove. It was possible to see that the houses were quite large and that most of the windows were heavily curtained in various kinds of nylon net. They had small front gardens planted with shrubs and a few decaying chrysanthemums. As she came nearer Dulcie saw that one house had a 'To be Sold' notice attached to the front wall. Fortunately it was next door to Mrs Williton's house, so that Dulcie felt justified in stopping and staring rather more intently than she could otherwise have done. The house for sale had nothing remarkable about it except a small stone squirrel, perched on a rockery in the front garden, a rather worn-looking little creature with its paws tucked up appealingly under its chin. But Dulcie was interested to notice that a good deal of bustle was going on next door – women, carrying shopping bags and parcels, were going up to the front door and walking in.

'Excuse me . . .'

Dulcie turned to see a tall dark woman with a long pale face at her side.

'That *is* Mrs Williton's house, I suppose, where everyone has been going in? I can't remember the number – my sister knew, but she and my niece have gone shopping this afternoon. Deirdre – my niece, that is, is expecting a baby.'

'Oh,' said Dulcie, rather taken aback, 'how nice for her!'

'And if it's a boy,' went on the woman in a fond tone, 'he's going to be an anthropologist like his daddy.'

'Goodness!' said Dulcie.

'That's just Digby's little joke, of course. He's my nephew by marriage of course – nephew-in-law, I suppose you'd say. Should we go in, do you think? I can't remember what time it said on the card – it must have got thrown away.'

'Yes, cards do tend to get thrown away,' said Dulcie, confused and a little excited, for so many women had been going into the house that it occurred to her that there was no reason why she should not join them.

'Let's venture then, shall we?' said the woman, sweeping Dulcie along with her. 'Mabel thought it would be in the drawing-room at the back – it's quite a big room.'

What would be in the drawing-room at the back? Dulcie wondered, not liking to ask and hoping that it was not essential that she should know.

'As a matter of fact,' said her companion, 'I have brought a few little things with me – some chutney and lemon curd, home-made of course – though it isn't exactly that kind of a sale. But every little helps, doesn't it, and it's such a good cause. Oh, look, it *is* half past three, not three o'clock, so we're not late after all.'

Dulcie looked and saw pinned to the front door a large hand-lettered poster. It said 'JUMBLE SALE – IN AID OF THE ORGAN FUND'. What a piece of luck, she thought, wondering for one wild moment if she could run back and snatch the stone squirrel from the garden of the empty house so that she too might have something to bring. But if she had brought nothing, she could perhaps buy.

'Ah, Miss Wellcome,' a little round woman had greeted Dulcie's companion, '*welcome*, if I may say so!'

'How good of you to have the sale in your drawing-room, Mrs Williton,' said Miss Wellcome, most fortunately identifying the woman Dulcie had come to see.

'Well, I thought it would be more convenient here,' said Mrs Williton, 'and after all it isn't as if it's an ordinary jumble sale – just among ourselves really, isn't it. How good of you to come,' she said turning to Dulcie. 'Are you new in the parish?'

'No, I mean, I was just passing and thought I might come

in. I can't resist a sale of any kind,' said Dulcie. 'And it did seem to be such a good cause, the organ,' she murmured.

'Yes, we all feel that Mr Lewis is worthy of a better instrument. You probably weren't in church last Sunday evening, so you didn't hear the little speech he made, so charming . . . And now I must get back to my stall – I've got my girlie helping me.' She turned to Miss Wellcome and said in a low tone, 'I expect Mrs Swan told you about *that*. Well, there it is – I always knew something like this would happen. I was afraid of it from the very first,' she added on a triumphant note.

Dulcie turned away, overwhelmed by the richness of the occasion. It was really more than she could possibly have hoped for. 'My girlie' – obviously Aylwin Forbes's wife – was, surely, the fair-haired young woman wearing a mauve twin-set, standing behind one of the trestle tables which had been arranged as stalls. Yet, thought Dulcie, going over to the stall, was she really quite young enough for that fluffy shoulder-length hair style? A closer inspection revealed that she was nearer thirty-five than twenty-five.

'How charming,' said Dulcie, boldly picking up a little pottery donkey drawing a cart. 'I can see that this is no ordinary jumble sale,' she added falsely, hoping that Mrs Aylwin Forbes would speak.

'No – people have really been very kind sending such treasures,' said Marjorie Forbes. 'It is sweet, isn't it.'

Impossible to tell whether she spoke ironically or not, Dulcie decided. Yet surely she could not have thought the object in question anything but tasteless and hideous?

'Why, it is a calendar!' said Dulcie. 'It would make a useful little present for somebody.' But who? she wondered, and then she realized, why, Miss Lord, of course. It was just the kind of thing she liked; indeed, she probably had one already. 'I'll have it,' she said, handing over half a crown.

'I'll just put a bit of paper round it for you,' said Marjorie, fumbling with a sheet of blue tissue paper. 'Oh, dear, his little head is poking through – the ears make it difficult to wrap.'

'It will go in my handbag,' said Dulcie, 'so please don't bother.'

'Oh, will it?' Marjorie went on struggling ineffectually with the paper. 'Perhaps that would be best.'

As Marjorie handed over the partially wrapped donkey Dulcie noticed that she wore a gold wedding ring engraved with a design of little flowers. Her fingers were rather stubby, with childish-looking short – perhaps bitten? – nails. It suddenly occurred to Dulcie that Aylwin Forbes had married beneath him – but why?

'There is tea over here,' said a voice at Dulcie's elbow, and she found Miss Wellcome standing by her. 'You take a plate and choose what you want, then pay for what you have – a good idea, I think.'

'Yes, isn't it – and rather like life,' said Dulcie. 'Except that there you can't always choose *exactly* what you want.'

'That's a very clever saying,' said Miss Wellcome playfully. 'You young women nowadays are so much cleverer than we were.'

'And yet,' said Dulcie, feeling that she knew what was coming, 'you were probably happier than we are.'

'Oh, I wouldn't say that. But life was simpler then. We made our own pleasures. Perhaps in some ways we were more serious – felt our responsibilities more.'

'Is that Mrs Williton's daughter talking to her now?' asked Dulcie, feeling her way.

'Yes, in the mauve twin-set. A lovely shade, isn't it.'

'Terribly difficult to wear, but it suits her. Does she live at home?'

'Not really – you see . . .' Miss Wellcome glanced around her and drew Dulcie aside into a corner. Then, lowering her voice to a rather melodramatic whisper, she went on, '. . . she has left her husband.'

'Oh. Did he . . . was he . . .?'

'Oh, *yes*. Quite a *libertine*, I believe.'

Dulcie's first impulse was to burst out laughing at the use of such an old-fashioned word, permissible, surely, only in the English synopsis of an Italian opera. The Duke in *Rigoletto* might have been so described, she thought. 'What did he do?' she asked. 'I mean,' she emended quickly, 'what was – or is – his profession?'

'Something in the literary world, I think. Not surprising, really, the kind of life they seem to lead there. I had a very interesting book out from the library not long ago – all about Lord Byron.'

'But surely he was rather exceptional?' Dulcie protested.

'Would you like a ticket for this raffle?' said Mrs Williton, appearing disconcertingly from nowhere. 'It is for a hand-embroidered duchesse set.'

'Thank you,' said Dulcie, taking a sixpence out of her purse, 'though I'm never lucky in these things.'

'But I must have your name and address, so that I can let you know if you *do* win – you never know!'

'Oh, well then . . . it's Miss Lamb, 17 Byron Road, S.W.19,' said Dulcie. She was surprised at her own fluency in deceit:

but it might be embarrassing if she really *did* win the duchesse set. 'And now I really must be going. I do hope you've made a nice lot of money.'

'It was good of you to drop in,' said Mrs Williton.

'Goodbye,' said Dulcie to Miss Wellcome, and hurried out into the hall, where she lingered for a moment, hoping to see 'something interesting', as she put it to herself. But there was only the evening paper stuck through the letter-box and a bill from the London Electricity Board lying on the purple-and-ochre tiled floor. It was greedy of her to expect any more when she had already received so much.

Outside it was already dark. Dulcie decided that it would be wiser not to walk across the common alone, and so turned up a road which she thought might lead to a bus stop.

Had she been a minute later in her turning she would no doubt have recognized the hurrying figure of Aylwin Forbes, coming along from the other end of Deodar Grove. He was carrying a bunch of chrysanthemums, which he had bought hastily at the flower shop by the station, feeling, with the force of some primitive taboo, that he must not enter the house of his mother-in-law empty-handed. The flowers were stiff and unnatural-looking, like washing-up mops, and each 'bloom' had cost one-and-three. Marjorie would have preferred a bunch of violets or a miniature cactus, but it had seemed more in keeping with his dignity to carry something large, and he had the feeling that it was his mother-in-law who needed to be propitiated. He supposed that he had behaved badly, or at least unwisely, and that it was up to him to make the first move. After all, he had known from the beginning that Marjorie could never enter into his work with him, but he had been touched and flattered by her show of interest and by the way she had listened when he talked. And the way she had looked – so fragile and appealing with her fluffy curls, almost a 'girl wife' – had been such a refreshing change from the frightening elegance, frowsty bohemianism, or uncompromising dowdiness, of those women who could really have entered into his work and would probably in the end have elbowed him out of it altogether. It was particularly ironical that it should have been Viola Dace, of all of them, who had brought about the break between him and Marjorie – the tears and protestations, the hurried packing of suitcases, even the grumbling taxi-driver, who doubted whether he could go 'all that way'.

One could hardly blame him, Aylwin thought, as he made his way along Deodar Grove. The stultifying oppression of the suburbs seemed particularly heavy on this early winter evening, with the darkness coming too quickly, and what light there had been scarcely able to filter its way through the layers of net curtains. Another ironical aspect of the situation was that Aylwin himself had been named after the title of the famous novel by Theodore Watts-Dunton, and it was near here that the poet Swinburne had been incarcerated by this friend in his later years. 'The brown bright nightingale amorous,' thought Aylwin angrily, seeing himself as that nightingale and blaming the whole thing on his mother-in-law, Mrs Williton.

As he approached the house he looked automatically for the stone squirrel, one of their now painful early little jokes, but it was too dark to see if it was still in the garden of the house next door. He noticed that the house was for sale, and wondered if the squirrel would be thrown in with the linoleum in the hall and what the house agents called 'f. & f.'.

And then, just as Dulcie had been, he was approached by a stranger, but a youngish, good-looking man with fair curly hair, who asked him in a rather prim voice, if number thirty-seven Deodar Grove was at this end of the road.

'It's this next house, with the particularly fine deodar in the front garden,' said Aylwin.

The young man laughed rather uncertainly, for he saw only a laburnum and what might have been a kind of prunus or almond tree. 'I hope I'm not too late,' he said. 'It's nearly five o'clock.'

'Too late?' Aylwin asked. 'For tea, do you mean?' What was this young man doing, going to the house at tea-time, as if he had been invited? A friend of Marjorie's, perhaps – but he could not place him among the youths at the tennis club who had been her suitors before he married her.

'Well, that and the sale,' said the young man, and then Aylwin saw what he meant. He read the notice on the front door – 'JUMBLE SALE – IN AID OF THE ORGAN FUND.' This was really too much! The things women did to men! Had anybody ever really made a serious study of the subject, of the innumerable pin-pricks and humiliations endured by men at the hands of women? How could he enter the house with flowers for his wronged wife when the place was crowded with women buying and selling jumble in aid of the organ fund!

'You see,' the young man explained, 'I'm the organist, and I feel the ladies will expect me to put in an appearance.'

'I'm sure they will,' said Aylwin, faintly ironical. He could imagine the entrance the young man would make, the pleased cries that would greet his appearance, the fresh tea that would be made, and his complacent acceptance of their tributes. No

87

doubt, like all men connected with the Church – his own brother Neville included – the organist would be at ease with ladies. He could see the phrase – *At Ease with Ladies* – as the title of a novel or even a biography.

Aylwin wished the young man good-night and walked on past the house, holding the flowers awkwardly in front of him. What should he do with them now? Was there anybody living in the district to whom he could give them, unobtrusively, of course, hardly seeming to do so? He thought for a moment, and then remembered that Viola Dace, who had so embarrassingly insisted on making the index for his book, had recently moved into the neighbourhood. He even had her address written in his diary. He would find a taxi at the station and take the flowers to the house – a landlady or servant would doubtless open the door, so there need be no embarrassing encounter.

Dulcie, walking from the bus stop and seeing the taxi stopping in the road, had no idea that it was coming to her house. Taxis usually meant Senhor MacBride-Pereira, or Mrs Beltane returning from a particularly exhausting shopping afternoon in Harrods. It was not until she reached her front gate and saw Aylwin Forbes standing on the doorstep that she realised the situation. And even then she did not, of course, know everything. Her one thought was that she must not meet him, so she walked quickly down the road past the house, an anonymous scurrying figure, just like a tired businesswoman returning home after a day's work.

Aylwin, meanwhile, had rung the bell and was waiting confidently for the landlady or servant who would appear and relieve him of the flowers. After what seemed a long time – especially as the taxi was ticking away in the road – the door was opened by a tall dark girl wearing tight-fitting black trousers and a yellow sweater.

'Oh . . .' Laurel exclaimed, obviously taken aback at the sight of such a good-looking man and such a very large bunch of flowers. 'I'm afraid my aunt isn't in yet.' But surely, she thought, he's come to the wrong house?

'Actually I brought these for Miss Dace,' said Aylwin, confused by the unexpected encounter with a pretty young girl and wretchedly encumbered by the flowers. 'But perhaps she doesn't live here? So stupid of me . . .'

'Oh, she does live here, but she isn't in either. Won't you come in? I don't suppose she'll be long.'

'Well, if I could just write a message . . .' He stepped into the hall and took a card from his wallet. What should he write? Something non-committal – the sort of thing one wrote to a woman who was undertaking the arduous and thankless task of making an index to a book. *With many thanks for all you are doing for me A.F.*', he scribbled. Really, it was the least he could do, he thought, quite forgetting what had been the original purpose of the flowers. He wished now that he had insisted on paying her for the work.

Laurel stood holding the flowers. 'I'll give them to her as soon as she comes in,' she said.

How charming she looked, holding the flowers like that! It seemed now as if this was why he had bought them – to see them held in her arms. *A l'ombre des jeunes filles en fleurs* . . . would she know what he was driving at if he were to quote that, or would it seem stupid and affected in the dark suburban hall, with the macintoshes and old shoes huddled together in the peculiarly unaesthetic hat stand?

'Thank you,' he said lamely. 'Good night!'

'Good night!' said Laurel, closing the door after him.

She put the flowers down on a chair and examined the card. So this was the famous Aylwin Forbes! He had seemed to her in their brief meeting the perfect 'older man', with whom young girls fell in love. '5, Quince Square, W.11', she read on the visiting card. And soon, when she had broken the news to her aunt, she was going to live in Quince Square herself! The prospect was so exciting that she nearly forgot to put the card back with the flowers. What on earth could Miss Dace, of all people, have been 'doing' for him, she wondered. Then she remembered – making an index for his book – it was at once comic and pathetic.

Dulcie, now scurrying back in the direction of her own house, nearly bumped into Aylwin as he was coming out of the gate, but he did not appear to recognize her. Just as well, she thought, remembering the strange and rather deceitful way in which she had spent the afternoon.

# CHAPTER TEN

In the days that followed, Dulcie found herself drinking endless late cups of coffee and accomplishing yards of knitting while Viola speculated on the significance of Aylwin having sent her flowers at that particular point in their relationship. Dulcie felt that she had become a kind of confidante, as in the plays of the great French classical dramatists, Racine and Corneille, which she had read in the sixth form at school. She supposed that it must be a role filled by many women, even today. Naturally she said nothing about her own feelings – her unworthy jealousy at the idea that Aylwin might be attracted to Viola as something more than a competent woman who could make a good index. For why else should he have sent her flowers? Gratitude for the work she was doing hardly explained this lover-like gesture. One could not blame Viola if she thought otherwise.

Yet Viola and Aylwin did not appear to meet very often. In spite of the flowers – or perhaps because of them – he made no move to seek her out. Viola's evenings were spent in her room surrounded by proofs and index cards, and, as far as Dulcie knew, he did not telephone her.

Dulcie had said nothing about her meeting with Marjorie Forbes, though she had admitted having seen the outside of the house. Viola would not understand her intense curiosity about all aspects of Aylwin's life and might easily be shocked to hear how she had managed to worm her way into the jumble sale.

One morning, about a fortnight after Aylwin had called with the flowers, Dulcie was sitting in the kitchen, waiting for Miss Lord to finish doing Viola's room, so that they could have their coffee. When Miss Lord eventually came down she was carrying the chrysanthemums with her.

'I think it's about time these were thrown away,' she said. 'Don't you, Miss Mainwaring?'

Dulcie hesitated. The flowers were certainly past their best, though, in the curious lingering way that chrysanthemums have, they were not exactly dead. Most of the leaves had withered, but some of the flowers might still pass, arranged with fresh leaves or massed together in a bowl. 'I don't think Miss Dace would like it if we were to throw them away without asking,' said Dulcie. 'You might change the water, though – it does look rather slimy.'

'I think it's very unhealthy to have flowers in a room where you sleep,' said Miss Lord rather huffily. 'Miss Dace is very untidy, isn't she? I wouldn't presume to put her clothes away for her, but it's difficult to do the room when they're lying all over the place.'

'Oh, I'm sorry. I must speak to her about it,' said Dulcie apologetically. 'Have one of these Abbey biscuits with your coffee. I know you like them. Where are you going for your lunch today?'

'Well, I might call in at the cafeteria in the High Street,' said Miss Lord, sounding a little brighter at the thought of lunch. 'I like it there. It's warm but not too squashed up – there's plenty of room between the tables. The only thing is that I *have* been unlucky there lately.'

'Unlucky?'

'Yes, with the beans – baked beans, you know. They didn't have any last time I went, and it rather upset me, what happened.'

'Oh?'

'The man in the queue *after* me asked for baked beans and *he* got them. He was laughing and joking with the girl who was serving – you know the way they do – I didn't say anything, but I was quite upset.'

'Yes, I know, that's what life is like. And it *is* humiliating. One feels a sense of one's own inadequacy, somehow, almost unworthiness,' said Dulcie thoughtfully. 'But then life is often cruel in small ways, isn't it. Not exactly nature red in tooth and claw, though one does sometimes feel . . . And what will you have for pudding today?' she asked, jerking herself back to reality by a sudden awareness of Miss Lord's pitying look at her vague philosophisings. If this is what education does for you . . . she seemed to imply. Well might one ask, 'But what will it lead to?'

'Deep apricot tart,' said Miss Lord, suiting her tone to the words.

The mid-morning post had brought two letters. They lay in the hall face downwards, waiting to be picked up. As always – and perhaps the feeling is universal unless one is expecting or hoping for a love letter – the thought of them gave Dulcie a slightly uneasy feeling. Then she saw to her relief that one of them was only Pontings' catalogue, and she rejoiced in the prospect of looking through it and marvelling at the splendid bargains to be had in the White Sale or in the buying up of fabulous stocks from some failed manufacturer. She saw also that the other letter was a tucked-in printed thing, so that could be nothing troublesome either.

But when she opened it she found that it was an invitation to attend the Private View of the works of a painter whose name was unknown to her, but which was to be held at the gallery off Bond Street where Maurice, her former fiancé, worked. Did he imagine, she wondered with a sudden rush of indignation, that she would find such an occasion at all congenial? That she could even bear to go to it at all? Life was at its tricks again, but this was a sharper cruelty than Miss Lord's discomfiture over the baked beans. She stood with her invitation in her hand, wondering why she did not immediately tear it up. But then reason took over and suggested to her that in all probability the invitation had been sent automatically because her name was on the gallery's list. It was possible that Maurice didn't even work there now.

When Viola came in she showed her the invitation and asked her if she would like to use it. 'I don't really want to go myself,' she added.

'Why not? I always think Private Views are rather amusing. Couldn't we go together?'

'Yes, perhaps I will come,' said Dulcie, imagining herself either plodding round in flat, comfortable shoes, or in more elegant agony, sitting on one of those round sofas in the middle of the room. Perhaps there was some kind of pattern in life after all. It might be like a well-thought-out novel, where every incident had its own particular significance and was essential to the plot. Seeing Maurice again, even if it were painful to her, might do something important to her self-confidence, even if only to make her ask herself, 'How could I ever have loved such a person?'

She felt quite excited when the time came and they were actually pushing open the red-handled swing doors of the gallery and stepping on to the soft black carpet that covered the passages and floors.

There was a young woman sitting at a table with catalogues spread out on it and a visitors' book open. Dulcie noticed the names of one or two art critics, but not, as she had hoped, that of Aylwin Forbes. And indeed why should he be here? He had no particular interest in modern art, as far as she knew. The young woman seemed a more elegant version of herself, rather as Dulcie might have looked if some woman's magazine had taken her in hand. The fair hair was elegantly folded into a kind of pleat at the back of the head, the eyes shadowed with blue, and the finger-nails painted with a pearly pink varnish. Dulcie turned away and sighed. It was a little upsetting to see what one might have been.

'Shall we start at the beginning and go stolidly round?' Viola asked.

'Oh, the pictures . . .' Dulcie roused herself to look at the walls, and saw with dismay that they were hung with geometrical shapes in ugly drab colours.

'Apparently this room contains pictures in his latest style,' said Viola, consulting the catalogue. 'The others are earlier works, so perhaps we should start in the other room?'

'This looks a bit more understandable,' said Dulcie, contemplating a black and white cat with a lemon in its paws. 'But is he really a good painter? This picture of onions and peppers and wine bottles, with the view of boats through the window – hasn't one seen this sort of thing rather often before? And what made him turn from these rather pleasant pictures to the dreary abstractions in the other room?'

'He feels he has gone through colour, as it were,' said a fat woman in a grey coat of some shaggy woollen material. 'His history is rather interesting. He comes from Herne Hill.'

'Indeed?' said Dulcie, feeling that this was the only possible response. Then, more characteristically, she added, 'But how splendid! I suppose he broke away from his background in the earlier pictures and then came to terms with it again – at least, I suppose the later pictures indicate that, don't they?'

'They seem like Herne Hill,' said Viola, for she had spent her earliest years in that neighbourhood. It was later that her father, with his love of Wordsworth, had taken a house in Sydenham, equally convenient for his office near Victoria and yet 'almost in the country'.

'Is the painter himself here today?' Dulcie asked.

'Yes – he is the young man in the speckled polo-necked sweater, standing over there.'

Dulcie hardly bothered to look in the direction indicated. It was boring, she thought, how young artists and writers still looked as one expected them to. How much more amusing it would have been had he appeared in a suit of one of the 'sub-dued business patterns' which she had read about the other day in Pontings' catalogue. 'I do hope some of the pictures have been sold,' she said, looking anxiously for little red stars and circles in the corners of the frames. It would be so dreadful if she had to buy one out of pity, though the cat and lemon was quite pleasant.

'Yes, three in this room are sold,' said Viola, 'and some of the abstracts, too. I think there is somebody wanting to talk to you,' she added.

Dulcie had not time to feel the overpowering agitation she had always imagined the meeting with Maurice might produce. It came upon her so quickly. She found herself saying, 'Why, hullo, Maurice, how nice to see you,' and then introducing him to Viola, who seemed to brighten up at the sight of such a young and personable man.

'We don't quite know what to make of all these pictures,' she said, and Dulcie allowed them to move a little away from her while Maurice explained to Viola the 'significance' of the painter's later work.

It did seem astonishing now, not that she could ever have loved such a person, for surely Maurice belonged to that category of persons who are always loved, but that he – so very much the opposite of everything that she was – could ever have considered marrying her.

He was of medium height, slender and brown-haired, with grey eyes and rather pointed features, the general effect being of softness and smoothness, yet with something hard underneath. He was wearing a heavy signet ring that Dulcie had not seen before. Perhaps he was now engaged to somebody else?

'Wonderful, seeing you again like this so unexpectedly,' he said softly, turning away from Viola, who was gazing at one of the pictures with the dutiful, slightly glazed, expression of a woman who has been shown what to look for by a distractingly handsome man.

'Wonderful?' she echoed. 'Didn't you know I'd had an invitation to the Private View?'

'I didn't really think, and even if I had known I shouldn't have expected you to come, in the circumstances.' He held up his hand and contemplated his nails delicately.

'Yes, I wondered if it would be too painful,' said Dulcie

honestly, 'but I thought that it might be a good thing for us to meet – and, as you see, it is,' she added, not looking at him.

'Is Miss – er – your friend living at your house now?'

'Yes, it's quite a good arrangement,' said Dulcie lamely: for of course to have a not particularly congenial woman friend living in one's house was hardly to be compared with being married to the man of one's choice – 'quite a good arrangement' was putting it almost too high. She experienced a sudden feeling of desolation, and heard Maurice saying something about lunch one day or a party he was giving, without taking in the significance of his words. She felt herself sinking down again into that state of lowness that she had hoped never to experience again. She heard Viola murmuring something polite, even saying that something would be 'delightful'. Her eyes wandered unhappily round the room and she could think of nothing but to escape as quickly as possible. It was ironical to think that she had even imagined that the visit to the Private View might have some special significance in her life.

'Goodbye,' she said, for already he was talking to somebody else.

'Goodbye, and let's meet again soon,' he called out.

'I think we'll go and have tea, shall we?' Dulcie suggested.

'Yes, but won't there be any kind of refreshment here?' Viola asked.

'There doesn't seem to be any sign of anything, does there, and we can hardly ask . . .'

Suddenly Dulcie grasped Viola's arm. 'Look,' she said in a whisper, 'do you see that clergyman? Isn't he like Aylwin? I wonder if it can be his brother?'

Viola looked. She saw a clergyman gazing at a painting of some angular-looking flowers in a lopsided vase.

'Well, Wilkins,' he said, going up to the artist, 'it looks as if you got out of bed the wrong side when you painted that one.'

There was some indulgent laughter on both sides and the clergyman then left the gallery, closely followed by Dulcie and Viola.

'He certainly has got a look of Aylwin Forbes,' said Dulcie. 'Can it be that he is going into that place to have tea?'

The clergyman was standing by a shop window, gazing at a display of cream cakes.

'Let's go in too,' said Viola. 'We need a cup of tea.'

They were lucky enough to find a table next to the one the clergyman had chosen, but once they were seated and had been brought their tea there was little they could do beyond stealing surreptitious glances at him and remarking again on his likeness to Aylwin Forbes. The fact that he had ordered coffee rather than tea and chosen a particularly elaborate and creamy-looking cake seemed to confirm their suspicions. But after whispering that surely a clergyman ought to be visiting or attending some kind of meeting rather than be sitting drinking coffee and eating cakes in Bond Street, Viola seemed to lose interest in him. It was Maurice she wanted to talk about.

'What a charming young man,' she said, rather gushingly. 'And so good-looking. Where have you been hiding him all this time?'

'I haven't exactly been hiding him,' said Dulcie, 'but it was a little awkward to get in touch with him myself. You see, I was once engaged to him.'

'*You* were engaged – to *him?*' Dulcie received Viola's unflattering though not unexpected exclamations of surprise with bowed head.

'Yes, the engagement was broken off about a year ago. Didn't I tell you about it?'

'Yes, you did mention that you had been engaged, but naturally I never *imagined* . . .'

'Naturally not – you wouldn't.'

'Did you have an engagement ring?' asked Viola in an openly curious tone.

'Yes. It was very pretty, a garnet in a circle of pearls.'

'Oh, antique.' Viola sounded slightly less interested. 'Did you keep it, after . . .'

'Yes. You see, *he* did the breaking off.' It was almost a relief to be honest about it after all these months – to face up to the fact that he just hadn't wanted to marry her, in spite of his way of putting it which had emphasised her goodness and sweetness and his own unworthiness.

'I see.' Viola could hardly be blamed if she sounded the tiniest bit satisfied at what she had heard. 'I suppose in those circumstances he could hardly expect you to return the ring.'

'No – but I didn't keep it. It wasn't that I couldn't bear the sight of it, but it seemed pointless to shut it up in a box, and I couldn't wear it, so I sold it.'

'You sold it?' said Viola, surprised, for it sounded so very unlike Dulcie to do such a thing.

'Yes.' Dulcie paused, and then went on, 'I had seen an advertisement in the *Telegraph* – an appeal for some distressed gentlewoman, a general's daughter living in very "reduced" circumstances – you know how I can never bear things like that.' She smiled apologetically. 'I sent the money there – it wasn't very much, but it brought some kind of relief. Oh dear, now I sound like Miss Lord and her television advertisements – so many things seem to bring "relief".'

'Look – Aylwin Forbes's brother has been joined by a companion,' Viola whispered.

'Goodness, yes – and wearing gaiters! Is he an archdeacon, do you think?'

'Ah, Gaythorne,' boomed the gaitered clergyman, in a voice that penetrated to the farthest corner of the tea-room, 'I thought I might find you here!'

Gaythorne, Dulcie thought, so he can't be Aylwin's brother after all. She felt quite ridiculously disappointed, and could hardly bring herself to listen with her usual interest to the conversation of the two clergymen, which was really most unsuitably catty.

'I suppose I'll see you at the induction this evening?' the gaitered one asked.

'Rather! Though it's really such a *very* western part of West Kensington that I can't imagine how one gets there.'

'They say he's an ex-chorus-boy or something – never done any pastoral work at all. I can't *quite* see him at St Jude's,' said the gaitered one in a gloating tone. 'I give him a year, at the most . . .'

At that moment a waitress came up to the table where the clergymen were sitting, with fresh coffee and another plate of cream cakes.

'I suppose we ought to be going,' said Dulcie, still conscious of her disappointment.

The afternoon had been a rather painful experience altogether; but later, when she was able to analyse her feelings, she realised that it was not her love for Maurice that had returned during their short meeting in the art gallery, but the remembrance of the unhappiness he had caused her. And that, she told herself stoutly, would soon pass.

# CHAPTER ELEVEN

Dulcie's sense of duty did not often drive her to visit her Uncle Bertram and Aunt Hermione, but it was getting near enough to Christmas for her to invite herself to supper and to take her presents with her to save posting them. If she went early – they had their evening meal punctually at seven – and left early, there would surely be a chance to walk past Neville Forbes's church, which a study of the map had told her was not so far away as she had feared. Her uncle and aunt were both churchgoers. Bertram was an Anglo-Catholic and had once held a position as lecturer at a teachers' training college; Hermione was more evangelical in her tastes to be different from her brother, Dulcie always felt – and had never had to earn her living. During the war she had worked in the Censorship, and now occupied herself by sitting on various committees and doing parish work.

It was a slightly foggy November evening when Dulcie got off the bus and turned into a road of Victorian houses approached by steep flights of steps. The one where her uncle and aunt lived had thick bushes of variegated laurels growing on either side of the front door. Dulcie rang the bell: but she knew that in the basement the cook-housekeeper, Mrs Sedge, would be preparing the evening meal and therefore unable to come to the door – and even if she had not been thus occupied it is doubtful whether she would have deigned to climb the stairs. After what seemed a rather long time the door was opened by Dulcie's Aunt Hermione, wearing her winter coat and a teacosy-shaped hat trimmed with brown fur.

'I'm so sorry, dear,' she said. 'I'm just in the middle of a telephone call. Do take off your coat and go into the drawing-room. There's a nice fire in there.'

Hermione returned to the telephone, which was in the hall, and Dulcie heard her say in a clear loud voice, as if she were speaking to somebody very far away, 'You are very much in our thoughts at this sad time. What a blessing that Maisie is with you – she will be a *tower of strength* . . .'

Dulcie went into the drawing-room, picturing Maisie as a tower of strength and wondering why her aunt had bothered to say the conventional thing about there being a nice fire in the drawing-room. She crouched down on the hearth rug by the sad smoking coals and began to look at some old copies of *The Field* which were lying in a heap on a brown leather pouf. She turned to the 'Answers to Correspondents' and read how to feed hamsters. She agonised with one who cried, 'Why do white maggots appear in the stems of my brassica plants?', but the query of a correspondent from – of all places – Montevideo, who wanted to know how he could stop a mat in his lounge from curling up at the edges, baffled her, and she found herself quite unable to picture either the 'lounge' or the mat in such an exotic setting.

'That was our vicar I was speaking to.' Hermione came into

the room and began taking off her coat. 'His sister passed away very peacefully this afternoon.'

'Oh, I see,' said Dulcie.

'Fortunately his *other* sister, the older one who lives in Nottingham, is with him.'

'You mean Maisie?' said Dulcie.

'Yes, and she will be a *tower of strength*, a real *tower*.'

'In a way it's better to be left with one's grief, to be allowed to indulge it, I mean. Was he fond of his sister?'

'Of Gladys? Oh, they were devoted, *quite devoted*.' Hermione gave these last words a particular emphasis as her brother Bertram entered the room.

He was a small, busy-looking man, shorter than his sister, with closely cropped grey hair.

'Hullo, Dulcie, my dear,' he said. 'May I ask who were quite devoted?'

'Why, the Vicar and his sister, of course,' said Hermione rather impatiently. 'He has just telephoned to say that the end has come.'

'You mean, his sister has died? *Requiescat in pace*,' said Bertram, crossing himself.

Hermione took off her hat with an angry movement and went to tidy her hair at the mirror over the mantelpiece. 'This looking-glass is so awkward,' she grumbled. 'Much too high up. And yet it seems hardly worth having it moved now, if we are going to leave this house.'

'Are you thinking of leaving?' asked Dulcie rather alarmed, for she saw them coming to live with her in their old age and the prospect appalled her.

'Well, the house has always been too big for us and it would certainly be too big for me alone.'

'Alone? But what's going to happen to Uncle Bertram?'

Bertram looked rather self-satisfied but said nothing.

'Oh, it's those monks of his or whatever they are,' said Hermione impatiently. 'They've agreed to take him in.'

'What, as a monk?' asked Dulcie incredulously.

'No, into their guest house or something like that.'

'I might eventually enter the community – take my vows, you know,' said Bertram. 'I should have to see how things went. But the guest house is very comfortable – I've stayed there before, of course – good food, central heating, no women . . .' He smiled at his sister and niece.

'No, I suppose there wouldn't be. Would you do some kind of work?'

'I suppose I could work. The abbey is famous for its pottery: obviously that must be made by somebody.' Bertram looked down at his hands doubtfully. 'Then there are the grounds to be looked after – acres of beautiful grounds with some very fine cedar trees.'

'I don't think those would need much attention,' said Hermione scornfully. 'Cedars live for hundreds of years.'

'Well, there is the vegetable garden. Weeds grow, even in a religious community. Or I could serve in the shop that sells the pottery and garden produce. Somebody has to do that.'

There was a rattling sound outside the door.

'I think Mrs Sedge is ready for us,' said Hermione, getting up. 'Shall we go into the dining-room?'

'Better not keep her waiting,' said Bertram. 'She doesn't like that.'

The meal was already on the table when they entered the room. A dish of mince with tomato sauce spread over the top seemed to be the main dish; boiled potatoes and 'greens' were on the trolley. Mrs Sedge, who had come to England twenty years ago from Vienna, had apparently retained little knowledge of her country's cuisine, if she had ever possessed it; Dulcie was always surprised at the thoroughness with which she had acquired all the worst traits of English cooking.

'Ah,' said Bertram, unfolding his table napkin from its carved wooden ring, 'boiled baby.'

Hermione stood tight-lipped, the spoon and fork poised above the dish. 'Dulcie, may I give you some mince?'

'Thank you – just a little.'

'That's what the lads always used to call it,' Bertram explained, perhaps unnecessarily.

'I should have thought that young men training to be school-masters would have been above such puerile jokes,' said Hermione tartly. 'You can hardly wonder that there is all this juvenile delinquency when the teachers themselves have so little sense of responsibility. *Quis custodiet . . .*' she began, but either the rest of the quotation evaded her or she thought it unnecessary to continue one so well known.

'Oh, they were up to every prank,' said Bertram complacently.

'I always think men are like a lot of children when they get together,' said Hermione. 'I suppose the monks will be just as bad.'

'I think people aren't always at their best when they are together in large numbers,' said Dulcie smoothly. 'I noticed at this conference I went to in the summer that everybody got rather childish. By the way' – she turned to her uncle – 'one of the lecturers there has a brother who is vicar of a church somewhere near here. The name was Forbes – I wondered if you knew him?'

'Ah, yes. That must be Neville Forbes of St Ivel's,' said Bertram.

'Yes, I think his name is Neville. But isn't St Ivel a kind of cheese?'

'Why, yes, so it is. Then perhaps it couldn't also be the name of a saint in the Calendar.' Bertram looked puzzled. 'Yet we have St Martin, an excellent marmalade, if I remember rightly.'

'Oh, l suppose St Ivel's could very well be the name of one of the sort of churches *you* like,' said Hermione childishly.

Dulcie sighed and took a sip of water. She had so often heard her uncle and aunt going on like this, bickering about unimportant things. Is this what growing old with somebody does to one? she asked herself. Would it come to this with anybody, perhaps even with Aylwin Forbes? She saw again the fluffy little woman in the mauve twin-set, wrapping up the pottery donkey . . . yes, certainly, even with Aylwin Forbes. But not, perhaps, with Maurice? There had been only rapture and misery there – impossible ever to tie him down to the breakfast table and the laundry list, or other fruitful occasions for bickering. Then she realised that it was herself, rather than other people, that she had been unable to imagine in such petty squabblings. She had forgotten the recent little disagreements with Viola, about clothes left dripping in the kitchen, the bathroom light left on all night, lack of co-operation in household tasks, even the merits of calf's – as opposed to lamb's – liver. Now she remembered them and felt humbler, for these were not even academic bickerings which one could regard afterwards with detached amusement.

The second course was stewed apple and semolina pudding, dishes which Mrs Sedge had mastered to perfection.

'I wonder what Maisie will be giving the Vicar this evening,' said Hermione thoughtfully. 'He will hardly feel like eating, of course. Nor will she.'

'No, but they will be urging each other to take something, as people do in these circumstances,' said Dulcie. Bereavement in some ways the most comfortable kind of misery, for there would always be somebody to urge; the unhappiness of love was usually more lonely because so often concealed from others.

'Macaroni cheese, perhaps,' Hermione went on, with what seemed unnecessary persistence. 'I know he likes that, and it is easily digested if there is not *too* much cheese.'

'I should think you know his likes and dislikes better than Maisie does,' said Bertram quite amiably. 'It's a pity that *you* can't be looking after him.'

'Oh, well, Maisie came at once – there was no question of anybody in the parish being asked.' Hermione had risen from the table and begun to assemble the dishes for clearing.

'I'll just go down and have a word with Mrs Sedge,' said Dulcie, picking up the dish of stewed apple.

'Yes, do, dear – she would like that,' said Hermione.

She would expect it, Dulcie thought, and take it out on Aunt Hermione afterwards if I did not go. She was something of a tyrant without having acquired the qualities of a 'treasure'. There was a graciousness in her manner as she rose to greet Dulcie and to accept her thanks for the delicious meal.

The kitchen was warm, and comfortable in a rather old-fashioned style, with deep basket chairs and a round table covered with a red plush cloth. The dominating feature of its decoration, apart from the television set, was a large highly-coloured print of the Duke of Edinburgh – the eyes stern-looking and of a brilliantly improbable blue. 'The light that never was, on sea or land', Dulcie always thought when she saw it. Its presence in the room was another indication of Mrs Sedge's 'Englishness', like her cooking and her acquisition of the traditional cook's title of 'Mrs', when she had never been married.

Lily Sedge – had the name originally been Lilli Segy, or Söj, or what? Dulcie wondered – had never really cared for cooking, if the truth were known. She had no idea how to make the strudels, torte and schnitzels for which her native land was famous; but twenty years ago, with her bad English, it had seemed easier to become a cook than a typist. As time went on she had made herself very comfortable, and even achieved a certain amount of power over her various employers. It seemed to be taken for granted that a Viennese woman would be a good cook, and it had not taken her long to learn the kind of easy dishes English people were accustomed to.

'You have met my brother, I think?' said Mrs Sedge, and Dulcie now saw that Bill Sedge (Willi Segy?) was standing in a corner of the room, bowing rather lower than an Englishman would have done and rubbing his hands together as if asking what her next pleasure might be. He, like his sister, had been fortunate in finding a comfortable niche for himself as the knitwear buyer in a chain of shops whose brilliant crowded windows were to be seen in many parts of London. 'I know what ladies like,' he would say, and he always made Dulcie in her subdued, greys and browns feel rather drab and unfeminine. At least, though, one did not have to worry about the Sedges; there was nothing sad about them. Indeed, they were a great deal less pathetic than many English people, and that was something of a relief.

'The evenings are drawing in,' said Bill Sedge.

'Yes, they are. I think they've really drawn in by now, haven't they?' said Dulcie. 'One is now almost thinking of them drawing out again.'

'In Vienna we did not notice such things,' said Mrs Sedge.

'But in Finchley Road one is always talking of the weather,' said her brother.

'Well, a Merry Christmas to you both,' said Dulcie, feeling that they had in some way got the better of her.

'And the same to you, Miss Dulcie,' they echoed.

Back in the drawing-room Dulcie exchanged Christmas presents with her uncle and aunt. A tea cosy and a tin of shortbread from them to her, and a bed jacket and a book about religious orders in the Anglican church from her to them.

'This is "just the job", as they say,' said Bertram, glancing through the book. 'I shall spend many happy hours with this book.'

'I think I ought to be going now,' said Dulcie, her thoughts on Neville Forbes's church. 'I know you like to get to bed early.'

'Yes, dear, but I think I shall telephone the Vicar again, just to find out if there is *anything* I can do.'

Dulcie hoped that he would find something, even if it was a thing he didn't really want doing at all. It was sad, she thought, how women longed to be needed and useful and how seldom most of them really were. It reminded her of Viola and Aylwin Forbes.

Once outside the house she broke into a run, both because of the coldness of the evening and the lateness of the hour – nearly nine o'clock. Was it likely that the church would be open now or that she would be able to glean anything from looking at the outside of it?

The road she had marked on the map seemed much longer than it had looked, and the church was not easy to find. Dulcie had imagined that as soon as she turned into the road it would be immediately visible, if only in the distance, a Victorian Gothic building with its own kind of nobility, its lacy spire towering above the houses. But she had come right up to it before she realised that the ordinary-looking red brick building in front of her was indeed St Ivel's Church. Only a notice-board, conveniently placed under a street lamp, with the times of services in faded gilt lettering and a poster announcing a whist drive, gave any clue. Then she looked up and saw that it had a little campanile, half hidden by trees, and that the windows were vaguely ecclesiastical in shape. She stepped into the porch, where another notice-board gave the service for the week typed on a printed form with little crosses at the corners. 'Confessions – Saturday 6.45', she read with a shudder. So it was High Church and Aylwin Forbes's brother might very well be unmarried.

Dulcie turned the heavy ring of the door handle. To her surprise the door opened; she had expected it to be shut at this time of the evening. What if some strange form of service were going on and she were trapped into taking part in it? But inside all was quiet; there was nobody to be seen, and yet she had a feeling that the building was not empty. Just inside the door was a marble stoup with some greenish – presumably Holy – water in the bottom. Dulcie dipped her finger in it and crossed herself, dropping down on to one knee as she had seen people do in Roman Catholic churches. Then, feeling that she had, as it were, a right to go in, she walked boldly up between the rows of chairs until she stood facing the altar. A few lights were on, and through the gilded rood screen she caught glimpses of bright Victorian stained glass and brass candlesticks on the altar. On her left was the organ, and she tiptoed up to it to examine the music lying on the stool – Rubinstein's Melody in F, 'O for the wings of a dove', 'Arias from *Cavalleria Rusticana*', and, surprisingly, a piano selection of *Salad Days*. Did these reflect the musical tastes of the organist, she wondered, trying to picture him, young and eager, perhaps riding a scooter. Round the corner behind the organ was a sort of choir vestry with blue cassocks hanging on hooks and piles of rather tattered-looking music stuffed into a bookshelf. There was a kind of mist hanging over the place, either fog which had seeped in from outside or the smoke of incense lingering from the last service. Dulcie groped for a light switch, and rather to her surprise found one. She was now able to see more clearly and to read a notice nailed to the door in front of her, which said 'Nobody, repeat NOBODY, is to tamper with the electric heating apparatus in here'. At the same time she was aware of a strong smell of paraffin. Puzzled, she tried the door, but it was, understandably, locked, so she switched off the light and returned to the main part of the church. The somewhat tetchy wording of the notice seemed out of keeping with the elegant italic hand in which it was written. Could it be the hand of Aylwin Forbes's brother, she asked herself. She wondered who might be tempted to 'tamper' with the heating apparatus – possibly the organist or the churchwardens; devout ladies slipping in for a moment's prayer and meditation might even be seized with an irresistible urge to do so.

Dulcie left the church with a vague prayer and a small coin for each of the boxes that invited her charity – sick and poor fund (in these days?); altar flowers; sanctuary fund; restoration fund (all churches seemed to have this, whatever their state of repair); and vicarage expenses. The last was rather obscure, and just because it was so, Dulcie put a shilling into the box.

She had just come out into the porch when she was aware of somebody – a woman, she thought, hurrying past her, opening the door and going into the church. Dulcie was certain that she was crying, though the handkerchief held over her face might have meant that she had a cold. She opened the door a crack and heard the sound of sobbing. It was difficult to know what to do, and Dulcie might have stood there undecided for some time longer had she not seen another woman making her way rather purposefully towards her.

'I've just come to put out the lights and lock up,' she said. 'Father Forbes would wish the church to be kept open for private prayer even at a time like *this*.'

'Oh? Has there been some trouble then?' asked Dulcie delicately.

'Trouble? Oh, my *dear*!' The woman made a little darting movement towards Dulcie, almost as if she were about to dig her in the ribs.

'I suppose people might break in and steal things if the church were left open all day,' Dulcie said, and yet she had a feeling that it was not that kind of trouble. Her thoughts ranged over the different varieties generally associated with the clergy and she began to feel that she had better have gone straight home rather than come here at what might be a painful and embarrassing time.

'We've never had people steal things here,' said the woman. 'We always leave it open till about ten o'clock every night – then I generally come over and lock up, or Father Forbes does – it all depends. I'm his housekeeper, you see.'

'He's not married?' asked Dulcie boldly.

'Oh, no!' The woman looked surprised at the question, as if Dulcie ought to have known that he was not married. 'But of course a good-looking man like that would have his difficult moments – only to be expected, seeing what women are, too. People are only human after all, be they male or female,' she added rather strangely.

Dulcie could not but agree. What does it mean, being 'only human after all'? she asked herself. It was generally said of a person who had committed some indiscretion or even sin. It looked rather as if Neville Forbes had got himself involved with some woman – perhaps a young Sunday school teacher, or even a married woman. 'I saw a woman go into the church just before you came,' Dulcie said. 'She seemed to be crying, and I wondered if I ought to go after her and ask what the matter was.'

'What the matter was!' echoed the housekeeper derisively. 'Well, I suppose there'd have been no harm in *asking*, as they say. I wonder what she'd have said, though.'

Naturally Dulcie wondered too, but the housekeeper had now turned towards the church and pushed the door open in such a way that Dulcie felt she was being dismissed.

'Bye-bye, dear,' said the housekeeper. 'I expect we'll be seeing you in church.'

Dulcie murmured something suitable. It did rather look as if she would have to visit Neville Forbes's church again, though in what capacity she could not as yet say.

# CHAPTER TWELVE

'"Trouble? Oh, my *dear!*"' said Dulcie. 'Those were the words she used. It seemed to have something to do with a woman who ran into the church crying. The housekeeper was one of those bright, friendly little women who are natural but harmless gossips. I'm sure she wanted to talk about the "trouble" but felt she ought not to.'

'I don't suppose it was anything much,' said Viola in her usual damping way. 'The clergy are always having women make scenes over them – one reads about it in the papers nearly every day.'

'Not in *The Times* or the *Manchester Guardian*, somehow,' said Dulcie rather doubtfully.

'No, of course not,' said Viola impatiently. 'But clergymen are rather at the mercy of women, aren't they; all this popping into church at odd times.'

'And people are only human after all, be they male or female – that's what the housekeeper said. Still, the Forbes brothers do seem to have a rather unfortunate touch with women. Do you think Aylwin knows much about his brother's affairs?'

'I can't think why you're so inquisitive. It isn't as if you'd even met Neville Forbes.'

'No, but it's like a kind of game,' said Dulcie. It seemed – though she did not say this to Viola – so much safer and more comfortable to live in the lives of other people – to observe their joys and sorrows with detachment as if one were watching a film or a play. 'Perhaps,' she went on, 'we might ask Aylwin to come in one evening – for a drink on his way home?'

'On his way home? But *this* could hardly be on anybody's way home,' said Viola scornfully.

'If he had been to Deodar Grove,' suggested Dulcie tentatively, 'it *could* be – almost. But then, if he had been *there*, it's perhaps hardly likely that he would want to go on anywhere else afterwards. Could we invite him to a meal? That might be better. I could ask another man,' she said, going rapidly through the list of her male acquaintances. But somehow none of those who first came to mind – Paul Beltane, Senhor MacBride-Pereira, her uncle Bertram – seemed at all suitable.

'Yes, that would be best. What about your – er – ex-fiancé – Maurice?'

'Maurice? Why, of course.' It would show him, she thought, not quite certain what it would show – perhaps that she could now bear to meet him in the ordinary course of social life – that she was a delightful hostess, a wonderful cook – that she knew people like Aylwin Forbes? 'And Aylwin Forbes,' she went on. 'Will you ask him or should the invitation come from me?'

'I don't think it matters. Perhaps I should ask him, making

quite sure that he realizes it is not to be *à deux*,' said Viola a
little bitterly. 'I suppose he will wonder why he is being asked.
I can't very well say it's because you want to find out about his
brother's "trouble".'

'But will he wonder? Surely men – and even women – can
accept a simple invitation without too much questioning?
Aylwin will think it is a simple tribute to himself. And after
all, we can always talk about indexes – this having some little
academic interest in common is a great safeguard. I suppose it
will have to be after Christmas, won't it?'

'Oh, *Christmas* . . .' Viola sighed, for she was to spend the
holiday with her parents at Sydenham. She regarded it as her
duty to go to them, while they, in their turn, felt they ought to
ask her though they would much have preferred to be by
themselves. At Christmas, Dulcie thought, people seemed to
lose their status as individuals in their own right and became,
as it were, diminished in stature, mere units in families, when
for the rest of the year they were bold and original and often
the kind of people it is impossible to imagine having such
ordinary everyday things as parents. Christmas put people in
their places, sent them back to the nursery or cradle, almost.
Where, she wondered, would Aylwin Forbes be spending
Christmas? Surely not in the house in Deodar Grove? Perhaps
he was one of those people who ignored it and went on working, regarding it as nothing more than an unusually long
weekend. After Christmas, if he came to dinner, it might even
be possible to ask him what he had done.

Dulcie herself was to travel home with Laurel on Christmas
Eve to spend the holiday with her sister Charlotte and her
family. It would be better than spending Christmas alone in
London, she knew, yet she felt reluctant to uproot herself and

be reduced in status to the spinster aunt, who had had an unfortunate love affair that had somehow 'gone wrong' and who, although she was still quite young, was now relegated to the shelf and good works. When Dulcie wondered, did one begin to take up good works if they didn't come naturally? When – and how? Then she remembered the evening she had gone to Neville Forbes's church, and his housekeeper saying 'Bye-bye, dear – I expect we'll be seeing you in church.' Perhaps it wasn't so difficult after all.

The day before they were to go, Laurel asked if she might bring her friend Marian to tea. Dulcie was delighted; she had always hoped that Laurel might bring her friends home, but the cosy student tea-parties up in the bed-sitting-room with the cooking on the gas-ring had not so far materialized. Laurel seemed to prefer to meet her friends in coffee bars or in *their* homes or lodgings, which were nearer the centre of London.

'You see,' Laurel said to Marian, rehearsing her beforehand, 'if we were to get the idea into her head now about my moving into a flatlet in your house and get her to realise what a good idea it would be, then she would be on my side at Christmas when we discuss it at home. My parents haven't the least idea about life in London, but my aunt is fairly reasonable – I think she'd see the point.'

As soon as Marian came into the room, Dulcie realised that she was an aunt, old, finished, fit only for the Scouts and their little jumble cart. Could it be that a generation was only ten years? Marian's elegant appearance and deferential, almost solicitous, manner towards her made Dulcie feel like a rather fragile old lady. Even the girl's voice seemed a little louder and more distinct than was necessary, as if she were speaking to a person who was slightly deaf. She was tall and slim, with fair hair done in a bun on top of her head and a side-swept fringe. Her dress was of the 'chemise' type, of a pale creamy brown shaggy material, adorned only with a string of beads that hung to her waist. On her feet were shoes with alarmingly pointed toes and stiletto heels.

'How do you do?' murmured Dulcie, taking the long slender hand that was languidly held out to her. 'It's so nice to meet one of Laurel's friends.'

'So kind of you to ask me,' said Marian. 'You're almost in the country here, aren't you. It seemed quite an adventure, coming all that way on the bus.'

'The Underground is really quicker,' said Dulcie a little sharply.

'Oh, but it always gives me claustrophobia being shut away down there with all those people – I've got quite a *thing* about it . . .'

'Marian has a lovely flatlet in Quince Square,' said Laurel a little nervously. 'I think I told you about it, didn't I?'

'Yes, with a cooker concealed in a cupboard,' said Dulcie. 'In a house full of young or old women? I suppose career women would be the right description.'

'That's rather an old-fashioned way of putting it, isn't it?' suggested Marian. 'One takes it for granted nowadays that women have careers. All sorts of people live in this house, anyway, and I don't think there's anybody over twenty-five. As it happens, one of them is leaving at the end of the year and we were wondering if Laurel . . .' she paused delicately.

'Could perhaps take the room?' Dulcie finished for her. 'Well, it would depend what her parents thought, wouldn't it. I'm only her aunt.'

'Then you wouldn't be – er – *hurt* if she left here?'

'Hurt? Oh, no – I'm not yet enough of an aunt to be hurt in that way,' said Dulcie laughing, glad to realise that she could still distinguish different degrees of hurt. It was surely something to be still alive and young enough to know what a real hurt could be, not like poor Miss Lord, who had been hurt by the man behind her having been served with baked beans when she had been refused. And yet how was she to square this sudden realisation with her conviction that it was so much safer and more comfortable to live in the lives of other people? In her confusion she was hardly conscious of Marian's voice, explaining something about shilling-in-the-slot meters and laundry and cleaning being included in the price of the room.

'. . . lots of meals out, of course. So one doesn't really cook very much.'

'Only breakfast and a hot drink at night perhaps,' said Dulcie, clinging on to reality. She began to wonder if she were not perhaps obsessed by the idea of these hot drinks.

'I don't really have breakfast,' said Marian.

'I don't suppose I should want to bother much with cooking,' said Laurel.

'Well, it's up to your parents to decide how you may live – until you're earning your own living, that is. It's not my responsibility at all,' said Dulcie lightly.

'But you do think it would be a good thing?' Laurel persisted.

'It might be . . . Isn't that the front door bell?'

In the slight confusion that followed, Marian left the house, teetering down the path to the bus stop on her stiletto heels, and Senhor MacBride-Pereira entered it, padding softly in his orange suede shoes. Dulcie took him into the drawing-room, wondering why he had called and if it was too early to offer him a glass of sherry. Then she saw that he was carrying in one hand, partly hidden behind his back, a round box done up in Christmas wrapping-paper.

'Plums,' he said. 'Plums of Elvas, from Portugal.'

'Oh, Elvas plums – how delicious!' Dulcie exclaimed.

'For you, Miss Mainwaring, a small token for this festive season and a return for *your* gift of Balmoral plums.'

'The Victoria plums I gave you in the summer? But those were from the garden,' said Dulcie, confused by the unexpected present.

'And these are from the garden of a distant relative in Portugal. They are picked individually and preserved by a special process. He is a cousin of some kind, many times removed, as you say; his grandfather and mine were second cousins.'

'I see,' said Dulcie, trying to work it out. 'It must be pleasant in Portugal now.'

'But better in Brazil. I look in your Sunday papers and I see the weather report – "Estoril: rain, 49–63 degrees". It does not say what it is like at Copacabana.'

'No, I suppose it's too remote for us.'

'Estoril is like Bournemouth,' declared Senhor MacBride-Pereira.

'Would you like a glass of sherry?' suggested Dulcie. 'I was just going to have some myself,' she added, hoping that this did not sound too unlikely.

'Thank you, that would be delightful.'

'Are you spending Christmas in London?'

'No, strangely enough I am going to Bognor Regis, where a lady of my acquaintance has a delightful "bungalow" – I believe you call it that?'

'Well, yes,' said Dulcie, unable to picture it exactly. 'A bungalow by the sea can certainly be delightful.'

'She – this lady of my acquaintance – will take me to the Midnight Mass at a fashionable church.'

'That should be nice,' said Dulcie, wishing that the sherry would improve her conversational powers. 'Nice' was hardly the word to use to describe a Midnight Mass, and indeed Senhor Macbride-Pereira was soon correcting her, though not for the reason one might have supposed.

'No, Miss Mainwaring,' he said, 'it is not nice – that does not describe what it is. In Latin America, and especially in Brazil, it is *not* considered nice for a man to go to church.'

'Oh, I see. You mean it's not done?'

'That is it – "*not done*" – I must remember that.'

Dulcie drank deeply of her sherry and was conscious that the front door bell had rung again. But Laurel would answer it.

This time it was Paul Beltane who entered the house. He wore a duffel coat and carried in his arms a large plant of some kind shrouded in white paper. A pinkish blossom peeped out from one corner, revealing that it was an azalea.

No doubt Dulcie had ordered one to take with them to her parents, Laurel thought, irritated at the idea of its awkwardness in the train.

'Hullo, Paul,' she said.

'I just came to wish you a happy Christmas,' he said, thrusting the plant towards her.

Laurel was reminded of the evening Aylwin Forbes had called with the flowers for Miss Dace, but this was for *her*.

'How sweet of you,' she said.

'I hope you'll like it.'

'Thank you – it's lovely.' She peered down inside the paper.

'An azalea – how pretty.' Her voice faltered a little, for suddenly she could see them all standing in the shop waiting to be bought. It was, in a way, doing him a kindness to take it off his hands. And yet why should not flowers from a florist be as exciting as flowers from any other man? Thinking this she looked up at him, about to say something else, to sound more grateful, when, to her amazement, she found herself enfolded in his arms, being roughly and passionately kissed.

'I shouldn't have done that,' he said at last, 'but I couldn't help it.'

'Oh,' she said, looking at him with new interest. Then she noticed his hands, slightly red from being in the cold flower water and now covered with scratches. 'Your poor hands!' she exclaimed, taking them in hers. 'What have you done to them?'

He smiled faintly. 'I've been making holly wreaths,' he said. 'There's always a big demand at Christmas.'

'For graves, you mean?'

'Yes, and people like to hang them on their front doors decorated with ribbons and things.'

'That's in the best part of Kensington, of course.'

'Yes . . .'

The drawing-room door opened and out came Dulcie and Senhor MacBride-Pereira, looking slightly flushed and dishevelled. But that, thought Laurel, seeing the glasses and decanter through the open door, was not because *he* had seized *her* in his arms in a passionate embrace.

# CHAPTER THIRTEEN

It was well into January before the dinner party, to which Aylwin and Maurice were to be invited, was finally arranged. It so happened that the evening chosen was also Laurel's last evening at Dulcie's house, before she left to 'take up residence', as it were, in the flatlet house in Quince Square. It had not been so difficult as had been feared, to persuade her parents to agree to the arrangement. Charlotte, Laurel's mother, revealed an unexpected and presumably long suppressed desire to live a 'bachelor girl's' life in London; the idea of a bed-sitting-room with a little cooker hidden away in a cupboard, a concealed washbasin and a divan bed piled with cushions was to her as romantic as an elopement to the South of France with a lover might have seemed to one of a different temperament. It was rather sad, Dulcie thought, that an apparently happily married woman should confess to a secret hankering for such a life. And yet, stealing a glance at her brother-in-law, at that moment preoccupied with classifying a pile of Masai warriors' spears and shields left to the local museum by a retired colonial servant, she could appreciate that perhaps a desire for escape was not so surprising. Many wives must experience it from time to time, she thought, especially those whose husbands smoked old pipes that made peculiar noises, and were so preoccupied with their harmless hobbies that they would hardly have noticed if their wives had been there or not. Dulcie herself had been asked about Marian and whether she seemed a suitable kind of friend for Laurel, but here she was at something of a disadvantage, for she could remember only the external details of Marian's appearance, like her little pointed feet, and could not say more than that 'there seemed to be no harm in her'.

'She'll find it expensive living on her own,' said Viola, when she and Dulcie were preparing for the dinner party.

'Yes, I suppose she will – and yet these girls do seem to manage somehow. I imagine they get taken out quite a lot. Laurel said that Paul Beltane was going to invite her to dinner – had actually done so, I think. And if she's in Quince Square – who knows,' she laughed, 'there may be crumbs from Aylwin Forbes's table.'

'It's hardly *that* kind of a table,' said Viola obscurely.

'You mean crumbs wouldn't fall from it? Or if they did they'd be swept up quickly and efficiently by those servants we heard listening to the television in the basement?'

'Well, yes. But I shouldn't think he's likely to invite her to a meal.'

'You never know what may happen after this evening,' said Dulcie gaily. 'Listen, that must be Miss Lord arriving. I do think it was kind of her to offer to help.'

'It makes a change from her routine – but she isn't going to wait at the table, is she? That seems to be carrying things a little too far. I told Aylwin it was going to be quite a simple dinner.'

'Did you?' said Dulcie, rather annoyed. 'Well, I suppose one could have a servant handing the dishes, whatever was in them.'

Viola had not offered any help, except that of arranging a few tulips and narcissi on the table. Dulcie had asked her advice about the food, but she had not seemed interested and only remarked that Aylwin had once said he didn't like tomatoes. Dulcie, therefore, had been careful to avoid any dish containing these 'love apples', as she now called them to herself, saying over the phrase 'Aylwin can't take love apples' with a good deal of enjoyment. But she had not repeated it to Viola, who did not seem to be amused by such trivialities.

'What are you going to wear?' Dulcie asked.

'Oh, my old black dress. It's really the only suitable thing I've got. I might do something to it.'

'Wear that Spanish shawl, perhaps?'

'Do you think it would look nice?' Viola asked doubtfully.

'Lovely – the only thing is that the fringe is apt to be awkward, getting into the food, isn't it?'

'I could slip it off when we were eating. What are you going to wear?'

'My old black.'

'I didn't know you ever wore black.'

'No, I don't in the daytime, but I have a black dress. I suppose in a way I'm the powder-blue-wool type, with a single string of graduated pearls – but I don't always act in character.'

'You haven't asked another man for Laurel – to make up the numbers.'

'No. I suggested asking Paul, but she seemed to think it wouldn't be a good idea – he'd probably be very shy. So we shall be two men and three women. But I shan't count myself,' said Dulcie hastily. 'I shall hardly be a woman at all, flitting backwards and forwards between the kitchen and the dining-room – looking to see if people have what they want, and all that sort of thing.'

'You will be playing the most womanly part of all,' said Viola. 'Laurel and I will seem insignificant by comparison.'

'Miss Lord will do the washing up, so perhaps I shall come into my own presiding over the coffee tray.'

'The silver coffee pot, of course, Miss Mainwaring,' said Miss Lord, who had just been cleaning it. 'It's a long time since you used *that*. This instant coffee, made in a moment in the cup with boiling water or milk, is all very well, but it hasn't got the *tone* of real coffee, has it. Not that it isn't deli-cious,' she added quickly, as if fearful that the manufacturers might overhear her disloyalty, so close was her contact with them through the waves of commercial television, 'and of course for people who live alone and busy housewives it's really the best thing.'

'What wine are we having?' asked Viola bluntly.

'A Clos Vougeot 1952,' said Dulcie. 'I asked the man at the wine shop to advise me, and of course we have dealt there for years, so I feel I can rely on him.'

'Yes, I think that is suitable with roast duckling,' said Viola.

'And I got some gin because Maurice doesn't like sherry . . .' Dulcie continued. She sensed that Viola was rather bored with the whole thing, and suddenly she too began to wish that her guests weren't coming and they could just have soup and cold ham or scrambled eggs on a tray by the fire.

Aylwin Forbes, on his way in a taxi because he had been unable to work out how one made the journey from Quince Square by public transport, was still wondering if he ought to have stopped somewhere to buy flowers for his hostess. Then he remembered that it was really more correct to do this *after* a dinner party. Miss Mainwaring – he really must try and find out if she had a Christian name – would no doubt have arranged her floral decorations by now. He pictured an Edwardian dinner table, with carnations in little silver vases and smilax trailing down the corners – like those illustrated in the old bound volume of *Every Woman's Encyclopaedia*, which had been a favourite childhood book in the lounge of his mother's hotel in the West Country. But of course it wouldn't be like that at all. The table would be rather bare, with mats showing Old Cries of London or Venice in the eighteenth century. Anyway, he couldn't be always arriving at this house with bunches of flowers, he thought, remembering the last time. It would be embarrassing, to put it mildly, if Viola thought they were for her. He wondered if the attractive young girl who had opened the door to him – Miss Mainwaring's niece, was it? – would be there. He hoped so, for he liked pretty young girls; it was, perhaps, a weakness that he shared with many of his middle-aged colleagues in the academic world, though not the sort of thing one could compare notes about.

The taxi was beginning to slow down in an effort to find the house.

'I think it's the one with the white wooden gate,' said Aylwin, leaning forward.

'Ah, yes, where the gentleman is going in now,' said the taxi driver, preparing to stop.

'No, not that one,' said Aylwin quickly, 'stop a little farther down, please.'

'By the green gate?'

'Yes, that'll do.' He was certainly not going to arrive on the doorstep at the same time as one of the other guests, especially when he had been able to see that it was a good-looking man, some years younger than himself – the niece's boyfriend, no doubt. He paid off the taxi driver and walked a little way down the road before turning back to the house with the white gate.

Maurice, standing on the doorstep about to ring the bell, was surprised and a little disturbed at the painful sensations he experienced at being once again on this particular doorstep. It was as if he had gone back in time to those days when he had loved Dulcie for her simple goodness, as he saw it – that goodness which he had decided he could not endure to live with all his life. He had not felt this when he saw her in the art gallery. There he had been conscious of *her* discomfiture, and irrelevant details like her thin legs and sensible shoes.

He rang the bell, wondering who would come to the door. His first thought, when it was eventually opened, was that he had come too early, for he saw the head and shoulders of a dark girl, apparently wearing only a vest, and was about to make some kind of apology when he saw that the 'vest' was a white dress of some knitted material, very bare about the neck and shoulders.

'Good evening,' Maurice said. 'I'm Maurice Clive.' Girls as young as this one seemed to be were of no interest to him; he found their freshness and exuberance exhausting and preferred 'mature' women, as he called them, whose knowledge of the world and of life matched his own. And yet Dulcie had not been one of these exactly; for although she knew life from her own rather odd angle, in other ways she had been as vulnerable and unsophisticated as a girl of eighteen.

'Do come in,' said Laurel. 'Would you like to hang your coat here?'

Maurice remembered the hatstand and his own reflection in the narrow looking-glass, placed for a man slightly taller than himself. He touched his soft brown hair and would have liked to do more to it, but Laurel was waiting, in her vest as he now thought of it, to show him into the drawing-room.

'I'm Miss Mainwaring's niece,' she said in a curiously formal way.

Miss Mainwaring's niece! he thought, as he entered the familiar suburban drawing-room with the comfortable, rather ugly furniture, rose-patterned loose covers, watercolour paintings in gilt frames, and rather too many china ornaments and jugs. Two women in black dresses were standing by the fire as if waiting for something to happen, as, indeed, they were. One was Dulcie, looking almost fragile and appealing in the paradoxical way that tall people sometimes can, the other a dark woman with trailing hair and a pink Spanish shawl draped uncertainly about her shoulders.

'Ah, Maurice, have some gin!' said Dulcie in a bright, nervous voice.

'Well . . .' he paused, confronted by what was obviously a new bottle bought specially for the occasion, 'what are *you* drinking?'

'We're having sherry,' said Dulcie. 'You remember Viola Dace, don't you,' she added, and was then conscious of her social error in having made the introduction the wrong way round. 'Viola, you remember Maurice Clive at the exhibition, don't you . . . those clever pictures . . . Cat with Lemon . . . and the abstract *shapes*. Were they all sold – or a good many of them? *Do* help yourself to some gin.'

Maurice helped himself rather generously and added a dash of water from a glass jug which stood on the tray.

He likes his gin, thought Aylwin, coming into the room just as Maurice was in the act of pouring.

'Good evening,' said Dulcie, 'so glad you were able to come. I think you know everybody except Maurice Clive. This is Dr Aylwin Forbes,' she explained to Maurice.

'I should think you must be pretty busy at this time of year,' said Maurice, 'with all this flu about.'

'Oh, he's not *that* kind of a doctor, ' Dulcie explained. 'Do help yourself to a drink.'

Aylwin, feeling all eyes upon him, poured himself a rather smaller gin than Maurice had given himself.

'Ah, I see. Then you must be one of the learned variety,' said Maurice.

'Yes, perhaps you might call it that. Learned but useless,' said Aylwin with a little laugh. 'I don't heal the sick, I'm afraid,' he added, almost as if he despised those who did.

'But you do such really worthwhile work in your own way,' said Viola fussily. 'It's so vitally important that the standard of true scholarship should be kept up, when you think of all there is to be contended with nowadays.'

'You mean television and the general lowering of standards everywhere?' said Maurice politely.

'Yes, that, among other things,' said Viola rather darkly. 'Aylwin's book on Edmund Lydden will be *the* definitive study.'

'Edmund Lydden,' Maurice repeated. 'Ah, yes.'

'Who is he?' asked Laurel, feeling that she was the only person young or old enough – in her case young to ask such a question.

'Edmund Lydden is – I suppose we should say *was* – one of

that little band of neo-metaphysical poets of the late seventeenth and early eighteenth centuries who have been
curiously neglected by posterity,' said Aylwin, beaming at
Laurel and wondering if he ought to explain the term 'neo-
metaphysical'. He would have liked to very much, but
through the open door he had just seen a woman in a green
nylon overall tiptoeing along the passage with what looked
like a tureen of soup. It would be a pity if his explanation
were to be broken into by the voice of a servant announcing
that dinner was served. He decided to keep it till they were
settled at the table or back in the drawing-room drinking
their coffee.

'I shouldn't have thought Edmund Lydden had left enough
poetry for it to be worth writing about him,' said Dulcie.
'There surely can't be very much?'

'That may be,' said Aylwin, 'but what remarkable stuff it is!
The "Winter" sonnets – unfinished, admittedly – and the
three Epithalamia, not to mention the fragments . . .'

'Ah, yes, the fragments,' murmured Viola, throwing him an
intimate glance.

'I suppose your book is to be published by one of the
University presses?' asked Maurice.

'Yes, by the Oxford University Press,' said Aylwin, in a full,
satisfied tone.

'They've been simply clamouring for it,' said Viola eagerly.

Dulcie smiled at the idea of anybody so dignified as she
imagined the Oxford University Press to be, 'clamouring' for
a book on a poet nobody had ever heard of. Then, suddenly,
she remembered the house in Deodar Grove and poor Marjorie Forbes. Would not Aylwin have been better employed in
putting his marriage to rights than in collating variant

readings in the works of this same poet that nobody had ever heard of?

'And I am doing the index,' said Viola with simple pride.

Aylwin was glad that the news of dinner being served interrupted this particular bit of conversation or he would have felt himself obliged to pay Viola some public tribute, to anticipate, as it were, the formal acknowledgment which would appear in cold decent print. The expression on his face as he looked at her was one of distaste, as if he were asking himself how he could ever have . . . and yet, really, when he came to think of it, he had *not*. There had been only that unfortunate evening when he had discovered her in tears in the British Museum reading room – the day before his wife Marjorie had gone home to her mother. He had taken her to his house for a drink – she had confided a vague unhappiness which did not by any means seem to justify tears in a public place – he had said something about Marjorie. 'We are two lonely people,' she had said, and he had been forced to agree. Then he had kissed her and put her into a taxi. That was all. Afterwards there had been the meeting at the Summer School and his unwise acceptance of her offer to make the index for his book.

'That must be an exacting task,' said Maurice primly.

There was a short silence. Dulcie began wondering whether she should offer another drink or get them into the dining-room, towards which she too had seen Miss Lord tiptoeing with the soup tureen.

'I think Dulcie wants us to go and eat,' said Maurice. 'Don't you?' he added in a lower, more intimate tone.

'Well, dinner *is* ready,' she said uncertainly. 'But do have another drink.'

'No, thank you, let us eat,' said Aylwin, feeling himself

taking command of the situation. Had he known exactly where the dining-room was he would have led the way there.

Dulcie sat at one end of the big mahogany table, with Aylwin on her right and Maurice on her left. Laurel sat next to Aylwin and Viola next to Maurice. There should have been a man, or some male presence, at the other end of the table to make things even, Dulcie felt. A clergyman would have served the purpose excellently and she thought what a pity it was that she did not know the vicar of the parish well enough to have asked him.

'My niece is going to live quite near you,' she said to Aylwin. 'Do you know a house in Quince Square which is turned into flats, or rooms for students and young people?'

'Ah, yes – that would be number six or number eight – just opposite my house. I often see young girls coming and going through the trees – A l'ombre des jeunes filles en fleurs,' he added, bringing out the tag of Proust he had wanted to use when he had seen Laurel for the first time. So she was going to live in the house opposite with the young girls! 'We may meet some time,' he added. He had wanted to ask her if she would come and cheer a lonely old man some evening, but could think of no way of expressing it that might not be misunderstood. Besides, he was only forty-seven and did not want to make himself sound ridiculous.

'Did you see the exhibition of Proust relics?' asked Maurice, showing that he had recognised the quotation. 'Such a jumble of things and yet so fascinating. It made one want to preserve one's own relics, just in case.'

'I think the relics of any woman could be just as interesting,' said Dulcie thoughtfully. 'Particularly if she had been unhappy, and who hasn't, and if she had kept things . . .'

> 'When my grave is broke up again,
> Some second guest to entertain . . .'

said Viola.

Laurel looked at the two women scornfully. If only they could realise how ridiculous and embarrassing they were! She began to clear away the soup plates rather noisily. There was something dreadfully depressing about the culture of middle-aged people.

'Would you like me to carve?' asked Aylwin when the duck was brought to the table.

'Well, thank you, but I think I can manage,' said Dulcie, seeing that Maurice was looking rather annoyed. 'Perhaps you would all start an animated conversation and not watch me too closely.'

'You would like me to pour the wine, wouldn't you,' said Maurice, rising from the table.

'Laurel is a charming name,' said Aylwin, obeying Dulcie's instructions. 'Women have such a choice of names. Literature, flowers, precious stones – one envies them.'

'You have no need to,' said Viola. 'Yours is most unusual. I suppose it came from Watts-Dunton's novel of that name?'

'Yes,' said Aylwin quickly. For the second time that evening he was reminded of the lounge of his mother's hotel and the odd selection of tattered-looking books in the glass-fronted bookcase in the lounge. As well as *Every Woman's Encyclopaedia*, there had been – indeed, there still was – *Aylwin*, by Theodore Watts-Dunton. 'And yours,' he added rather spitefully, 'is not Viola, with her willow cabin, but the Violet by a mossy stone. How sad Wordsworth's women are – Alice in her tattered cloak – Lucy, in her grave, and oh the difference!'

'And Barbara in the churchyard, with the rain plashing, was it, upon her stone,' said Maurice. 'Though of course that's not Wordsworth,' he added hastily.

The duck was well cooked, Dulcie noticed with relief, as she sliced the rich brown meat and crisp skin. Viola had suggested it might be stuffed with olives, but Dulcie had preferred the conventional sage and onions and the traditional accompaniment of apple sauce and green peas to anything more exotic.

'This reminds me of home,' said Aylwin, looking down at his plate with pleasure.

'Home?' Dulcie echoed. Did he mean his home with Marjorie, or something more remote – little-grey-home-in-the-west kind of thing? And he did come from the West Country, too. She bent her head to hide a smile, for home was no laughing matter.

'Yes, duck was my favourite dinner when I was a boy,' he explained.

'When you were a boy,' Viola repeated with a kind of wonder.

'Yes, I was once a boy,' he admitted. He did not feel that he need go into the hotel background or reveal that his family had had much better food than the guests. That was only to be expected, when you came to think of it, but no good could come of such frankness.

'A splendid wine, Dulcie,' said Maurice. 'I must congratulate you on your choice.'

'The wine merchant helped me,' Dulcie admitted.

'Good! I don't think women should be too knowledgeable about wine,' said Aylwin.

'I only like white wine,' said Laurel.

'Imperial Tokay or a delicate Liebfraumilch,' said Aylwin, thinking what a pleasure it would be to initiate her into the joys of drinking. 'Or perhaps a Bernkastler Doktor . . .'

'Well, as long as it's sweet and not too heavy,' said Laurel indulgently.

'You'll soon grow out of liking sweet wines,' said Viola rather waspishly. She was embarrassed and disgusted by Aylwin's behaviour towards Laurel. One could see now why he had married somebody like Marjorie. She remembered the evenings she had sat up, her eyes dazzled and exhausted by the little slips of paper when she was making the index for his book. He would never realise what hard work it had been. She could feel her eyes filling with tears of self-pity. What would happen if they began to course down her cheeks? she wondered. Nobody would notice except Dulcie and she would offer some homely remedy or ask if she was getting a cold. She looked up and saw that Maurice was watching her with a half-smile on his lips.

'I'll take some of these things out into the kitchen,' she said quickly. She stood up with a dish of peas, the pink shawl slipping from her shoulders.

In the kitchen Miss Lord was sitting at the table, polishing some little glass dishes.

'Dainty, aren't they,' she said. 'Just the thing for the sweet. That orange mousse will look lovely in them. Oh, Miss Dace, your shawl! It must've dipped in the soup. Give it to me and I'll wash the fringe.'

Viola returned to the dining-room.

'. . . Easter in Tuscany,' she heard Aylwin say.

'How I should love to go to Italy!' Laurel sighed.

After the mousse they had cheese and a bottle of her

father's port, which Dulcie had found in the cellar and decanted into one of the decanters which had stood empty on the sideboard since his death.

'I suppose we should leave the gentlemen to it,' she said, in her naive way.

'No, we will help you to clear the table,' said Aylwin, getting up.

'I'd really rather you went into the drawing-room and then I will bring the coffee in there,' said Dulcie.

Aylwin, Viola and Laurel did this, but Maurice stayed behind.

'I remember where some of these things go,' he said, opening a drawer and putting the table mats into it.

'Can they still go in the same place after all this time?' said Dulcie.

'It doesn't seem so long to me, now that I'm here again,' said Maurice. 'I've been putting mats away in spirit so many times.'

'What *are* you talking about?' Dulcie frowned, trying to find room for another dish on the trolley.

He came up to her and put his arms around her. She stood there without moving, the dish still in her hand, but his nearness was disturbing and she turned her head away when he made as if to kiss her.

'Oh, Dulcie, perhaps it was a mistake, our breaking it off like that!'

*Perhaps?* she said to herself. He might have sounded a little more sure. After all, it was he who had done the breaking – he who had said that he was unworthy of her love. Did he now consider that he was worthy? Or that her own standard was less high?

'It was all for the best,' she said stiffly. 'We shouldn't have been happy together.'

'Not then, perhaps. But now it might be different . . .'

'It's too late now.'

'You mean there's somebody else. This Dr Forbes? Aylwin,' he said mockingly.

Dulcie smiled at the idea. She remembered 'Some problems of an editor' and herself rushing forward with the smelling salts; then her researches in the public library and the dark walk to Neville Forbes's church.

'I shall never marry now,' she said.

'Oh, come Miss Mainwaring, I wouldn't say that,' Miss Lord's voice rang out in the hall. 'Oh, I beg your pardon,' she said, backing out of the doorway. 'I didn't realise you had anybody with you. I thought you were just talking to Miss Dace. I shouldn't like you to think that I was eavesdropping in any shape or form.'

'That's all right, Miss Lord,' said Dulcie, feeling for her embarrassment but not knowing what to say to improve matters.

'There you are,' said Maurice, when Miss Lord had left the room. 'Quite hopeless, aren't you.'

Dulcie smiled, but there was really no pleasure in feeling that he might be persuaded to come back to her. She had only to encourage the idea to lose him again, and the second loss might well be more painful than the first.

'There are plenty of girls,' she began, not really wanting him to agree that there were, but of course he did.

'It's only that you're different, somehow,' he added. Yes, she thought, older and duller and with the added interest of being somebody to be won back again.

'The others will be wondering if they're ever going to get any coffee,' she said, hurrying out to the kitchen.

Maurice went back to the drawing-room, where Aylwin had started his little dissertation, postponed before dinner, on what he called 'the neo-metaphysicals', but only Viola seemed to be listening, and now the arrival of the coffee interrupted him yet again.

Dulcie had been wanting to ask him about his brother Neville, and now, with the anxieties of the meal safely behind her, she found the courage to begin.

'By the way,' she said casually, 'haven't you a brother who's a clergyman?'

'I *have* a brother in Holy Orders, certainly,' he said rather reluctantly.

Dulcie was a little discouraged by his cautious tone and tried to remember quickly whether it was possible that she could know about this by legitimate means, as it were. Then she was back in the cloakroom of the learned society with the washbasin cluttered up with flowers for an invalid and heard again the tall woman saying that she had been curious to see Aylwin Forbes because he happened to be 'our vicar's brother'. So it was all right to know about Neville and quite unnecessary to reveal that she had made a special journey to the public library to look him up in *Crockford*.

'Somebody told me at the conference last summer,' she explained, 'and I have an uncle and aunt who live quite near his church. I happened to go past it once.' 'Happened to go past' could describe any sort of manoeuvre, really: she wasn't telling a lie in describing it in those words.

'We don't see much of each other,' said Aylwin. 'Just because somebody is one's brother it doesn't necessarily mean that one finds him particularly congenial.'

'Blood isn't always thicker than water, then,' said Maurice.

'Well, it's hardly a question of that,' said Aylwin a little testily.

'And just because he is a clergyman it doesn't necessarily mean that one should pretend to feel more than one does,' said Viola, as if she were rising in Aylwin's defence.

'No, of course not. Perhaps one expects more of the clergy than of other men, but really he has been rather troublesome lately. My mother and I have had a good deal to put up with.'

'Ah, your mother,' said Dulcie, hoping for more. She pictured a rather conventional kind of mother, elderly, of course, with white hair, and lace at her throat. But were mothers like this nowadays? Anyway, old Mrs Forbes was somewhere in the West Country, putting up with a good deal from the Rev. Neville Forbes. It was an unusual picture, but the details were blurred. And now Aylwin had changed the subject and they were somehow back at the neo-metaphysicals again. Dulcie, while appearing to listen, was going over in her mind the various ways in which a clergyman son might be 'rather troublesome'. The possibilities were infinite, and not all of them could be discussed in the present company. It seemed that she would have to go to his church again; this time it would probably be better to attend a service . . .

Soon after this the party began to break up. Maurice, it seemed, lived in Highgate now, and had a long journey. Aylwin found himself resenting the way he took his hostess's hand in both of his, as if he had some special claim on her, but was glad that he appeared to ignore Laurel almost completely.

'My *dear* Dulcie,' Maurice murmured, 'so very sweet of you. A *lovely* evening . . .'

So her name was Dulcie. Aylwin registered this fact for the

first time, and when he came to say goodbye he made a point of using it, not to be outdone by the younger man.

'Thank you, Dulcie,' he said, 'for a most delightful evening. And a memorable dinner.'

Dulcie hardly knew what to say, so surprised and pleased was she at his use of her Christian name. And yet there was nothing so very special about it, when they were all on quite friendly terms. It was just the contrast with the chilly 'Miss Mainwaring' that delighted her. She wondered when she would dare to call him 'Aylwin'.

# CHAPTER FOURTEEN

Every morning now Laurel drew back her curtains as if she were flinging open the shutters on to a prospect of the Bay of Naples or some soaring mountain peak in Switzerland instead of just the dripping February trees of Quince Square. Life was what one called 'intoxicating', from this moment of waking, through all the stages of getting up and making her own breakfast on the little concealed cooker, to the final rush to the bus stop, sometimes in company with one of the other inhabitants of the house. These consisted of various other young girls, like Marian and herself, two Africans who were studying at the London School of Economics, a young man who worked in a bank and did morris dancing in his spare time, a young actor and his friend who were always pressing their suits in the ironing room downstairs, and one or two as yet unidentified young men who wore bowler hats and looked rather alike, so that Laurel thought there might be any number of them or only one.

Aylwin Forbes, watching from an upper window of his house, had once seen Laurel leaving the hostel, and after that he often found himself at the window at about that time. He decided against a chance morning encounter at the bus stop, however. He was not at his best in the mornings and would, he thought, be totally incapable of making sparkling conversation with the young girls who, this year, were dressed in bright shaggy coats and sweaters which made them look like delicious furry animals.

The coming of spring found him in a state of indecision about everything. His book was finished but he had not yet started a new piece of work. The thought of Marjorie still nagged at his conscience – it was at this time of year that they had first met – but he made no attempt to visit the house in Deodar Grove. He imagined his mother-in-law vigorously washing the net curtains and turning the house upside down with spring cleaning. Perhaps Marjorie would be helping her, or giving tea to that organist he had met on the doorstep on the afternoon of the jumble sale. His thoughts turned quickly away from her; it was she who must make the next move. As for the other woman in his life – if somebody who is making an index for one's book can be so described – he was relieved to think of her living with that nice Dulcie Mainwaring, and felt that he need not worry about her any more. The index was finished, she had been fulsomely thanked in the foreword, and that was that.

Having decided against a chance morning encounter with Laurel, Aylwin began to wonder whether a chance evening encounter might not be arranged. The days were drawing out now and he could easily be walking round the square in the twilight at about the time the young girls were coming home. For the first time in his life he began to wish that he was an animal-lover, that he had a dog who needed to be taken out for an evening walk. A vigorous, bounding animal, from whom the girls might need to be protected, might be the best, and he imagined himself apologising for Nigger's or Rover's – he had conventional ideas of dogs' names – muddy paws soiling one of the fluffy coats. Or, again, a smaller animal, one who might be petted and exclaimed over, should also be considered. But then, advantageous though the possession of a dog might be, what was he going to do with it when he was not using it to walk round the square? He disliked animals in the house and it was too much to expect the servants to have it with them all the time. The only solution would be to ask that nice Dulcie Mainwaring to look after it, but then the animal would be too inaccessible to be available when it was needed.

As it happened there was no need even to consider getting a dog. The encounter took place quite naturally one evening when Aylwin himself was returning from his publishers and Laurel from her secretarial college. They found themselves getting off the same bus, with Laurel's friend Marian, and the three of them walked into Quince Square together.

Laurel introduced Marian rather confusedly. They had enjoyed several jokes about Aylwin, as women, even the youngest, will about men, and an unexpected meeting with him was somewhat unnerving.

'You were just going home,' he said rather lamely. He, in his turn, found Marian somewhat unnerving – such a sharp little face above the fluffy orange coat, a contrast to Laurel's gentleness. 'Have you had a good day?'

'Yes, thank you,' they answered politely.

'Have you?' asked Laurel, aware that any kind of comparison of their 'days' must sound ridiculous. It was beyond her to imagine what his would be like.

'I always think one needs a drink at this time,' he said, as they approached his front door.

'A drink?' said Marian in a surprised tone, and Aylwin realised that they were so much younger than he was that they could have hardly any points of contact between them. Their gay, birdlike little days would not *need* drinks at the end of them, like some kind of restorative, as the days of grown-up people like himself did. Really, one could sympathise with those elderly ladies who kept brandy in the house for 'medicinal' purposes only.

'Well, a drink is sometimes nice,' said Laurel, a little apprehensively.

'Will you excuse me, Dr Forbes? I have a date this evening and must hurry and change.' Marian's little pointed toes and stiletto heels, so precariously supporting the fluffy orange bundle of her body, were away and into the door of the hostel before either Laurel or Aylwin realised what had happened.

'Then perhaps –' Aylwin turned to Laurel and smiled – '*you* would like to come and have a drink with me if you aren't doing anything better?'

Poor lonely man, Laurel thought with a rush of pity, using to herself the words he had not dared to utter himself for fear of ridicule. Would they go to a pub or to his house? she wondered. Presumably his house, as it was so near.

'I should like to very much,' she said.

'My house is just opposite. I had been hoping I might see you some time. And how is your aunt?'

'Aunt Dulcie?' she asked in a rather surprised tone. 'Oh, very well, I think. She usually is. I don't see so much of her now, of course.'

They were going in through the shiny painted door and

climbing flights of stairs softly carpeted in red. Dark oil paintings, sinister because the subjects were not easily discernible, adorned the walls. Aylwin went on ahead and flung open a door.

'My library,' he said.

There were certainly a great many books, the kind that looked as if they might be a false façade, swinging back to reveal a cocktail cabinet. Laurel peered at them, more for something to do than from any particular interest; the bindings were beautiful but the titles meant nothing to her.

'Very obscure English poets,' said Aylwin apologetically. 'The sort of things I've spent my life studying.'

'Goodness!' said Laurel, wishing that Marian were with her to make some pert and amusing comment.

'What would you like?' he asked, waving his hand towards the drinks which were decently set out on a small table near the gas fire.

Laurel hesitated, wishing that he would suggest something. 'This is quite a pleasant sherry,' he said, picking up a decanter. 'Or there's gin, of course, or even whisky – but I don't suppose you'd like that.'

'Probably not,' said Laurel rather sadly. She accepted a glass of sherry and stood looking round the room, holding the glass in both hands.

'Well, here's to your very good health,' he said stiffly, feeling that it was not quite the thing to say to one who looked such a picture of health anyway. He would have liked best to sit and gaze at her, not saying anything for, delightful though they were, these young girls were not for talking to – but he tried his best to make suitable conversation, asking again after her aunt, inquiring about her work and how she was enjoying life in the hostel.

While he struggled with conversation Laurel's eyes had strayed to a large table which was littered with papers.

'You are looking at the proofs of my book,' he said. 'It's now in its final stages.'

'That's the one Miss Dace has been helping you with?' she asked.

'Well, yes, in a sense. She has only done the index,' he said meanly.

'I should find that kind of work terribly boring, I'm afraid,' said Laurel confidently.

'Yes, it's a dreary job – one I simply can't imagine you ever having to do.' He smiled.

'But somebody has to.'

'Yes, somebody has to. But there are people trained to do such things.'

'Like performing seals,' giggled Laurel, who was not used to such large glasses of sherry as Aylwin provided.

But he seemed to think her little joke terribly funny and they both laughed rather more than was necessary. In the back of his mind Aylwin may have felt a little guilty, thinking of women he knew who made indexes – that nice aunt of Laurel's, and poor Viola, of course – but this was not the moment to remember them.

'Your glass is empty,' he said, his hand on the decanter.

'I don't think I ought to have any more,' said Laurel. 'Or perhaps not a full glass. I really ought to be going now.'

'Must you?'

He stood with the decanter poised over her glass, and Laurel, looking up at him, thought in a variation of Dulcie's words when she had bent over him at the lecture, why, he must have been very good-looking once. And now the lines round his eyes and the few silver threads that her sharp eyes detected in his golden hair touched her heart, so that she felt rather pleasantly sad and remembered a line from a poem she had read in some anthology –

*His golden locks Time hath to silver turn'd –*

and, when one came to think of it, he must be rather old – getting on for fifty probably. She was rather sorry now that she and Marian had mocked him.

He bent down towards her, almost as if he were about to kiss her. A feeling of panic came over her and she cried out inside herself, Oh, Paul, Paul . . . but at that moment there was a knock at the door and a dark foreign-looking maid stood in the doorway.

'Please sir, Mrs Williton is here. She will speak with you.'

Down in the hall Grace Williton stood in front of a mirror, ornately framed in gilt cupids, and straightened her pink felt hat. She had decided to wear her new hat with her grey costume for this visit to her son-in-law. He would have got her letter yesterday, warning him of her visit. She was glad that the maid had said he was in. That showed that he was not shirking his duty – for once, she added sarcastically. But sarcasm was not normally within her range. She liked to think of herself as a straightforward sort of person. 'People always know where they are with me,' she would say rather smugly; it never occurred to her that people might not always want to know such things.

She began to climb the stairs, wondering as she did so if the carpet was brushed every day and if moths lurked in the darkness of the treads; She had never felt at home in this house and she never would. Neither had Marjorie, if it came to that.

'Dr Forbes is in the library,' said the maid, backing away from the door so that Mrs Williton could go in. 'I'll say you have come.'

'Well, Aylwin,' she began uncompromisingly, feeling as always what a ridiculous name he had.

'Why, Grace, this *is* a surprise!' he brought out, feeling that while 'Grace' was not quite right, 'Mother' was impossible.

Mrs Williton had not at first seen Laurel, who was over by the table, displaying an unnatural interest in the proofs of Aylwin's book.

'May I introduce Miss – er – Mainwaring,' said Aylwin, who had temporarily forgotten Laurel's surname.

Laurel looked up in surprise, not at first recognising herself under her aunt's name. She saw a little dumpy woman in a grey suit and pink felt hat, her gloved hands clasped tightly together.

'Mrs Williton – my mother-in-law,' Aylwin explained.

'How-do-you-do,' Laurel murmured, smiling because of the sherry and the unlikeliness of Dr Forbes having such a banal thing as a mother-in-law. 'I was just going,' she added.

'Let me see you down, then,' said Aylwin. 'You will excuse us, Grace? I shan't be a moment.'

'I didn't know you had a mother-in-law,' said Laurel brightly, as they were going down the stairs.

'Well, it isn't the kind of thing one reveals – or conceals, for that matter,' said Aylwin, unhappy that the evening should be ending in this slightly ridiculous way. 'I'm sorry she should have chosen to call just now.'

'But I had to go anyway,' Laurel reminded him.

'You must come again. Goodbye!' He took her hand and kissed it lightly. Laurel, astonished and inclined to giggle, ran out into the square.

Upstairs Mrs Williton prowled uneasily round the room, beating her still gloved hands together. She noticed the two sherry glasses and the almost empty decanter. Plying a young girl with drink, she thought, assuming that the decanter had been full at the start of the evening. It was disgusting. She had always known that her son-in-law-was a man of loose moral character, but never before had she been confronted with the actual proof of his degeneracy. What might not have happened had she not chosen to arrive at that moment! And in a library, too, surrounded by great literature! She removed her gloves and took out her spectacles to peer at some of the titles of the books surrounding her – such fine old leather bindings, but the gilt lettering was a little difficult to read. *The Rosciad, Night Thoughts, The Pleasures of Imagination, The Bastard* – could it be? She peered more closely; it looked like 'Bastard', or was it perhaps 'Bustard', a kind of bird? . . . She turned away from the books shocked and confused. What made the whole thing even more shocking was that Aylwin should be carrying on in this way when he must have known from her letter that she would be arriving at any moment. And yet that too was typical of him. The man was – what was that word that Miss Wellcome had used when they met in the library that day and she had been returning a book about Lord Byron? – a *libertine*, that was it. She repeated it to herself, saying it almost out loud.

'Sorry to keep you waiting, Grace.' Aylwin almost bounded into the room. 'Do sit down and we'll have a drink. What would you like?' He fetched a clean glass from the table and stood for perhaps the third time that evening with the decanter poised.

'No, thank you. You know I never take spirits,' said Mrs Williton, pursing her lips.

'Well, sherry isn't "spirits",' – he seemed to emphasise the word in a sarcastic way, she thought – 'But I dare say we've got some tomato juice or something like that downstairs. I'll ring for it.'

'No, thank you – I don't want anything. You got my letter?'

'No, I didn't. You wrote to me, then?'

'Yes, the day before yesterday. It should have arrived by now.'

'The evening post is here.' He went over to the table. 'But I haven't had time to look at it yet.'

'I'm not surprised,' she said grimly.

'Let me see – ah, yes, here it is. But my dear Grace, you put Quince Square, S.W.11! The correct address is W.11, you knows. No wonder it was delayed! It's probably been to wherever S.W.11 may be – Balham or Barnes or Battersea – who knows.' He tossed off the names with a light contemptuous air, as if it was scarcely believable that people should actually live in such places. 'Shall I read what you say or would you rather deliver your message in person?'

'I only said I was coming to see you.'

'Why didn't you telephone?'

'It was better to write.' Mrs Williton had a deep mistrust and fear of the telephone, which she would use only in the gravest emergency. 'Now that I'm here, all I want to ask is what you propose to do about Marjorie.'

'What *can* I do?' Aylwin poured himself some more sherry. 'She left me, after all. I even tried to visit her once, which is more than she has done.'

'When was that?'

'You were having a jumble sale in aid of the organ fund,' said Aylwin drily. 'It seemed not quite the time to call.'

Mrs Williton's grim expression softened for a moment, then her lips tightened again into a hard line.

Thinking of that handsome young organist, no doubt, said Aylwin to himself.

'I'm sorry you felt unable to come into the house,' she said. 'Perhaps if you'd given us some warning . . .'

'The whole point seemed to be to come *without* warning – on the impulse of the moment.'

'It is always unwise to act on an impulse,' said Mrs Williton.

'Yes, I rather agree with you,' he said. Had not his own marriage been that kind of an action? And Marjorie's leaving him, also?

'Couldn't you and Marjorie have a talk with your brother?' Mrs Williton suggested. 'After all, a clergyman must see so much of this kind of thing – he would surely be able to help.'

'Neville has seen rather *too* much,' said Aylwin. 'He's quite unable to manage his own affairs, let alone advise other people.'

'Our Father Tulliver is very wise,' she persisted. 'How would it be if you were to spend Easter with us? He could probably spare a moment to see you – I'm sure he would, though Easter is a very busy time for the clergy, as you know.'

'I'm afraid that's impossible. I have made arrangements to spend Easter in Tuscany this year.'

'*Tuscany?*' The mingling of incredulity and horror in Mrs Williton's tone made him wonder what she imagined he was going to do.

'Yes, in Tuscany,' he repeated. 'A part of Italy, you know – delightful in April.'

'Oh, Italy!' Her tone was contemptuous now. Italy and libertines seemed to go together quite naturally. Tuscany had sounded more sinister. Perhaps because the word reminded her of 'tusks', she had thought vaguely of elephants and Africa, or something farther back in the dark ages – mammoths, she believed. It was all very confused. She eased the pink hat slightly off her brow, where it was beginning to give her a headache, and stood up.

'I can do nothing here,' she said wearily.

'Well, I'm sorry you feel that,' said Aylwin pleasantly. 'Why didn't Marjorie come herself? How *is* she, by the way?' he continued chattily as they made their way downstairs. 'And what are you doing for Easter? Why not arrange to have a few days at Taviscombe – I'm sure my mother would be glad to have you. The hotel isn't usually very full at Easter.'

And being related by marriage we should be taken on reduced terms and given poky little rooms at the top of the house, thought Mrs Williton grimly. Still, it was an idea. A breath of sea air would do her girlie good. Perhaps not at Easter, though. One did not want the upset of a strange church over the Festival, and then there was Father Tulliver's Easter offering. She preferred to put it in the bag herself rather than send it to one of the churchwardens. One could never be *absolutely* sure that it would get to Father Tulliver that way, though of course it was ridiculous to feel that, really – they were both perfectly honest . . .

Mrs Williton walked briskly from the house without looking back. She had remembered noticing a tea-shop near the Underground station and she made her way towards it for that cup of strong reviving tea which Aylwin had not offered and which her pride would not have allowed her to demand. Here she sat, strength flowing back into her with the sweet brown liquid, while a big jolly-looking woman from the West Indies cleared away the used crockery and wiped over the table top with a huge dusky hand. It was about half past six in the evening and other solitary people sat, reviving themselves after their day or summoning up the strength to go home. Most of them looked as if they had problems worrying them – a novelist or a sociologist might have felt very near the heart of reality at that moment. But Mrs Williton was neither of these things. She finished her tea and made her way down into the station. As she stood uncomfortably in the District Line train, she began to wonder why Marjorie had married Aylwin, and when no answer suggested itself she went on to wonder why anybody married anybody. It only brought trouble to themselves and their relations.

# CHAPTER FIFTEEN

The morning of the Sunday chosen by Dulcie and Viola for their visit to Neville Forbes's church was warm and spring-like.

It was the Fourth Sunday in Lent – Refreshment or Mothering Sunday – and Dulcie wondered if Aylwin had sent a present to his mother in the West Country. She somehow imagined that he had not. It was difficult to imagine him among all the cards and suitable 'gifts' that had suddenly blossomed in the shops. Dulcie preferred to think of him ordering a case of wines to be sent or choosing a piece of antique jewellery in a dark little shop.

During the morning she wrote some letters and went out to post them just before lunch. As she was returning, a taxi stopped in the road, and out got Mrs Beltane, holding Felix in her arms, followed by a good-looking elderly clergyman, carrying a bunch of narcissi. Felix, released from captivity, bounded along the pavement, yapping excitedly, and Dulcie stooped down to pet him. She was surprised and not a little curious to see Mrs Beltane with a clergyman. It seemed not to be quite in character, for, as far as she knew, Mrs

Beltane never went to church. She was of that school which prefers to worship in a garden or some lovely 'spot': indeed, she would probably have maintained, if challenged, that one is nearer God's heart in a garden than anywhere else on earth.

'Good morning, Miss Mainwaring – and *what* a lovely morning! May I introduce Father Benger?'

Dulcie shook the clergyman's hand and murmured something, rather confusedly, for she was dazzled by the brilliance of Father Benger's silver wavy hair, surely blue-rinsed like Mrs Beltane's?

'A great pleasure,' he purred, taking her hand in a soft, intimate clasp and smiling to reveal a set of almost too natural-looking white teeth. Dulcie had the feeling that he was not an Anglican or Roman priest – although he was addressed as 'Father' – nor did he seem like a Nonconformist minister. There was something slightly phoney about him, and Mrs Beltane's next words confirmed her suspicions.

'Where is your church?' Dulcie asked politely.

'Well, it isn't exactly a *church*,' explained Mrs Beltane, 'but a large room – an *upper* room – most beautifully furnished, in the best of taste. Very near Harrods, as a matter of fact. A few of us meet together, you know, for quite a simple service, though there *is* incense, and candles too, and today the most beautiful spring flowers, *exquisitely* arranged. And afterwards, cocktails in Father Benger's flat.'

'I thought churches didn't have flowers in Lent,' said Dulcie bluntly.

'Oh, well, this isn't an *ordinary* church,' said Mrs Beltane.

'We feel,' said Father Benger, in a slightly reproachful tone, 'that the most beautiful things should be offered to God regardless of the time of year.'

'Yes, of course,' said Dulcie hastily.

'And Felix enjoyed the service too, didn't you, darling?' said Mrs Beltane, gathering him up in her arms.

Felix yapped vigorously.

'All animals are welcome – within reason, that is,' said Father Benger. 'We look to St Francis of Assisi as our patron. My own name happens to be Francis,' he added.

'It sounds most interesting,' said Dulcie politely.

'Perhaps you will join us one day,' said Mrs Beltane, in the rather perfunctory tone in which social invitations not meant to be accepted are sometimes issued, and to which the only suitable reply is a murmur. 'I had hoped to persuade Senhor MacBride-Pereira to come, but he has some idea that it is beneath a man's dignity to go to church.'

'Ah, yes, in Latin America – perhaps in Brazil particularly – it is considered "not *nice*" for a man to go to church,' said Dulcie, remembering her own conversation with him.

'If all men had that idea where would the church be today?' asked Mrs Beltane, with an admiring glance at Father Benger.

'The labourers are still few,' he said, with understandable complacency. 'I wonder if there is a shortage of priests in Latin America?' he asked, turning suddenly to Dulcie.

'I'm afraid I don't know,' she faltered. It wasn't the kind of thing one would be likely to know, she felt. 'One always imagines that these Latin countries are swarming with priests,' she added.

'Well, Felix made one more little man for your congregation,' said Mrs Beltane, kissing his blue curly head.

Felix's little black beady eyes looked fiercely out at the assembled company.

'Mother, lunch is ready,' said Monica, appearing in the doorway, looking rather harassed.

'Ah, our good Martha,' said Father Benger.

He and Mrs Beltane moved slowly into the house, as if conscious of being the ones who had chosen the better part.

Dulcie went in to her own lunch. She wondered if they would be having chicken – something reared in the dim light of a broiler house as artificial as Father Benger's 'church'. She and Viola were having lamb, which had roasted to perfection in a slow oven, made fragrant with sprigs of rosemary.

At lunch, she asked, 'You *are* coming to Neville Forbes's church this evening, aren't you?'

'Yes,' said Viola, 'if you want company. I suppose it may be quite interesting.'

Later that day, as they got off the bus and walked along the road to the church, Dulcie said, 'I feel I ought to call and see Uncle Bertram and Aunt Hermione. Perhaps there will be time after the service. "Solemn Evensong and Benediction",' she read from the weather-beaten brown notice-board, which was easier to see than at her first visit. 'What a lot they're giving us!'

'Oh, it's the usual kind of service in Anglo-Catholic churches,' said Viola in a superior tone.

'Oughtn't you to be wearing a hat – or don't they mind about that sort of thing nowadays?'

'No, I never wear a hat. I have a black lace mantilla which I wear when I want to cover my head. It's more becoming.'

'Surely one shouldn't think of whether it's becoming or not,' said Dulcie, regretting her last year's dingy blue felt hat. She hoped Viola wouldn't wear a mantilla for the service –

it might make them look conspicuous, and that was the last thing she wanted. Those who go to church for other reasons than worship should sit unobtrusively towards the back, observing but not observed. Perhaps the dingy felt hat, being a kind of protective colouring, was not a bad idea after all.

They entered the church, taking hymn-books and prayer-books from a shelf by the door. There were not many people there, so it was easy to choose a seat at the back. A middle-aged man, wearing a hearing-aid, was sitting two rows in front of them. He must have heard or sensed their entrance, for he looked quickly round at them, and when Dulcie had got up from saying a quick prayer, she was disconcerted to find that he had disappeared. Nor was she reassured when some instinct made her turn round and she saw him now sitting behind them. There was the usual sprinkling of elderly ladies, one of whom came fussing up to them with more hymn-books, and several young men and girls sitting together in a group.

The organ began to play some indefinite music and Dulcie and Viola waited eagerly for the entrance of a handsome clergyman who looked like Aylwin Forbes. A choir of about a dozen men and women wearing purple robes now came in, and behind them a tall shuffling clergyman, bald and wearing heavy horn-rimmed spectacles. He looked disappointingly unlike Aylwin, and bore no resemblance to the handsome clergyman they had seen in the Bond Street tea-shop. No doubt Neville Forbes was the elder of the brothers! Dulcie thought, really quite a lot older, and with none of Aylwin's good looks. Still, disappointing though this was, it should not make him any the less interesting. Indeed, it was perhaps even more interesting that such a plain-looking man should have been, in Aylwin's words, 'rather troublesome'.

'This *can't* be him,' whispered Viola, as a droning voice began the service.

'He must be a lot older than Aylwin,' Dulcie answered.

She recognised most of the service as being like an ordinary Evensong, though there was some business with incense and putting out of candles at the beginning of the Magnificat.

At last the time for the sermon came. The text was given out: 'Let him that is without sin among you cast the first stone.' That seemed suitable, Dulcie thought, for none of us is without sin, but could it be that it had some more particular application here? Had there then been noticeable casting of stones in the parish of St Ivel? Many people – especially non-churchgoers – often accused those who went to church of uncharitableness, and it seemed from the veiled references in the sermon that something of that kind had been happening now. 'One of our number not with us this evening' – 'an unhappy business' – 'The old saying "Charity begins at home"' – certain phrases in the rather rambling sermon reminded Dulcie of her encounter with the vicar's housekeeper on her first visit, and the weeping woman running into the church. 'Trouble? Oh, my *dear*' – had this sermon any connection with that? Supposing this man in the pulpit were not Neville Forbes? The more she thought about it the more convinced Dulcie was that he was not. 'One of our number not with us this evening' must be Neville, and he had gone away somewhere, perhaps with the weeping woman. Dulcie tried to remember whether she had seen any headlines in the cheaper daily papers lately of the 'Secret Life of Vanished Vicar' type, but she could not remember having noticed anything in Miss Lord's *Daily Mirror*. Now she could hardly wait for the service to be over, and when it was, she found herself lingering in the pew, hoping that somebody would come up and speak to them.

'Well, that seems to be that,' said Viola. 'What an odd sermon Neville Forbes preached, though I suppose that kind of thing's suitable for Lent. Has there been some scandal in the parish, do you think?'

'I don't think he is Neville Forbes,' said Dulcie, 'but we must find out definitely.'

'Good evening,' said a voice, louder and more confident than theirs. 'I don't think I've seen you here before. I hope you'll both come and have a cup of tea in the hall? We always do have one on Sunday evenings, even in Lent.'

Dulcie turned and saw the vicar's housekeeper standing at her side, dressed in purple – perhaps for the solemn season – and holding a pint bottle of milk, about two-thirds full, and a packet of lump sugar. At the same time the man with the hearing-aid crept past them carrying a brass dish of collection money, pausing for a moment as if to listen to what they were saying.

'Thank you, we should love to,' said Dulcie, before Viola could refuse.

'Come with me, then,' said the woman, and they followed her up the aisle and past the organ, where Dulcie had been on her previous visit. The air was thick with incense here, and a couple of servers in scarlet cassocks were hurrying about putting out candles and taking things off the altar. It seemed odd and a little unsuitable to be taken 'backstage' in this way, Dulcie felt, averting her eyes as one of the servers began to remove his cassock and put on a very secular-looking leather jacket. One should not perhaps ever witness the change from the sacred to the profane, and how very profane it seemed when she noticed that another server was wearing jeans.

'The hall is through here,' said the vicar's housekeeper, opening a door. 'Very handy for the church, you see.'

'What is that noise?' asked Viola. 'It sounds like dance music.'

'Oh, it is! The boys and girls always put on their favourite records on Sunday evenings. Of course it's all a terrible noise to me – I don't know one of these crooners from another!'

'I don't think they even call them crooners now,' said Dulcie, but her remark was lost in the blare of sound that hit them as they opened the door of the hall. Inside the young people were dancing with abandon and enthusiasm and the noise was deafening. How was one ever to carry on any sort of conversation against such a background, Dulcie wondered in dismay.

'Your vicar preached a very good sermon,' she shouted.

'Goodness, dear, *that's* not the vicar!' came the answering shout. 'That's a locum who's come to help us out.'

'To help you out?'

'Yes, Father Forbes isn't here. Oh, good, here's tea!'

A young girl, with her hair done in a ponytail and wearing black stockings, came towards them, carefully carrying a tray with cups of tea on it.

'Thank you, Shirley,' said the housekeeper, offering tea to Dulcie and Viola, who each took a cup. 'Do you like sugar, dear?' she turned to Dulcie and handed her a pink plastic apostle spoon with which to scoop sugar out of a jar.

'Is Father Forbes ill, then?' asked Dulcie, fearing that the subject might be dropped.

'Well, not *ill*. But it all got too much for him – that business with Miss Spicer.'

'She was the woman who was crying in church that

evening,' said Dulcie, more to herself than to anyone in particular, and indeed the music was still so loud and raucous that she was surprised when the housekeeper answered her. Obviously she must be conditioned to this atmosphere.

'That's right, dear,' she said. 'She fell in love with Father Forbes. Well, she's not the first to do that – he *is* good-looking, you know – although I say it,' she giggled, as if being his housekeeper made it somehow immodest and unsuitable for her to praise him. 'But he's a celibate, of course.' Here her tone took on a sterner, more vigorous note. 'And anyone can see that. It sticks out a mile.'

Dulcie caught Viola's eye and she wanted to laugh, though one could see what she meant. Celibacy so often *did* stick out a mile, and not only among the clergy.

'Did she,' asked Viola tentatively, '*say* anything – I mean, how did people know about her falling in love with him?'

Dulcie could see an anxious look on Viola's face, almost as if she hoped to profit from Miss Spicer's mistakes or to say to herself, Well, at least I didn't do *that*.

There was a respite from the music at this point – a record was being changed – and the unaccustomed silence seemed to be waiting for the housekeeper's answer, which came ringing out.

'Oh, she said she loved him – waylaid him one night after Benediction – a week or two ago, now – must have been *before* Lent, Quinquagesima, I believe. Anyway, she followed him back into the vicarage – I remember, I'd hurried on ahead because I had a cauliflower cheese in the oven, and I was just going to make some toast when I heard her voice in the hall, or rather *his* voice.'

'What was he saying?' Viola asked.

'Oh, I didn't hear, really,' said the housekeeper. 'I suppose the kind of things men do say when women get troublesome in that way.'

Are there then 'things' that men invariably say in such situations? Dulcie wondered. Does it happen all that often? Perhaps more to the clergy than to other men, and perhaps they, being practised speakers anyway, would find the 'things' easier to bring out. The housekeeper's use of the word 'troublesome' to describe Miss Spicer's behaviour reminded her that Aylwin had also used it to describe his brother, which seemed a little unfair. But perhaps Aylwin did not know all the circumstances. 'Of course we know Father Forbes's brother,' she said, anxious to indicate in some way that she and Viola were worthy to receive the rather shocking confidences that were being poured out.

'You know his brother, do you?' said the housekeeper. 'I thought you probably had some reason for coming here.'

Dulcie was relieved that this appeared to be a sufficient reason. With quiet persistence, she asked, 'And where is he now? Father Forbes, I mean.'

'Oh, in the West Country, of course. Gone to his mother. She has a hotel in Taviscombe, you know.'

'A hotel? In Taviscombe?' Dulcie tried to keep the excitement out of her voice. 'No, I didn't know that.'

'Eagle House Private Hotel,' said the housekeeper. 'Quite a little goldmine, I should think.'

'And Miss Spicer?'

'Well, she's still here. of course – can't leave her mother. Old Mrs Spicer's over eighty now and getting a bit difficult. Keeps falling out of bed,' said the housekeeper, with a callous little laugh. 'So she couldn't be left.'

'How dreadful,' said Viola in a faint tone, seeing the whole pathetic picture – spinster tied to elderly mother and falling in love with handsome celibate priest.

'Of course it was a pity it all had to blow up now in Lent,' the housekeeper went on. 'It couldn't have happened at a worse time, with all the Easter services coming on. He *has* left us in a hole.'

'It seems odd that he had to leave,' said Dulcie. 'One would have thought he could have coped somehow.' Unless he wanted to spare poor Miss Spicer's feelings – could it have been that? 'I suppose he'll come back?' she added.

'We don't know. He can't very well just go off like this or the Bishop would have something to say – I mean, if he's gone for more than a week or two. We get these odd priests to help out but they're not really satisfactory.' She lowered her voice and looked quickly round the hall. 'This one now, for instance, he stays out till all hours, wasn't in till after midnight last night, goodness only knows what he was doing.'

'That does seem strange,' Dulcie murmured, wondering as she said it if it really was strange. After all, a grown man could surely stay out after midnight without exciting comment – there might be many reasonable explanations.

'And one we had used to go down to the larder in the night and forage around,' the housekeeper continued. 'He ate up some cold brussels sprouts – would you believe it!' she laughed derisively. 'And he tampered with the heating apparatus in church – couldn't seem to leave it alone.'

'That seems to point to some dreadful kind of frustration – eating cold brussels sprouts in the middle of the night and tampering with the heating,' said Viola thoughtfully, but the idea was beyond the range of the housekeeper's imaginings, so that it was not developed as fruitfully as it might have been.

'Well, I do hope Father Forbes will come back to you before Easter,' said Dulcie, putting on her gloves. 'I really think we ought to be going now – thank you so much for the tea. It's been a most interesting evening,' she added, somewhat obscurely.

'Oh, you must come again,' said the housekeeper. 'Perhaps when Father Forbes is back – I'm sure you'd like *him*.'

'Yes, I'm sure we should,' said Dulcie to Viola, as they hurried away down the ill-lit road past what she thought of as 'mean' little semi-detached houses. 'But what a rich evening!'

'Yes,' Viola agreed, 'even *you* could hardly want more than that. It seems a bit late for you to go and see your uncle and aunt now, doesn't it?'

'Yes, perhaps it is, and anyway I don't feel in the mood for seeing them now. Shall we go and have a meal somewhere so that we can get used to the idea of the Eagle House Private Hotel and all that?'

'Yes, let's do that. There's something strange about that church,' Viola said. 'Did you notice the way that churchwarden kept creeping up behind us. Yet he didn't speak to us afterwards.'

'No, there was no sign of him in the hall. He disappeared – into the vestry, I suppose – to count the money. It's like a church in a Graham Greene novel, or even an early John Buchan – the kind of place that might be a cover for some sinister activities. And this Father Neville Forbes – does he really exist? What *proof* have we that he does?'

'Only the housekeeper's word, and Aylwin's, of course. I suppose if we were to go to this place where his mother has the hotel . . .' Viola suggested tentatively.

'You mean to Taviscombe – for Easter, perhaps . . .' Dulcie stopped in the middle of the pavement, her eyes shining with excitement.

'Hush, Dulcie,' said Viola sharply. 'People are looking at us.'

They had now reached a street of shops where the buses went.

'That man there, arranging things in that shop window,' Viola went on. 'He's smiling at you. Do you know him? I should hardly imagine so.' Viola made as if to hurry on, but Dulcie stopped her.

'Why, it's Bill Sedge,' she exclaimed. 'He's the brother of my aunt's housekeeper.'

'What's he doing in a shop window at this time of night?'

'Oh, he's the knitwear buyer for this chain of shops. I suppose he's arranging the window ready for Monday morning. It would be only polite to stop and speak to him for a minute.'

The dapper shirt-sleeved figure of Bill Sedge, wearing felt over-shoes and carrying a bough of artificial cherry blossom, now appeared in the shop doorway.

'Miss Dulcie, what a pleasant surprise! I have just finished arranging my display of spring knitwear from Florence and Vienna. I felt I had to do it *myself* – this is a very special collection, a real *scoop*.'

'It looks very nice,' said Dulcie feebly. 'Viola, this is Mr Sedge – his sister works for my aunt.'

'Viennese cooking, you know,' said Bill Sedge, taking Viola's hand and bowing low. 'I hope you ladies will join me for a cup of coffee? There is quite a good little place near here. Excuse me a moment, I will get my coat and lock up.'

'Just look at those petticoats,' said Viola self-consciously, as they waited by the shop window, 'all those frills and froufrou – not quite *us*, somehow.'

'A New Temptation,' Dulcie read from a card fixed to a black lace strapless brassière. 'For whom, one wonders.'

'Perhaps we ought to be looking at Mr Sedge's knitwear,' said Viola, going to the other side of the window, 'that will be more suitable. I suppose we couldn't very well refuse to have coffee with him.'

'No, hardly – and he is quite an amusing little man. He and his sister have had a hard time of it, but of course they are all right *now*,' said Dulcie firmly.

'*Andiamo!*' cried Bill Sedge gaily, propelling them across a zebra crossing. 'You have had your evening meal? No, I think not! Then we need more than coffee.'

They protested mildly, but he obviously enjoyed ordering Wiener schnitzels and a bottle of wine, joking with the waitress in German, for all the world like an English businessman in a City restaurant.

He seemed to be rather taken with Viola, who, much to Dulcie's surprise, was listening to his conversation with every appearance of interest.

'One of my spring colours is just *your* colour,' he was saying. 'How can I describe it – a shade of blue, almost *violet*, I might say.'

'How strange,' Viola murmured, looking at him rather intensely. 'I was christened Violet.'

'*Ein Veilchen auf der Wiese stand
Gebückt in sich und unbekannt,*'

quoted Bill Sedge softly.

Really, the ridiculousness of men! thought Dulcie, wondering now why she had been surprised that Viola should be listening to his conversation with every appearance of interest.

I suppose if somebody quoted poetry at me I should have just such an expression on my face, she thought, looking away from Viola. Aloud she said, 'That must be a sort of German version of "A violet by a mossy stone".'

'Well, hardly,' said Viola with a superior little smile. 'And it does sound rather better in a foreign language,' she admitted.

'I really ought to be going home now,' said Dulcie, when they had finished their coffee. She did not quite know what to do about Viola, who could perhaps follow later, escorted by Bill Sedge. Dulcie herself was quite prepared to slip quietly away and humbly join the nearest bus queue.

But Bill Sedge's manners were equal to the occasion.

'You must allow me to escort you both,' he said firmly. 'It is not very nice for you to be out alone at night like this.'

'Oh, but one so often is,' said Dulcie in confusion, and then wondered what kind of an impression she had created. 'We had been to church.'

'And was there no man at this church to take you home? If you had not met me, what might have happened!'

What might not have happened! Dulcie thought, plunging still deeper into confusion. 'I don't think one expects men to escort one home from church,' she said. 'I didn't really notice anyone there who could have done.'

'Except the churchwarden who crept up behind us,' laughed Viola, 'and he was busy counting the money.'

'We will take a taxi, I think,' said Bill Sedge masterfully.

When they were comfortably installed in one, Dulcie allowed her thoughts to wander to the Eagle House Private Hotel. She had as yet had no opportunity to meditate on the richness of the name or to consider in detail the possibility of going to Taviscombe for Easter. Tomorrow she would write for the tariff. Did one have to enclose a stamped addressed envelope, she wondered.

'We like to cater for ladies of taste as well as for young girls,' Bill Sedge was saying. 'I think you will be just crazy about some of our spring knitwear.'

The phrase 'just crazy' did not seem to suit Viola, but after he had gone she said to Dulcie that she had liked him very much.

'Shall you go and look at the spring knitwear?' Dulcie asked with a sparkle of amusement.

'Oh, that's not the point,' said Viola impatiently. 'How often does one meet an Englishman with such charming manners – who makes one feel – well – a *woman*?' she brought out at last.

'Well, not often, I suppose,' Dulcie agreed. 'He certainly is very charming, but he makes me feel slightly ill at ease – almost as if I were a woman *manquée*, if there could be such a thing – you know, something lacking in me.'

'Oh, well, that's hardly *his* fault.'

'No,' Dulcie agreed. 'Mine, of course.'

# CHAPTER SIXTEEN

It was generally on Palm Sunday that the cloths were put on the tables in the dining-room at the Eagle House Private Hotel, ready for the Easter visitors. Having a clergyman son, Mrs Forbes found that it was easier to have the kind of routine that went with the Church's year. At the same time the big stuffed eagle in the hall – from which the hotel took its name – was given its annual cleaning with one of the Hoover attachments. The fierce-looking king of birds submitted himself to various indignities at the hands of a bustling woman. There were, of course, many other things to be seen to, the refurbishing of the residents' lounge being perhaps the most important. The picture in the brochure, 'A Corner of the Residents' Lounge', gave little idea of the true flavour of the room, which visitors discovered for themselves, when a wet day or an idle moment after a meal gave them the opportunity of savouring it.

This year, however, the routine had been a little upset. To begin with, it was not till the middle of Lent that Mrs Forbes discovered that the table-cloths in the dining-room had not been removed since the end of the summer season. This was because they were new plastic ones and so did not need to be sent to the laundry. Then, like a kind of omen in classical literature, the eagle had seemed to resent his annual cleaning and had 'attacked', as it were, the woman wielding the Hoover attachment and given her a nasty scratch with one of his claws. The third unusual happening was the arrival of Mrs Forbes's son Neville, coming up to the door in the dusk one evening, his black clerical raincoat over his arm and a small suitcase in his hand. For a clergyman to leave his parish, even though it could hardly be described as 'a busy London parish', in the middle of Lent was surely most unusual. Mrs Forbes found herself wishing that it had been Aylwin, who would at least have made himself more useful about the place, as well as being her favourite son. Neville could hardly even be called upon to wait at table, for he insisted on wearing his cassock all the time, and even had he worn only an ordinary dark suit and his clerical collar he would still have looked a little unusual, taking the dishes from the hatch and bringing them to the tables. Besides, people just did not like a clergyman wandering about in a hotel; it was to be hoped that he would have gone back before the Easter visitors arrived.

He did not at first tell his mother why he had come home so suddenly. Every morning he was out early, murmuring something about having 'the use of an altar', just when Mrs Forbes had thought it would be a good chance for him to have a nice lie-in. She gathered that he was taking some of the weekday early services – Masses, he called them – at one of the town's churches, the one people described as having been 'spoilt' because of the present vicar's Romish tendencies. But although he had said nothing about his reasons for coming,

Mrs Forbes guessed that it must be, in her own words, 'trouble with a woman', for it had happened before. What began as a pleasant friendship between priest and parish worker all too often blossomed – or should one say degenerated? – into love on the woman's part. And even now Neville seemed quite unable to deal with it. He should either marry or go into a monastery, thought Mrs Forbes firmly, though even marriage would not prevent the female members of his flock from falling in love with him. Still, a strong-minded woman could be a powerful deterrent to all but the most determined. It was a pity that Aylwin had not chosen a more suitable wife. Marjorie was a sweet girl but totally unfitted to be the wife of a man in Aylwin's position, and now that marriage seemed to be going wrong.

Mrs Forbes picked up a letter from Marjorie's mother, Mrs Williton, and hesitated a moment before opening it. She was sitting in the little office where the business of the hotel was conducted, a small cosy room behind the reception desk. She was a gaunt-looking woman, with a large nose and piercing eyes; her handsome sons did not seem to take after her. This morning she was still wearing her usual winter costume of tweed suit and fur-lined boots on her thin, white, old woman's legs, which today were stockingless. When she went out she would put on the ankle-length musquash coat and deerstalker-type hat which hung behind the door. She was a well-known figure in the town and was often to be seen walking on the moors. Indeed, people used to wonder how the cooking at Eagle House could really be 'under personal super-vision of Resident Proprietress, Mrs Horatia M. Forbes' (as it said in the brochure), when she was so often not there at meal-times.

At last Mrs Forbes opened Mrs Williton's letter.

'Dear Mrs Forbes,' it read – for they had never become 'Horatia' and 'Grace' to each other – 'I expect you will not be surprised to hear from me, or perhaps you will be, seeing all that has happened. The fact is I went to see Aylwin in Quince Square, but he is quite adamant in the course he is pursuing. His own pleasure is all he seems to care about and he tells me that he is spending Easter in Tuscany, a part of Italy, which brings me to the point of this letter. I should like to bring Marjorie to Taviscombe for a few days after Easter, as the sea air might do her good and we could have a talk about things. We would come on the Tuesday or Wednesday after Easter if that suits you and you have a room free, as I expect you will have *after* Easter. Let us hope the weather will have improved a bit by then . . .'

Mrs Forbes tossed the letter aside and opened another.

'Dear Madam,' it ran, 'I should be obliged if you would send me a copy of your tariff, for which I enclose a stamped addressed envelope. Yours faithfully, Dulcie M. Mainwaring.'

Mrs Forbes put her hand into one of the pigeon-holes of her untidy desk and took out the little folded card which described the hotel and gave a list of charges, now out of date. As she put the tariff into the envelope she noticed that it had a threepenny stamp on it. No need for such extravagance, she thought – a piece of wet blotting paper or the steam of a boiling kettle would soon deal with that. 'Printed matter only needs a twopenny stamp,' she murmured to herself. Her voice had a soft West Country burr which, having lived all her life in Taviscombe, she had never lost.

She then turned her attention to Mrs Williton's letter. It would be quite convenient for them to come after Easter –

indeed, they could have come *for* Easter without any great inconvenience. The visitors who came to Taviscombe to see the sea, the primroses, or whatever delights it happened to offer, did not all flock to the Eagle House Private Hotel, which was rather inconveniently situated for the beach ('Close to sea and shops' the tariff said, but it could have been closer to the former), and did not have bathing costumes hanging from its windows in summer or drifts of sand and buckets and spades in the hall. Mrs Williton and Marjorie could have one of the back rooms looking out over the recreation ground, which would be suitable to them as relations who could not be expected to pay much. Aylwin would, of course, not have thought of their paying at all, but Mrs Williton's independent spirit made her insist on at least a token payment. 'After all,' she would say to Mrs Forbes, 'it is your livelihood. Marjorie and I wouldn't feel comfortable if we didn't pay you anything.' Not that they were much more comfortable paying, but of course one could only think that kind of thing – it was the feeling of moral rather than physical satisfaction that Mrs Williton needed.

'Well, Mam,' said Neville, appearing in the doorway. The childish abbreviation sounded strange coming from a cassocked priest, but Mrs Forbes did not notice it. 'What are you up to now?' he asked indulgently.

'I was just wondering what room to give Marjorie and Mrs Williton.'

'Well, there's plenty of choice surely at this time of year, isn't there?' he said with a little laugh.

'Yes, there's choice all right. What do you want to go about in that old black cassock for?' she asked rather irritably.

'It's the uniform of a priest you know,' he said seriously.

'You'd find many in London who went about in their cassocks.'

'Oh, *London* . . .' She made a contemptuous gesture. 'You look like some old monk. Still, I suppose it saves your other clothes – like wearing an overall. Nev, I wish you'd have a talk with Aylwin. He and Marjorie don't seem to be getting on at all well, and she's a nice girl, really.'

'It was a most unsuitable marriage,' said Neville primly. 'I'm afraid Aylwin didn't really consider whether she would share his interests – he fell in love with a pretty face.'

'Like that woman falling in love with you, dear!' said Mrs Forbes with a sudden hoot of laughter.

Neville flushed. He could not help knowing that he was exceptionally good-looking, but he did not like to be called 'pretty', even by his mother. Perhaps unconsciously – though who can be sure of this? – he glanced over towards the mirror and saw a face similar in features to that of his brother Aylwin, but less careworn, the hair fairer and curling round the temples like an angel in an Italian Renaissance painting. 'Miss Spicer didn't – er – fall in love' – he brought out the words with difficulty – 'with my appearance.'

'Oh, don't you go stuffing your old Mam with that kind of rubbish! Women are all alike in the spring,' said his mother with a chuckle. It seemed for a moment as if some ribald West-Country proverb or quip was about to come out, but perhaps the sight of the cassock silenced her, for she contented herself by pulling him towards her and telling him that one of the buttons was loose.

'You look just like your Dad,' she said affectionately, 'though I sometimes think Aylwin's more like him. What a pair you are, the two of you, with your women!'

'Mam, really! You make it sound so much worse than it really is.' Neville smiled protestingly.

'Just to think that I should have two boys like you – one a professor and the other a clergyman. Who would've thought it!'

'Aylwin isn't really a professor,' said Neville pedantically.

'Oh, well, whatever he is – Doctor of Philosophy or something. I'm sure he *ought* to be a professor and will be one day,' she said lightly. 'And you'll be a bishop – fancy that!'

'I should think that's most unlikely.'

'Just look and see if that coffee's boiling, will you dear? I like it to boil a bit.'

Neville went over to the gas-ring in the hearth on which a saucepan of coffee was standing. 'You don't need to *boil* it,' he said, 'just heat it up.'

'Boiling makes it stronger,' said Mrs Forbes obstinately.

'No, it doesn't really,' said Neville. 'I hate boiled coffee.'

'Well, I always boil it for the visitors – it seems to look a bit darker when it's boiled. You have to think of these things, you know.'

'Yes, of course.' Having been brought up in the hotel business Neville saw nothing unusual or even dishonest in trying to make little, or almost nothing, go a very long way.

'Will you be here for Easter, Nev?'

'Yes – I've arranged with the Bishop not to go back till afterwards. He was most understanding.'

'What – you didn't *tell* him? Not about Miss Spicer coming at you like that?' Mrs Forbes's hooting laugh rang out somewhat discordantly to her son's sensitive ears.

'No, I didn't tell him all the details, of course. I implied that

I was in a rather overwrought nervous and mental state, without going into exactly what happened.'

'*Mental!* You be careful, Nev, or they'll be taking you up Dene Vale.'

Neville shuddered when she named the big mental hospital which served the district. It had always been a place of dread since childhood, when he had heard grown-up people talking in hushed tones about somebody being 'up Dene Vale' without knowing what it really meant.

He had imagined, when he made his decision to leave London for a while, that coming to his mother would be calming and soothing, and so, in a sense, it was. Her very lack of understanding of his problem had a quality of restfulness about it.

'It may be that I shall have to marry her,' he said, almost to himself. 'We could have her mother at the vicarage, of course, there's plenty of room.'

'*Have* to marry her?' echoed Mrs Forbes, and Neville realised that for a countrywoman the phrase might have a very definite and in this case totally misleading significance. 'Nev, what've you been up to?'

Neville smiled uncertainly, resenting her tone – as if he were a boy of seventeen instead of a grown-up man and a priest at that. 'I meant that it might make things easier all round, and I dare say she'd make quite a good wife,' he said doubtfully.

'I thought you didn't hold with marriage.'

'I don't really, for a priest, but there could be situations where one might have to sacrifice one's principles for the happiness of another person.'

'Well, I don't know, I'm sure. Isn't that old coffee boiling yet? I expect it'll all come out in the wash,' she laughed. 'If you're going out, you might post this letter for me – a lady in London, wanting to see the tariff.'

'All right.' Neville took the letter and turned it over to read the address. 'Miss Dulcie Mainwaring, 149 Lincoln Road, London, S.W.13,' he read. A rather pleasing handwriting. Presumably she had sent a stamped addressed envelope – otherwise his mother would not have sent her a copy of the tariff.

# CHAPTER SEVENTEEN

When Aylwin kissed Laurel – and he had at last managed to achieve this one night after he had taken her to the theatre – it was different from when Paul did. Aylwin murmured romantic phrases and his hands moved with practised skill. He has done this many times before, she thought, wondering if she would tell Marian afterwards, or whether things had reached the stage when one no longer confided everything to one's girl friend but preserved an enigmatic silence. He had said something about his wife as they drove home in the taxi – not that she didn't understand him but that *he* didn't understand *her*, which was a new line and rather effective. It seemed as good a reason as the more hackneyed one for him to demand Laurel's sympathy. And next week he was going to Tuscany. She must think of him, a lonely man going round looking at churches. Laurel saw him in her mind's eye as a tiny figure against one of those miniature brownish Italian landscapes, glimpsed through casements in the works of the great masters.

When she got back to the hostel she found Marian in her

room. Her face was white and ghastly-looking from the mask-like preparation she had painted over it 'to draw out impurities' and, in addition, wore a look of resentment under the mask.

'Your friend Paul rang up,' she said. 'I was just leaving you a message. That's the third time you haven't been in.'

'Oh, I must go and see him some time,' said Laurel smiling vaguely.

'You and your men,' said Marian, half scornful and half jealous. It was annoying that Laurel, the country mouse whom she had initiated into the sophistications of London life, should have two such good-looking admirers while she herself had only the constant and boring devotion of the young bank clerk who lived on the top floor. 'Was the play good?' she asked.

'Not really. He hasn't got anything new to say and one gets so tired of the same old hates and bees in the bonnet being trotted out all the time.'

'Does *one?*' asked Marian rather acidly. 'I'm afraid I wouldn't know. I filled your hot water bottle,' she pointed out, lingering in the doorway.

'Oh, thanks.' Laurel started to take off her black dress, first tying a chiffon scarf over her face.

'Did he kiss you?'

'Of course!' The answer was muffled because Laurel was now half-way out of her dress.

'Well, people don't always. I thought you didn't want him to, anyway.'

'One can change one's mind. He's rather sweet and I feel sorry for him.'

'Because his wife doesn't understand him?' mocked Marian.

'I expect she does,' said Laurel, not revealing what he had said. 'Surely no man seriously claims that sort of thing nowadays?'

Marian left the room, her curiosity unsatisfied. She had thought of offering Laurel a hot drink, but perhaps it was not the appropriate beverage to round off an evening of illicit kisses from a married man, she thought sanctimoniously, climbing into bed with her mug of Bournvita. She sat upright, drinking it, a virtuous and rather comic little figure, with her white masked face and her hair neatly bound up in a blue turban.

Laurel fell into bed in a confused state, her hair unbrushed and her face only very sketchily washed. While Aylwin was in Tuscany would be a good time to see Paul, she thought.

The next day she decided to combine a visit to the flower shop with going to supper with her aunt Dulcie. It was really the only place where she could be sure of seeing him, she thought, as the bus took her from the best part of Kensington to the not-so-good, where mourners ordered bleeding hearts of red and white carnations for their departed loved ones.

As she approached the shop she began to feel nervous. Somebody else might be there, which would be embarrassing, though if he were alone she would have to think of conversation straight away and that might be worse.

The window was full of daffodils and irises, with a few early tulips and presumably late chrysanthemums. The barrage of dwarfs and stone animals was still there, as were the white-painted pot-holders and other objects whose purpose was more obscure. The shop was empty. She could see dimly that Paul was at the back making a wreath or a bouquet.

'A North Kensington wedding, I suppose, with all that fern,' said Laurel gaily, but he did not seem to hear, and as that kind of remark is difficult, if not impossible, to repeat, she was reduced to silence, and he said rather formally, 'Good evening. What can I do for you?'

'Oh, nothing, really.' Laurel glanced around nervously at the massed yellow of the daffodils. Could this be the young man who had seized her in his arms and kissed her so forcefully? 'I only came to say I was sorry I wasn't in last night when you rang up,' she mumbled.

'Why last night particularly?' he said unhelpfully, taking up a white carnation and thrusting a piece of wire through its heart.

'Well, I mean the other times too, when I haven't been in.'

'You never do seem to be in.'

'I've said I'm sorry,' said Laurel rather indignantly. 'It just so happened that I was out those particular evenings when you rang. Once it was something I *had* to go to. Miss Mickleburgh's presentation,' she finished defiantly.

For the first time a smile played around the corners of his mouth.

'Who's Miss Mickleburgh?'

'She was headmistress of my old school – but she lives in London now, so we had the presentation here.'

'And what did you present her with?'

'A Wedgwood dinner service and a travelling clock.'

'Heavens! Will she be doing all that dining and travelling in her retirement?'

'She isn't retiring, exactly. Well, she is but she's getting married.'

'Surely that's rather unusual?'

'Yes, I suppose it is. She's rather old – about fifty – but she's marrying a retired admiral, so that's all right.'

Paul stuck what seemed to be the last carnation into the bouquet. 'Are you going home to see your aunt?' he asked. 'We might travel together.'

It was the rush hour and they got separated on the bus, coming together again like lovers after a long parting. They walked hand-in-hand down the road and were seen by Senhor MacBride-Pereira to stop and kiss rather indiscreetly near one of the street lamps, which cast a sickly glow over their young fresh faces. Then they parted and went into their respective houses.

Orpheus and Eurydice? thought Senhor MacBride-Pereira. Now what have I seen – an end or a beginning? Romeo and Juliet, Paolo and Francesca, or just two young lovers of today, a suburban idyll? He had been sitting in his top-floor front room, reading Eça de Queiroz and eating grilled almonds from a bag at his side, dipping absent-mindedly but steadily into it until the bag was empty. In the summer he would eat sugared jordan almonds, delighting especially in the mauve ones.

Yesterday evening, at about the same time, he had come home with a parcel from the Scotch House, containing the kilt in the MacBride tartan which he had ordered, to be worn secretly in his room at first before he ventured outside in it. He had long wanted to possess such a garment and was eager to parade before his looking-glass in it, but first it would be prudent to draw the curtains, he decided. Going to the window, he had seen the lady from next door with the fish's name – Miss Dace – being handed out of a taxi by a gentleman who had kissed her hand in the Continental fashion. The things I see! he said to himself. With a young girl and a boy perhaps it is nothing or of little importance, but with a by-no-means-beautiful woman getting on in years, who knows what it might not be!

Inside her house Dulcie was in the kitchen making lemon marmalade. The window was open at the bottom and the outside sill held several saucers in which sticky deposits of the marmalade at various stages of the boiling had been placed. Dulcie took up the latest one and tilted it anxiously to see if the surface wrinkled.

'Not yet,' she sighed rather tragically. 'Last year it was twenty-five minutes. Why is it taking longer now?'

'Of course,' said Viola, who had been sitting at the kitchen table reading *Encounter*, 'I'm not a great marmalade eater at the best of times.'

*Not a great marmalade eater* . . . Dulcie repeated to herself in a kind of despair. 'And when would the best of times for eating marmalade be?' she said aloud.

Viola did not answer.

Another five minutes passed and the marmalade was again tested. It really seemed as if the setting point had been passed now. It would go like a kind of syrup.

'People blame one for dwelling on trivialities,' said Dulcie, 'but life is made up of them. And if we've had one great sorrow or one great love, then who shall blame us if we only want the trivial things?'

Viola murmured something, but Dulcie knew that she did not really understand. Lately she had begun to admit to herself that Viola had turned out to be a disappointment. In a sense, Dulcie felt as if she had created her and that she had not come up to expectations, like a character in a book who had failed to come alive, and how many people in life, if one transferred

186

them to fiction just as they were, would fail to do that! So perhaps it was not so surprising after all. Viola was just a rather dull woman, wanting only to be loved. Presumably Bill Sedge would marry her – for things seemed to be going that way – and take her to live in Finchley Road, and she would forget all about making an index and searching for facts in libraries and correcting proofs of other people's books.

'You *are* coming to Taviscombe for Easter?' she asked uncertainly.

'Oh, yes. Bill thinks I ought to get away.'

'I expect he said the sea air would put roses in your cheeks,' she said, absent-mindedly rather than cattily.

'Yes, he did,' said Viola rather coldly, raising a hand to her cheek. 'And I have been feeling a bit off-colour lately.'

There was a plopping sound as the evening post fell through the letter box on to the floor.

'I did hope for a postcard from Tuscany from Aylwin,' said Dulcie, examining the circulars and bills. Then she saw her own handwriting and felt a faint tremor of excitement. It would be – it must be – the tariff of the Eagle House Private Hotel.

'The birthplace of Aylwin Forbes,' she said, opening the envelope. 'I suppose he was born there – perhaps not literally, but we know it was his childhood home.'

The front of the little folded card showed what might be described as an artist's view of the hotel. He – or more likely she – had, as so often, seen his subject illuminated by 'the light that never was on sea or land'. It appeared to be a kind of Gothic castle, standing back from the road in such spacious grounds that the wrought iron seats seemed a little out of keeping. Outside the gates stood an Edwardian type of motor car.

'Oh, do you think Lord Berners ever stayed there?' said Dulcie rapturously. 'I suppose some grateful guest – a lady, I think – drew this. She happened to have her sketching things with her.'

'I wonder when it was done,' said Viola rather sourly. 'Years ago, I should think. I don't suppose it looks a bit like that now.'

'No,' Dulcie agreed. 'It dates from the time when ladies had time to do sketching and things like that. But this "A Corner of the Residents' Lounge" seems to be a photograph. It would look more real if they had somebody actually sitting in it. It looks rather unlived-in as it is – so does this photo of "One of the Bedrooms".'

'They could hardly show somebody in bed.'

'No – though I shouldn't mind volunteering to be photographed if I was given due warning. It would make a good picture to have somebody sitting up in bed drinking early morning tea. But how can one think of Aylwin Forbes there – that's the impossible thing!'

But Viola's thoughts were on another subject. Had he really meant it when he said that she had brought something into his life that he had never had before? She supposed he might have done – anyone could say a thing like that, really, and it could be true in the most uninteresting ways. But when it was murmured in a mixture of German and English it had an air of greater sincerity. Of course the whole thing was absurd, when one came to think of it. This dapper little refugee, not quite as tall as she was – after somebody like Aylwin – surely not! She remembered him in the shop window that Sunday night, arranging the knitwear among the boughs of artificial cherry blossom. And yet, as she had said to Dulcie, he did make her feel that she was a woman, and that – in these pushing, jostling days of the so-called equality of the sexes – was a great deal. Perhaps all love had something of the ridiculous in it. Look at Aylwin, even, collapsing like that at his lecture, and Dulcie's former fiancé, Maurice, with his absurd pronouncements on art and literature. One came across it all the time.

# CHAPTER EIGHTEEN

When it came to the point, Dulcie showed a surprising reluctance to book rooms at Eagle House straight away. At the same time as she had written to Mrs Forbes for her tariff, she had also obtained a list of hotels and boarding houses from the town's information bureau, and she proposed that they should stay the first night at one of these and then move into Eagle House, having first had a look at it from the outside, as it were.

'As long as we know that Aylwin is *definitely* in Tuscany,' she said, 'it'll be all right. If only he would send a postcard!' And at that moment, as if in answer to a prayer, the telephone rang. It was Laurel, and at the end of their conversation she let fall casually the information that she had had a card from Italy – 'from Dr Forbes. A picture of a church.'

'How nice!' Dulcie said. But privately she thought it would have been more suitable if he had sent one to Viola and herself. After all, Laurel was only a child. Still, it was kind of him to feel himself responsible for her cultural education.

'He wouldn't *mind* us going to stay at his mother's hotel,' said Viola. 'He'd probably expect us to. I can't think why you're making such a fuss.'

'Oh – don't you know how it is! One goes on with one's research, avidly and without shame. Then suddenly a curious feeling of delicacy comes over one. One sees one's subjects – or perhaps victims is a better word – as being somehow degraded by one's probings . . .' Dulcie stopped, her face flushed, then went on, 'And going to Neville's church – it had to be done, but I suppose, in a way, it isn't right to go to a church for such a reason. And then to find out *that* about him – it was like a judgment.'

'But it wasn't our fault. It would have happened whether we'd gone there or not. In fact, it had already happened. Our going or not going had nothing to do with it.'

'One wonders how it all started,' said Dulcie rather desperately. 'I mean, my interest in the Forbes family.'

'At the conference, I suppose.'

'Yes, that must have been the beginning. If Maurice hadn't broken off our engagement, I shouldn't have gone to it and seen Aylwin, but then, being the sort of person I am, it might have happened anyway . . .' she broke off in confusion.

'But going to Eagle House will be just rather amusing,' said Viola soothingly. 'There couldn't be anything upsetting there.'

'No, I suppose not. Oh, let's have a cup of tea!' Dulcie took the kettle to the sink and began to fill it in a kind of frenzy. 'And which of all these other hotels shall we stay at on the first night? Blencathra, Strathmore, Lomond House – how curiously Scottish the names of boarding-houses always are! Moranedd and Min y Don – those are Welsh, I suppose. Here's Eagle House, but it doesn't say anything special about it. The

Anchorage – "bright Christian atmosphere" – should we try that?'

'We might,' said Viola doubtfully.

'Yes,' Dulcie agreed, equally doubtful. 'Why is it that one suspects a place that actually *claims* to have a bright Christian atmosphere? What is one afraid of?'

'A certain amount of discomfort – and that the Christianity will manifest itself in unpleasant and embarrassing ways,' said Viola.

'And that one will have to endure the company of those who call themselves Christians. Shall we risk it? It seems to be almost opposite Eagle House, judging by this map – and the Welsh and Scottish places might be worse.'

In fact, the window of their room looked out on to the turning down which Eagle House lay. It looked smaller and darker than the artist's impression, and there was no motor car of any description outside. Dulcie stationed herself at the window until darkness fell and nothing more could be seen.

'Perhaps it isn't really open for Easter,' she said, 'but we shall have to find somewhere else to go tomorrow.'

They had been extremely lucky, so the manageress informed them to get in at The Anchorage for this one night. 'We are fully booked for Easter,' she informed them. 'It is really our speciality,' she added somewhat obscurely.

She was a tall, neat-looking woman of about forty-five, wearing rimless glasses and a very clean white nylon overall, which made her look like a dentist's receptionist. She had a high-pitched, tinkling laugh, perhaps the 'bright' part of the Christian atmosphere.

'Do you know a hotel called Eagle House?' asked Viola casually.

'Oh, my goodness!' The tinkling laugh rang out. 'You wouldn't want to go there! I've heard it's very old-fashioned inside.'

'A Mrs Forbes is the proprietress,' said Dulcie.

'Yes, old Mrs Forbes. She's quite eccentric.' She pronounced it 'essentric', which gave the word a new significance. 'And there's been talk about the place – things that go on there.'

'Things? But it's not licensed, is it?' asked Dulcie naively.

'No – but there's something about it. I see that clergyman son is back – the good-looking one. Now why should a clergyman leave his parish at a busy time like this?' The manageress's eyes, disconcertingly magnified through the rimless glasses, gave Dulcie a penetrating stare, under which Dulcie's own glance faltered, and she found herself stammering, 'Well, er – I don't know, really. There might be all sorts of reasons. Perhaps to give a bright Christian atmosphere to the hotel for Easter,' she added naughtily.

'He certainly won't give it that by going about in his cassock,' said the manageress firmly, apparently taking no offence at Dulcie's remark. 'And of course, it isn't necessarily a *clergyman* who provides a Christian atmosphere in a place. Oh, no! Quite the contrary, sometimes. A lot of dismal Desmonds some of them are!' The laugh rang out again.

'Is there a Mr Forbes?' Dulcie asked.

'Well, there must have been, mustn't there? But we don't see him about now. I suppose he's passed on,' she added comfortably.

'Oh, how I'd like a drink,' said Viola, when the manageress

had left them, to attend to some domestic matter. 'I really think we shall have to go out and buy something to drink here.'

'You mean gin?' asked Dulcie, in a rather fearful tone.

'Yes, why not?' Viola's tone had almost a note of challenge in it.

'No reason, really. It just seems rather depraved to drink it in one's bedroom.'

'How old-fashioned you are in some ways, Dulcie,' said Viola impatiently.

'Yes,' Dulcie agreed humbly. 'I suppose I am. People obviously do these things all the time now. I feel a wine might be more appropriate – there's something rather pleasing about the idea of sitting up in bed drinking wine. There might even be special vintages recommended for drinking in the bedrooms of unlicensed hotels.'

'Here's a shop open,' said Viola. 'You'd better leave this to me.'

'Good evening, ladies!' A dark, good-looking man seemed to be lying in wait for them, almost, behind the counter. He stood against a background of bottles, many of unfamiliar and intriguing aspect.

Dulcie longed to ask him for something suitable for drinking in the bedroom of an unlicensed hotel, and she was sure he would have been equal to the challenge, but she kept silent, allowing Viola to ask for a quarter-bottle of Gordon's gin. Only when he was wrapping it up, respectfully as if it were medicine, did she say anything.

'Perhaps we should have a corkscrew?' she suggested nervously.

'A corkscrew? Oh, madam,' the salesman laughed quite pleasantly, 'you won't need *that*, I can assure you.'

'Really, Dulcie,' said Viola when they were outside the shop, 'you did make me feel a fool. Surely you know how a gin bottle opens?'

'I know you don't need a corkscrew for champagne,' said Dulcie, 'but I'd forgotten about gin.'

'Dinner is at a quarter to seven,' said Viola, 'which is much too early. I can hear the gong now.' She gulped down her gin and water. 'I suppose this is the kind of place where they don't like you to be late.'

There was silence as they entered the dining-room and were shown to a table for two near the door. The window tables were occupied by an elderly couple and what looked like a family party – mother and father and two daughters and a boy of about fifteen, who glared resentfully round the room. At a small table by herself sat a fierce-looking, white-haired woman, extremely thin and surprisingly sunburnt considering the time of year. Her collar bones stood out sharply from the neck of her low-cut blouse – there was something almost aggressive about so much burnt flesh. Two women of about their own age, and a clergyman with his mother, judging by the similarity of features (beaky nose and small pursed mouth), sat at two tables in the centre of the room. A third table was unoccupied, but laid hopefully with the appropriate china and cutlery.

The silence in the room was broken only by the sound of water being poured out into glasses – perhaps the most dismal sound heard on an English holiday, and having nothing in common with the musical trickle of spring water rippling over stones in a mountain stream. The elderly couple in the window had a bottle of lemon barley water on their table. Dulcie thought of the little bottle of gin upstairs and wondered if it could be smelt on their breath.

A plate of bright tomato soup was put before her, and the waitress handed a basket piled with very small squares of white bread.

'You take bread?' she said fiercely, revealing that she was a foreigner and not the gentle, slow-speaking West Country girl that might have been expected. That in itself was saddening and disillusioning. Dulcie wanted to remark on it to Viola, but she left it too late, so that the soup-drinking – under cover of which she might have spoken – was finished, and the unnerving silence again descended on the room.

After a moment the clergyman took up the water jug and began to fill glasses for himself and his mother.

'Don't do that, Clive,' came a whisper from one of the window tables, as the mother admonished the fifteen-year-old.

At last, and it was fitting that he should be the one to break the silence, the clergyman made an audible remark. Addressing the white-haired lady, whose table adjoined his, he said tentatively, 'This must be a change from Uganda, Miss Fell.'

It was less than he deserved that she should be a little deaf, so that he was forced to repeat his not very brilliant observation, whose inanity she emphasised yet further by saying in a loud bright voice, 'A change from Uganda – it certainly is!'

'What a lovely title for a novel that would be,' Dulcie whispered, 'and one can see that it would be almost easy to write. The plot is beginning to take shape already . . .'

'I suppose one should say *Bu*ganda to be strictly accurate,' laboured the clergyman with unnecessary pedantry, but his efforts had not been in vain, for now a general conversation started between the tables.

It seemed that Miss Fell was a missionary, a sister of the

owner of The Anchorage. She was on leave, or 'furlough', as she called it, from Uganda, where she was headmistress of a girls' school.

'I hope you got your walk before the rain started,' she said to the clergyman's mother.

'Yes, we went quite a way. In fact, we *saw* the castle in the distance, but of course we couldn't have gone in.'

'No, it doesn't open to the public till Saturday,' said Miss Fell. 'I often wonder what old Miss Forbes would have thought, to see all those people traipsing through the rooms. It's really a mercy she can't.'

Some thin slices of meat were now served, and little dishes with just enough vegetables for two were placed on the table. Remembering that it was Friday – and Good Friday, too – Dulcie glanced to see whether the clergyman was having fish. But he was not, and did not appear to object to what was put before him. Dulcie was disappointed, having hoped for some spirited protest or whispered conference between him and the waitress. She supposed he must be rather Low Church.

'Old Miss Forbes,' repeated Viola in a low tone, and of course Dulcie had noticed it too. It was odd how a name would crop up when one happened to be interested in it. 'I suppose that's the castle you see from the train,' Viola went on.

'Yes, we must go and look over it,' said Dulcie. 'You never know, there might be some connection.' She would have liked to join in the general conversation and find out more about it, but the subject had now been left, and walks in the neighbourhood were being discussed.

It was at this point that somebody came to the unoccupied table, but as she was a woman of about forty, ordinary-looking and unaccompanied, nobody took much notice of her. As it happened, she was a novelist; indeed, some of the occupants of the tables had read and enjoyed her books, but it would never have occurred to them to connect her name, even had they ascertained it from the hotel register, with that of the author they admired. They ate their stewed plums and custard and drank their thimble-sized cups of coffee, quite unconscious that they were being observed.

The thought of the small 'lounge', crowded with chairs and tables, was insupportable, so Dulcie and Viola went up to their bedroom. Sitting aimlessly in bedrooms – often on the bed itself – is another characteristic feature of English holidays. The meal was over and it was only twenty-five past seven.

'The evening stretches before us,' said Viola gloomily. 'What shall we do with it?'

'I should like to have another look at Eagle House,' said Dulcie. 'It's dark now and we must decide whether we're going to stay there or not, as they can't have us here.'

'I don't want to stay here,' said Viola. 'Let's go boldly to Eagle House and see if they can take us.'

'They might be in the middle of dinner now,' said Dulcie doubtfully.

'Well, we can wait a little – we could always go into one of the hotels and have a drink.'

'Another?' said Dulcie nervously. 'But I can see now that it's a way of passing the time.'

'There's a big hotel on the sea front,' Viola suggested. 'There might be a bit of life there.'

They put on their coats and went down the road that led to the beach. The distance was what The Anchorage in its description claimed it to be – 'sea 500 yds'. It was dark and quiet there, for the tide was out and nothing was to be seen but wet glistening sand and large stones.

'I suppose they have fairy lights strung along these trees in the season,' said Viola rather sadly.

'It must look quite gay,' Dulcie agreed.

An elderly man with an Aberdeen terrier passed them. 'It must be strange to live at the seaside all the year round,' Viola observed. 'Look – there's the hotel I was thinking of – the Bristol. It seems to be the biggest one. Shall we go in?'

'Yes, but let's peer first,' said Dulcie. 'This is the dining-room, obviously.'

A middle-aged couple, looking like people in an advertisement – she in pearls and a silver fox cape over a black dress, he in a dark suit – sat at a table in the window. A waiter bent over them – 'deferentially', Dulcie supposed, helping them to some fish – turbot, surely? Its white flesh was exposed before them. How near to the heart of things it seemed!

'What is that sauce one has with turbot?' Dulcie asked. '*Du* something or other. I suppose this is only one course of dinner at the Hotel Bristol. I feel quite hungry again. Do we go in by this side door – where it says "American Bar"?'

'I suppose so.' Viola pushed open the door and led the way. A young man in a white coat stood behind a bar polishing glasses; otherwise it was empty. Some small tables had on them dishes of olives and potato crisps. Dulcie and Viola sat down at one of these.

'Two gins and tonic, please,' said Viola, in a rather high voice as if she were nervous: and indeed, it did seem quite an ordeal to break the silence, like getting up to ask the first question after a lecture.

'It's like a poorly-attended church,' whispered Dulcie. 'Or even a cathedral.'

'I expect it's pretty lively in the season,' said Viola doggedly.

The barman finished polishing glasses and began to read a newspaper. It was a relief that he did not show any signs of wanting to make conversation.

They finished their drinks rather more quickly than they had intended, said 'Good night' to the barman, and found themselves again by the dining-room window.

'They're eating roast duck now,' said Dulcie. 'I can hardly bear it. I think we must go to Eagle House now and book our rooms.'

'You're sure we want to stay there?' asked Viola doubtfully.

'I don't know about "want",' said Dulcie, 'but we're going to. I can feel it. The whole thing now has the inevitability of Greek tragedy.'

They walked on in the dark until they came to Eagle House. Seen at close quarters and at night there was something strangely impressive about it, so that the artist's picture did not seem so much exaggerated as they had at first thought. There were indeed little turrets and narrow Gothic windows and the general effect was one of size and mystery, increased by the fact that the place seemed to be in total darkness.

'Perhaps they are all at dinner, round the back somewhere,' Viola whispered. 'Is this the main entrance?'

'It's the sort of door that looks as if it's never opened,' said Dulcie. 'Or only when a Stuart king ascends the throne of England. But *this* door seems to be open and there's a dim light on inside. We'd better go in here. It seems to be a kind of lounge,' she added, tripping over a small footstool. The floor seemed to be littered with them, like toadstools. 'I don't recognise *this* from the photograph.'

'What extraordinary pictures!' Viola exclaimed. 'Coloured prints of the Pre-Raphaelites, aren't they? "The Death of Guinevere"!' she read, peering at one of them. 'Where on earth did they get these?'

'There's a room leading out of here. Ah, *this* is it – the Corner of the Residents' Lounge in the photograph!' cried Dulcie enthusiastically. She approached a glass-fronted bookcase and opened one of the doors. 'Novels by Marie Corelli and Florence Barclay. *Kelly's Directory of Somerset for* 1905. *Aylwin* – of course! that's where he got his name. And a bound volume of *Every Woman's Encyclopaedia* for 1911 – that's the one I've got.'

'Dulcie, we can't stay here like this,' said Viola firmly. 'We must find somebody to ask about booking rooms. There seems to be a kind of reception desk through here – perhaps somebody will come if we wait.'

'Listen,' said Dulcie. 'I can hear voices through that door.'

They were quiet and heard a woman's voice with a pronounced West Country accent and a cultured man's voice engaged in conversation.

'Yes, I could,' said the man, 'but I don't feel that's a very good way to start married life. I'd rather make my own choice, if it has to be. Did you hear somebody outside? I'll go and see who it is.'

'You'd better leave that to me, Nev,' said the woman. 'You wouldn't know what to say.' She laughed roughly. 'Good evening, ladies. What can I do for you?'

Actually confronted by Mrs Forbes, Dulcie could think of nothing to say, so surprised was she by her air of total unlikeness to Aylwin. It was Viola who inquired about the rooms.

Dulcie was peering behind the desk to the room leading away from it, where a clergyman in a cassock was standing facing her. Neville Forbes at last, she thought. Is this why we have come here?

'I see that dogs are not allowed in the public rooms,' she said impulsively, for he had come out as if to speak to her.

'Aren't they?' He turned to where she was reading from a printed notice. 'Oh, I see. Well, I expect we could make an exception for yours.'

'I haven't got one,' Dulcie blurted out.

'We are going upstairs to see the rooms,' said Viola sharply. The four of them ascended a wide staircase, covered in dark red Turkey carpet. Mrs Forbes led them along a corridor, lined with closed doors and with engravings of violent battle scenes on the walls. It was all as quiet as the grave – as if nobody had ever penetrated behind the doors, which must surely conceal some dreadful secret. At last she stopped at one, which she unlocked from a bunch of keys, and stood aside for Dulcie and Viola to go in.

A double bed, covered with a white honeycomb quilt, dominated the room. Had the brochure said 'hot and cold water in all bedrooms?' Dulcie wondered, for she could not see any. And a double bed! Viola would never stand for that. But this is Aylwin Forbes's mother, she told herself firmly, impossible though it may seem. They would have to accept what she offered.

It was with shame and relief that she heard Viola, who was perhaps less conscious of the sacredness of the relationship, protesting and saying to Mrs Forbes in a firm tone, 'I'm very sorry, but this room won't be at all suitable. We should want one with two beds and hot and cold water – or two single rooms.'

Mrs Forbes was silent for a moment, but a crafty look had come into her eyes.

'It would be more expensive,' she said at last. 'And there'd be a double lot of sheets. You wouldn't believe the price of this old laundry here, robbers they are.'

'Yes, laundries are expensive, I know,' said Dulcie, anxious to please, but feeling at the same time that it was hardly fitting for a hotel proprietress to fall back on this kind of excuse for not offering her visitors single rooms. 'Are all these other rooms taken?' she asked, indicating the closed doors on either side of the corridor.

'Oh, those. Not taken, really, but people might come.'

'Yes, but if they haven't in fact come, surely we could have two of them,' said Viola rather impatiently. 'You mean they haven't actually been *booked* by other people?'

'Well, I wouldn't like to say that. People come for the stag hunting. Fifty sitting down to dinner – and all that washing up! Many's the time Aylwin and Nev have given a hand in the kitchen when they were lads.' Mrs Forbes cackled with laughter. 'And the ladies in evening dress and diamonds – oh, it was a sight.'

'And furs, too, Mother,' said Neville, who had appeared at their side. 'I'm afraid my mother is apt to live in the past at times,' he said in a low voice, turning to Dulcie. 'She does very little business now, except sometimes in the summer. But there's a woman who comes in to cook and clean, so we could make you tolerably comfortable. You could have two of these smaller rooms.'

Dulcie was still bemused by the picture of Aylwin and Neville as lads, giving a hand in the kitchen, and left it to Viola to clinch the deal with Mrs Forbes.

'We'd better get the beds made up,' said Neville, and Dulcie wondered if he himself would be doing it. She imagined him tucking in the sheets rather untidily and getting blanket fluff all over his black cassock.

'We shan't want to come till tomorrow night,' said Viola firmly, 'but perhaps we could move our things in the morning?'

Dulcie peeped into one of the rooms they were to have. It looked cheerless and unlived-in, though there was a basin with the possibility of hot and cold running water. But now a new anxiety came over her – one inherited from her mother: was it certain that the beds would be properly aired? A *damp bed . . .* she could hear again the horrified tone in which these words were pronounced. Damp beds – rheumatic fever – death: this was the natural sequence of events, with all the horror of a Victorian novel.

'Then that is settled,' Neville was saying pleasantly. 'We shall expect you tomorrow.'

# CHAPTER NINETEEN

'I suppose the *newer* graves would be in the town cemetery, wherever that may be,' said Dulcie thoughtfully, as, having 'vacated their rooms' at The Anchorage and left their things at Eagle House, they climbed the hill leading up to the parish church.

'What do you mean exactly?' Viola asked.

'I mean the late Mr Forbes – he must be buried somewhere,' said Dulcie firmly. 'And probably in Taviscombe.'

'Perhaps he was killed in the war.'

They had come to a granite obelisk, surrounded by railings and carved with the names of local men who had lost their lives in the two wars.

'There's no Forbes here,' said Viola after scrutinizing the lists.

'We can look in the churchyard, then, and inside the church. And I suppose we could find out where the cemetery is and go there.'

'Goodness,' said Viola faintly. 'I hope we find it here.'

They entered the churchyard through the lich-gate. On

either side of the path stood crooked rows of gravestones, delicately ornamented with cherubs' heads and skulls, now worn away and overgrown with orange lichen.

'Not *here*, of course,' said Dulcie dreamily, running her finger over the surface of a stone.

'Where, then?' asked Viola impatiently. 'All these graves seem to be old.'

'These are newer – 1887 and 1891 – but still no Forbes. You'd think the *name* would crop up.'

'Perhaps he came here from somewhere else,' Viola suggested.

'Good morning!' A jolly voice, belonging to a jolly-looking man wearing a pepper-and-salt tweed suit and a high, old-fashioned clerical collar, greeted them as they rounded a corner of the church.

Dulcie and Viola returned his greeting.

'I suppose the *newer* graves would be in the cemetery and not in this churchyard,' said Dulcie, forgetting her shyness in her pre-occupation with her quest.

'Oh, nobody's been buried here for about forty-five years – except for old Miss Forbes a year or so ago,' said the clergyman. 'And of course that wasn't in the churchyard, exactly. They opened up the family vault for her – terrible business,' he chuckled. 'Found there wasn't room for her after all!'

'So what did they do?' Viola asked politely.

'Had to tell the others to move up! They did find room in the end, but it was a tight squeeze. I keep thinking we ought to have a "House Full" notice put up, so that those who come after us won't have to go to all that trouble again.'

How strange, Dulcie thought, that the name of Forbes

should crop up again. And yet it wasn't really – the Miss Forbes who had been buried in the vault must be the Miss Forbes who had once lived in the castle that Miss Fell was talking about at dinner. It would have been easy to verify this, but again a curious delicacy held her back. Nor could she bring herself to ask whether there was any connection between this Miss Forbes and the proprietress of the Eagle House Private Hotel. There might be some clues inside the church, but now that the vicar, or rector, had attached himself to them they would doubtless have to endure a tedious 'conducted tour', for he was inviting them to look round the church, which contained, he promised them, several 'unusual' features.

'The ladies are starting the Easter decorations, so the place is a bit of a shambles,' he said apologetically, as they stepped over bundles of greenery in the porch. Bunches of daffodils were crammed into containers and a commanding-looking woman, carrying a trug full of polyanthus, seemed to be directing operations.

'Ah, there you are, Benjamin,' she said rather ominously.

'Just a moment, dear. These ladies are visiting the church – I just want to show them one or two things.' He turned to Dulcie and Viola. 'This little pamphlet – no charge – will tell you what to look out for,' he said. 'The main feature, as far as I'm concerned, is the unique oil-fired system which heats the church – the only one of its kind in the West Country, I think you'll find.'

'That must be very convenient,' said Dulcie politely.

'Oh, it's a real blessing. And we've got the same at the vicarage –' he lowered his voice – 'a substantial legacy from a grateful parishioner. *Constant* hot water, of course . . .'

Dulcie reflected for a moment on the curious obsession of the clergy with paraffin, almost as if it were some kind of holy oil. And which was the holier – the pink or the blue?

'Radiators *and* open heaters – we've got a 500-gallon storage tank. I dare say you noticed when you came in? Behind the yew trees.'

'Surely that is a *Norman* font?' said Viola rather sharply.

'Yes, I believe so,' he said, indifferently. 'Yes, Miss Brewis, what is it?'

An indignant-looking lady – an obvious crank – had come up to him, holding a bunch of celandines.

'Your wife has seen fit to reject my humble offering,' she said. 'And yet one of our greatest English poets did not disdain to immortalise it. A *wild* flower it may be, but there are many in this church who could learn something from it. Now she said to me, "Miss Brewis, we do not usually have *wild* flowers – that is *not* our custom here" . . .'

Rather meanly, Dulcie felt, she and Viola moved away, leaving the vicar to deal with the celandine lady.

'Look – this must be the Forbes family monument,' said Viola. 'Rather disappointing, don't you think?'

'Yes,' Dulcie agreed. 'I'd hoped for splendid recumbent figures with children and dogs lying under a great canopy. This is obviously Victorian.'

'Here's a tablet to Archibald Forbes – killed in the South African War,' said Viola. 'But that doesn't tell us anything.'

'Don't you think Aylwin and Neville might be of noble lineage?' said Dulcie, as they walked away from the church. 'They both have fine features.'

'Yes, but Mrs Forbes is obviously of humbler birth. The name must be just a coincidence.'

'I wonder where the cemetery is,' said Dulcie. 'It might be on the map at the back of the guide.'

'Couldn't we sit down and have coffee somewhere before we go and look for it?' Viola pleaded. 'My feet are beginning to feel tired. And I want to get a postcard to send to Bill.'

'Oh, yes. You mustn't neglect him,' said Dulcie perfunctorily. The idea of sending postcards to real people was very far from her mind at that moment.

'This café looks quite nice,' said Viola.

'Yes, and if we can get a window table we shall have a good view of the main street.'

The café was over a shop, a large rather bleak room, apparently full when they entered it, but luckily an elderly couple at a window table were just paying their bill. Dulcie and Viola slipped into their places with almost indecent haste, so that the woman gathered her plastic macintosh around her with a little gesture of indignation, and swept out after her husband with a hostile backward glance.

'*Black* coffee for me,' said Viola. 'It seems to be very weak, unless it's tea the people over there are having.'

Dulcie opened the map, while Viola gave their order to the waitress.

'The cemetery is marked!' she cried out excitedly. 'And it doesn't look very far from here – we could easily manage it before lunch. Is the cemetely far from here?' she asked the waitress when she brought the bill.

'About twenty minutes' walk, madam. You go straight up the main street and it's just past the gasworks – on your left. You can't miss it.'

'She didn't seem to think it an odd question,' Viola commented. 'Do people often ask for it, I wonder?'

'Perhaps at Easter, taking flowers to relatives' graves and that kind of thing. Cremation is so much more anonymous, isn't it.'

'Yes, but better – though in a way one likes to think of people visiting one's grave,' said Viola, as they trudged on. She had bought a postcard for Bill Sedge and was wondering rather anxiously what to write on it and whether she should end up with 'Love'.

The gasworks towered up before them; then the houses became more spread-out, and suddenly they were in the open country and the cemetery was on their left – a sloping field, spiked with white gravestones, looking like teeth in the distance, stretching as far as the eye could see.

Even Dulcie's heart sank at the sight of so many.

'Do you think they're classified or arranged in some way?' she asked, as they opened the gate. 'They might be in order of date, perhaps.'

'This one's 1904,' said Viola, 'and this one next to it 1927. I suppose the more recent ones must be all together.'

'But don't people – or their relatives – choose plots? I mean, one might want to be buried under those yew trees, or up on the hill.'

'Yes, I see,' said Viola hopelessly.

'Let's sit down on this seat and think out a plan of campaign,' Dulcie suggested. 'It would probably be better if we separated – each one covering a different bit. Otherwise, we can't possibly go over the whole area.'

'Oh, good heavens,' Viola burst out, 'we'll never be back in time for lunch at this rate! I really can't think why you don't ask Mrs Forbes or Neville outright where the grave is. We don't even know that he's buried in Taviscombe at all.'

'Well, now that we've come we may as well look,' said Dulcie. But she too was beginning to feel a little discouraged. How, indeed, did they know where the late Mr Forbes was buried?

'Do we,' she asked in sudden confusion, 'even know that he's dead?'

'Oh, Dulcie, *really* . . .' Viola looked at her watch. 'It's nearly quarter past twelve.'

'I suppose they have services in that little chapel,' said Dulcie, who had started to walk about and peer at random, but without much hope, at a few tombstones. 'Or is it just a little Gothic building, perhaps with toilet facilities, where people can get water for the vases when they do the graves?'

'Those figures in the distance up on the hill look like a painting – especially with the cypresses behind them,' said Viola.

'Little knots of mourners bringing flowers to the graves for Easter,' said Dulcie. She was beginning to feel rather sad, as if she really had a loved one of her own buried there. And yet it was like a kind of pilgrimage, and so almost a duty, that they should find Mr Forbes's grave. 'There's a woman over there – or is it a man? digging or something. I suppose we could ask – he would probably know the more recent graves . . .'

'Dulcie – *look*! Isn't that Neville and Mrs Forbes up there on the hill?'

'It is!' Dulcie exclaimed. '*They* must be bringing flowers like everybody else. What shall we do if they see us?'

'I don't suppose they will – but for all they know we might have a relative buried here.'

'Yes, but I think I'd feel safer hiding behind something,' said Dulcie, moving to the other side of a large marble angel with outstretched wings. 'They can't see us now. Oh, how *right* a cassocked priest looks moving among gravestones!' she whispered fervently, as Mrs Forbes and Neville passed in the distance. 'And how wise Anglo-Catholic priests are to wear their cassocks so much. I suppose they'll be hurrying back now, if Mrs Forbes is to supervise the cooking of lunch.'

Dulcie and Viola walked quickly up the hill to where they had seen Mrs Forbes and Neville standing, and soon came upon the grave they were looking for. Indeed, it stood out conspicuously from those around it, for the stone was of a very dark grey veined marble, whereas all the others were white. It was a double grave, the space below the stone being filled in with green chippings, which looked like bath salts. Two vases of fresh daffodils stood among the chippings.

The stone was engraved with gold lettering, which read as follows:

Sacred to the Memory of my Beloved Husband
GAISFORD ARTHUR BRANDRETH FORBES
Who Departed This Life
April 11th 1924 Aged 42 Years
*Joy has faded but Love will stay*
*Until we meet again one day*

The tears came into Dulcie's eyes and she wished Viola had not read out the pathetic little verse in a rather scornful tone, but perhaps that too concealed emotion of some kind.

'You'd think,' said Dulcie at last, 'that with a clergyman son there would be some kind of Christian message on the stone.'

'Well, it's over thirty years ago – and perhaps Neville hadn't decided to be ordained at that time. After all, he would only be a boy.'

'What a grand name it is – Gaisford Arthur Brandreth Forbes,' said Dulcie. 'Surely he *must* have been of noble birth?'

They were walking back now, hurrying, with occasional backward glances in case a bus might be coming. But none did.

'Shall we be able to face Mrs Forbes and Neville at lunch now?' Dulcie wondered. 'Won't it show in our faces, what we've been doing?'

But when they reached Eagle House the dining-room was empty. They went in and sat tentatively at a table in the window which was the only one properly laid, with the napkins folded into fancy shapes, and a vase of daffodils – of the same variety as those they had seen on the grave – in the centre. An elderly woman at once appeared and began to serve them. It was evident that they were the only people lunching there that day, which made them feel both glad and sorry. There was no sign of Mrs Forbes and Neville, and this was perhaps a relief.

'No doubt they are eating a vastly superior meal behind closed doors,' said Viola.

After the inevitable tomato soup, however, the lunch was not at all bad. It was at least different from the unimaginative meals of places like The Anchorage.

'Stag's liver,' declared the woman as she put two plates down in front of them.

'Goodness,' said Viola faintly, 'one would really rather not know.'

But it was very good, and there were plenty of vegetables. It was followed by an excellent steamed treacle pudding and a cup of strong Nescafé. This last, had they but known it, had been made by Neville himself, ignoring the protests of his mother, who had wanted to give them the remains of her mid-morning coffee, 'well boiled'.

They had just finished their meal when he came into the room, still wearing his cassock.

'I hope Mrs Newcombe gave you enough to eat,' he said. 'My mother usually leaves it to her to do the cooking these days.'

'It was very nice, thank you,' said Dulcie, her eyes not meeting his, for she was remembering the scene in the cemetery.

'You're amused by these pictures?' he went on, seeming to follow her glance, which had now settled on a large sepia reproduction of a Roman banquet scene.

Dulcie was embarrassed, being unable to judge by his tone whether he was amused too. She was relieved when he explained with a laugh that the whole lot had been bought at an auction sale by his maternal grandfather for ten shillings.

'So this hotel belonged to your mother's father,' said Viola thoughtfully.

'Yes – my father married into it, if you see what I mean.'

This interesting piece of information was received in silence, each woman giving it her own interpretation. They got up from the table and Neville followed them out into the hall, where Mrs Forbes was sitting at the reception desk, study-ing the bookings of long ago or fitting in present imaginary ones.

'And what are you going to do this afternoon?' Neville asked.

'We'd thought of going to look over the castle. I believe it's open to the public now, isn't it?' said Viola.

''Tis a dirty old place,' said Mrs Forbes suddenly, lapsing into her native speech. 'What you want to go there for?'

'Well, Mother, it's quite interesting,' said Neville soothingly – 'though,' he added, turning to Dulcie and Viola, 'the oldest bits have been smothered by some unfortunate rebuilding. But if you're at all interested in Victoriana you should certainly see it.'

'Half a crown to go in, they charge,' cackled Mrs Forbes. ''Tis robbery.'

'You can get a bus from the end of the road,' said Neville, ignoring his mother. 'I hope you'll enjoy it.'

'Odd, isn't it,' said Viola, as they sat in the bus, 'the way he's just here, apparently doing nothing. How does it solve the problem of poor Miss Spicer and her love for him?'

'Not to mention her aged mother,' said Dulcie. 'I suppose he's waiting till things calm down – if things like that ever do.'

'Mrs Forbes didn't seem to want us to go to the castle – I suppose it must seem rather shocking to the older people – this opening one's house to strangers. Particularly when it's the local gentry.'

'Interesting, wasn't it, what Neville said about his father marrying into the hotel, as it were,' said Dulcie thoughtfully. 'You know, I'm wondering if he *did* perhaps have some connection with the castle. The grand name on the tombstone – *that* ought to give us a clue.'

They got out of the bus behind three elderly ladies in well-cut tweed suits and severe felt hats, one of whom, when she turned round, was seen to be startlingly bearded.

The castle was approached by a steep path leading up

through wooded grounds. It looked dark and rather sinister, seen through the trees, most of which were evergreens. They climbed the steps up to it and went in by a heavy oak door, inside which was a small table with tickets, guide-books and postcards laid out for sale. They discovered that a guide was at that moment taking a party round, but both were impatient to start exploring on their own account, so they started to walk through the rooms without waiting for the next conducted party.

The rooms were furnished in a luxuriantly Victorian style, and filled with such nostalgic trivia as waxed fruit under glass, paper-weights, shell and seaweed pictures, and stuffed birds. It was difficult to imagine anybody now living in such rooms, though they possessed a certain gloomy cosiness lacking in the austerely beautiful eighteenth-century rooms of the more admired 'stately homes'.

It was when they were leaning over the red cord to study a particularly striking arrangement of pressed seaweeds that Dulcie's attention was caught by a rather interesting-looking couple, who had come close enough for their conversation to be overheard. They were a tall, elegantly-dressed woman of about thirty-five, with a fur stole draped casually over her dark-grey suit and a frivolous little pink velvet hat, and a younger, smaller man, with dark hair cut in a medieval style, who was rather oddly dressed in tight-fitting blue jeans and an orange heavy-knitted cardigan. He had a flat, rather common little voice, which kept up a non-stop flow of conversation.

'But, Wilmet,' they heard him say, 'how do they keep them *clean*? Those yellow curtains must be ever so dusty if they're never taken down. That guide said the brocade was over a hundred years old. *I* call it disgusting.'

'Yes, specially woven in Lyons,' said his companion. 'Don't you think it's a beautiful design?'

'I'd rather have something contemporary that could be sent to the cleaners, or you could wash yourself in Tide. Then you'd know it was *really* clean,' said the young man smugly.

'Oh, Keith, you really are absurd!' The young woman laughed. 'You're quite obsessed with things being clean – like those people in television advertisements.'

'Well, *I* think it's important,' he said defiantly. 'How can you have a really nice home if things are dirty and dusty?'

'I suppose the answer is that one couldn't ever imagine this place being described as "a really nice home",' said the young woman.

'Does anybody actually live here now?' asked Dulcie, plucking up courage to address her, conscious though she was of her own shabby tweeds and heavy shoes in contrast to the other's elegant appearance.

'Yes, the family has one wing which isn't open to the public – but of course they're only distant relations of the people who used to live here,' said the young woman in a pleasant, friendly tone. 'When old Miss Forbes died it passed to them, and they apparently decided to try and make a bit of money out of it.'

'Weren't there any nearer relations?' Dulcie asked.

'There was one, but he was rather naughty,' giggled the young man.

The young woman smiled indulgently. 'Perhaps "naughty" isn't quite the word. But it seems that the younger son of the last generation of Forbeses – a nephew of the old lady – made an unsuitable marriage, which was all the more distressing because the elder son had been killed in a motor accident.'

'How do you mean – unsuitable?' Dulcie asked.

'He married the daughter of somebody who kept a hotel in the town – quite a common sort of person,' said the young man primly. 'He was cut off with a shilling.'

So that was it, Dulcie said to herself. Marrying beneath them seemed to be a characteristic of the Forbes family. No wonder Mrs Forbes thought the castle 'a dirty old place'.

'It all sounds like a Victorian novel,' said Viola, disbelieving.

'Yes, doesn't it,' the young woman agreed, 'but we were assured that it was true. The guide who took us round told us. We felt we had to give him an extra large tip for such an unexpected piece of entertainment.'

'Oh, but it's sad, really,' Dulcie burst out. 'People may be – people *are* – still living who played a part in the story.'

'Yes, I suppose they are,' said the young woman, but at this point she was approached by two other men – one an obvious husband-type and the other tall, fair and handsome.

'Ah, there you are, darling,' said the husband. 'I've brought the car up the drive. We thought you'd probably be worn out after all your sightseeing, didn't we, Piers.'

*Piers*, thought Dulcie, with an envious glance at him.

'Do you *know*,' said the dark young man, 'they never take those curtains down to wash them? Would you believe it!'

They seemed to melt away, the young woman throwing a vague smile towards Dulcie and Viola as, cherished and secure with her three men, she moved away from them.

'No wonder she's tired in those ridiculously high heels,' said Viola sourly, as they waited for the bus back. 'What odd people they were! Like characters in a novel.'

'This whole afternoon has been rather like a novel,' said

Dulcie, 'I feel as if I'd been rushed through to the end without having read the middle properly. Can you imagine Mrs Forbes as a young girl, being wooed by handsome young Mr Forbes from the castle?'

'It's impossible to imagine some things,' said Viola wearily. She was thinking of the little bottle of gin in the bedroom cupboard.

'The extraordinary thing is,' Dulcie went on, 'that these things have always been so, and yet it's only our knowing about them that has made them real.'

'You could say that about anything,' Viola objected.

'It's the fourth dimension, isn't it, or something like that. I wish sometimes that I knew about philosophy. Did you see that portrait on the staircase?' Dulcie was quickly down to earth again. 'Couldn't you see a likeness to Aylwin there?'

The bus came and they got on to it. When they got back to Eagle House Mrs Forbes was in the hall, doing something to the eagle. 'Moulting, he is,' she said. 'I think the moth's got him, in the neck here. My father was proud of this old eagle.'

Dulcie and Viola crept up to their room, hardly knowing whether to laugh or cry.

# CHAPTER TWENTY

Mrs Williton and Marjorie, as was their invariable custom when travelling, had arrived at Paddington an hour too early for the train. There was therefore nothing to do but to go and have a cup of tea. They had brought their own with them to have on the train, though Marjorie would have liked to have tea in the restaurant car, where there was always the possibility of a romantic or interesting encounter. After all – though this was hardly the time to dwell on it – had she not met Aylwin in very similar circumstances?

'I'll keep an eye on the luggage, dear, while you fetch the tea,' said Mrs Williton, who had found two places at a table. While Marjorie queued at the counter, her mother's eyes never left the two small suitcases and the canvas shopping-bag that they had brought with them. She did not realise that the other travellers were much too preoccupied with their own luggage to entertain any idea of stealing hers. She always imagined that some lurking stranger was lying in wait, eager to snatch away the cases if her glance should stray from them for a moment. But he'd probably be disappointed in what he found, she thought with grim satisfaction, remembering the woollen dresses, grey pleated skirts, handknitted twin-sets, and blouses (in case the weather got warmer), which they had packed.

When the train came in they went to their reserved seats, which were in a carriage not too near the engine (in case there should be an accident) and, of course, in the second class. Aylwin had always tried to persuade Marjorie to travel first class, but Mrs Williton's natural thriftiness would not hear of this. Money could be put to better uses – the organ fund, for example. Again, Marjorie would have liked to travel first class. The possibilities of a romantic encounter were as great in a first class carriage as in the dining car – greater, even. One never met anybody interesting travelling second class.

Their seats offered some advantage, however – to Mrs Williton if not to Marjorie. They were on the corridor side, so that Mrs Williton could slip easily and comparatively un-noticeably to the lavatory. This meant, however, that she would not have control of the window, but, as she whispered to Marjorie, 'You can't have everything.'

As they entered the carriage, a silent middle-aged couple were already preparing to occupy the window seats, and the man was in the act of getting up and shutting the window. This was very disquieting, and Mrs Williton foresaw a tense atmosphere all the journey. She would be worrying about whether she was getting enough air, and then, if she *did* pluck up her courage and ask for the window to be opened, it might become too draughty. She sat down stiffly on the edge of the seat, like a bird on an unfamiliar nest.

Marjorie opened her favourite woman's magazine and turned to the serial, hoping to lose herself in it. She did not really want to go to Taviscombe at all, thinking it a dull place and being rather afraid of her mother-in-law. She had reached a state of apathy about her marriage and her feelings towards Aylwin were a mixture of fear, dislike, and boredom. Coming back to live with her mother in the house facing the common had seemed, at the time, 'an important step', and she had waited in almost pleasurable anticipation to see what would happen next. But nothing had happened – there had been no dramatic move on Aylwin's part, and her mother's friends, after their first ghoulish curiosity had died down, had accepted her living there just as they had done before she married. Indeed, it was useful to have Marjorie at home again to help with church activities, and some people even forgot that she had ever been married and started to call her 'Marjorie Williton' again.

In theory, of course, divorce was not approved of in Mrs Williton's circle, though where one's own daughter was involved, and where her husband had turned out badly, was, in fact, a 'libertine', it was a different matter. Mrs Williton had even gone as far as suggesting that Marjorie should see a solicitor about the possibility of divorcing Aylwin. But when it came to presenting evidence it did not seem to amount to very much; perhaps it was not really 'adultery' – kissing a woman who had been helping him with his book – entertaining a young girl to a glass of sherry – the solicitor, wise and kindly though he undoubtedly was, made it all sound rather ridiculous. He hadn't exactly said 'I'm afraid you must do better than that,' but he had implied it. The only hope now was Italy – Tuscany, Mrs Williton thought, lingering on the sinister associations she had given the name.

The journey passed quickly. The window was opened and

shut several times, almost amid laughter, the couple in the window proving most accommodating. The furtive sandwich-eating and the bringing out of the flasks of tea was accomplished with hardly any embarrassment. At last the train began to move more slowly, and on their right the sea came into view and was greeted with exclamations all round. It looked grey and cold, and the couple in the window remarked that they wouldn't care to bathe in *that*, thank you. Mrs Williton thought how much cosier it would be to stay in one of the bright-looking little holiday chalets than in the gloomy Eagle House Private Hotel. At Taviscombe station they had to take a taxi, though she resented the extravagance as she always did, but there was no bus that went near enough.

Mrs Forbes was waiting in the hall when they arrived.

'That old eagle,' she said, pointing to the bird, ''tis losing its feathers.'

If Mrs Williton and Marjorie thought this a strange form of greeting they were by now used enough to Mrs Forbes not to show it.

'Well, Marjorie, how are you, dear?' she went on obviously making an effort to behave like a normal mother-in-law. 'And how's my lad? Not been behaving himself too well by all accounts,' she added, with what seemed to Marjorie a leering smile.

To hear Aylwin called 'my lad' and to have his conduct dismissed in such a phrase was making altogether too light of the whole matter, Mrs Williton thought indignantly.

'Perhaps we could see our room,' she said rather stiffly. 'There'll be plenty of time to talk afterwards. Are you full with visitors?'

'Not *full*, as you might say. I've got Nev here and two very nice young ladies, but I don't reckon to do much business these days. Bed and breakfast in the season and evening meal if they want it – I've made my bit, you know, though between you and me I'm not going to tell those robbers in the Income Tax where I've put it,' Mrs Forbes rambled on. 'Oh, here's Nev – he'll take your luggage.'

Neville Forbes appeared, smiling pleasantly. The sight of him in his cassock did much to reassure Mrs Williton and she felt, as Dulcie had in the cemetery, not only the appropriateness of a cassocked clergyman among tombstones, but his essential rightness anywhere. If only it could have been Neville that Marjorie had married! she thought regretfully.

'This isn't the room we usually have, is it?' she remarked as Mrs Forbes opened a door. But what did it matter? It was, if anything, a rather pleasanter room.

'Well, people might come, you never know these days,' said Mrs Forbes vaguely, as if she believed it less and less. 'I'll leave you to unpack now. Dinner is at half past seven.'

In their room Mrs Williton and her daughter turned to each other in the way that people left together in a hotel bedroom do. Mrs Williton held up a towel with a frayed edge, Marjorie commented on the pink plastic tooth mugs and turned back the eiderdowns to count the number of blankets on the beds.

'It's nice to have a proper wash,' said Mrs Williton, running water into the basin. 'You can't really wash your hands on the train – those little pieces of soap never lather properly and the water's never hot.'

'I wonder who the two young ladies are,' Marjorie said. 'It seems funny to think of anyone staying here from choice.'

A heaviness of spirit had descended on her and she was feeling how much better it would have been to have stayed at home. As she unpacked she wished she had brought different clothes with her – the pink twin-set rather than the mauve, a nicer dress to wear in the evenings, and her new raincoat instead of the old one she had thought good enough for Taviscombe.

'I wonder who the people who have just arrived are,' said Viola to Dulcie.

'Yes – I'd almost got to thinking of Eagle House as our own private place.'

'Like the grave,' said Viola.

'Ah, yes, where none embrace,' said Dulcie, catching the allusion. 'Well, evidently not Neville,' she added absently, for she was still shaken by the revelations at the castle, since which nothing had seemed quite real.

'Perhaps they'll be at dinner,' said Viola. 'It will seem awkward in the dining-room with other people there. Do you think we'll have to make conversation?'

'It'll be difficult if they're in the opposite corner.'

'I expect we shall all be put in the window,' said Viola, 'the kind of cosiness I *don't* very much like.'

But when the gong, rung by Neville, boomed out there was no sign of the other visitors. Over roast lamb and bottled gooseberries and custard, Viola speculated as to what could have happened to the new arrivals. Dulcie was less interested in their whereabouts than in the idea of Mrs Forbes bottling gooseberries, which she found impossible to imagine.

'But Dulcie,' Viola persisted, 'if they aren't eating in the dining-room, where *are* they eating? I suppose they've gone out.'

'Surely not on their first evening? You don't think they could be dining with Mrs Forbes and Neville?'

'They might be. I think they were women, judging by their voices.'

'I know,' said Dulcie, 'it's Miss Spicer and her mother come to claim Neville. *They* would naturally have dinner with him and Mrs Forbes.'

'Oh, of course,' said Viola. 'But don't forget that the mother is said to be over eighty and bedridden.'

They finished their meal and drank cups of coffee, which, as Viola commented, tasted as if it had been well boiled. They decided to go and sit in the lounge for a while and browse among the books in the glass-fronted bookcase.

'Oh – how nice!' The exclamation startled them a little, and they saw that the newly arrived visitors had just come out of Mrs Forbes's private sitting-room. 'We've met before, haven't we? What a funny thing, seeing you here!' Marjorie confronted Dulcie in such a way that there was no possible escape.

For a moment Dulcie thought of denying that she had ever met Marjorie, but while she hesitated Marjorie was enthusiastically recalling the occasion of their meeting – the jumble sale in aid of the organ fund in her mother's house.

'You bought that rather sweet little Italian pottery donkey, didn't you. I remember I had such a time wrapping it up – the ears would keep poking through the paper,' she laughed.

Her mother stood by with a pleased expression on her face. To hear somebody recall the happy occasion of the little sale – and it *had* been a success, over £20 profit – was the nicest thing that had happened since their arrival in Taviscombe. She and Marjorie had had a trying meal, with Neville not seeming to know what to talk about, and Mrs Forbes going on about the moulting eagle and how well her 'lads', as she would insist on calling them, had done for themselves. It was impossible even to touch upon Aylwin's disgraceful behaviour, for whenever Mrs Williton tried to hint at it Mrs Forbes would bring out a story about some person in Taviscombe who had behaved in a similar, generally worse, manner some thirty or forty years ago. Both Mrs Williton and Marjorie were beginning to be very sorry that they had come. Even the prospect of sea air was not particularly attractive, for the weather was dull and rainy and a brisk tap on the barometer in the hall showed that it was falling.

'Yes, I think I do remember you,' said Dulcie, trying to gain time.

'I'm Marjorie Forbes,' she said eagerly, 'and this is my mother, Mrs Williton.'

'I'm Dulcie Mainwaring, and this is my friend Viola Dace,' said Dulcie in return.

'Funny – I had the idea your name was different,' said Marjorie. 'A shorter name, but I can't remember now what it was.'

'Oh, you must be confusing me with somebody else,' said Dulcie quickly, hoping that the false name she had given at the sale would not be remembered.

'And how do you like Eagle House?' asked Mrs Williton, with a note of challenge in her voice.

'It has great atmosphere, I think,' said Dulcie.

'It certainly has that,' said Mrs Williton, not quite knowing how to take the remark.

'Mrs Forbes is my husband's mother,' said Marjorie, as if to forestall any too frank expression of opinion.

'Oh, then Eagle House must be a very special place for you,' said Dulcie, much too gushingly in her nervousness. It seemed so odd to think of Aylwin being the husband of this dim young woman in the pale blue wool dress, with a single string of pearls and diamanté flower spray brooch. She seemed so totally unsuitable. Was it Aylwin's father coming out in him, she wondered. And yet Mrs Forbes, even if she had been beneath him socially, was so much a personality in her own right. What was the explanation? Dulcie supposed that, for some reason or other, he must have fallen in love with her; it was as simple as that.

The four ladies parted with mutual expressions of goodwill.

'I expect we'll be seeing you about the place,' Marjorie said.

'How strange that she didn't appear to recognise me,' said Viola, when she and Dulcie were alone.

'Well, you haven't met often,' said Dulcie, 'and probably emotion has somehow blotted out your appearance – you know – you are something she didn't want to remember.'

'It was *I* who felt the emotion,' said Viola indignantly. 'In fact it's still rather painful for me to meet Aylwin's wife. It brings it back to see how utterly unsuitable she is. How could he *ever* . . . but what's the use of asking.'

'No, some men seem to make a habit of choosing the wrong women,' said Dulcie thoughtfully. 'I suppose it's because sub-consciously they don't really want what's good for them.' She remembered Maurice in the early days of their engagement saying that she was good, 'like bread', but who wanted bread all the time? Following up the analogy, she tried to think what Marjorie was like – some kind of fancy cake or 'pastry' seemed to suggest itself immediately, the kind of thing one might start and not be able to finish. 'Rather embarrassing, really, that *they* should be here,' she said to Viola. 'Will they begin to wonder about us, do you suppose?'

'No,' said Viola. 'Anybody might come to Taviscombe, and The Anchorage could only take us for one night. Don't forget that.' She took a letter from her bag and began to read it, smiling to herself in the irritating way that people sometimes do when they are secretly pleased by something. Dulcie supposed it was from Bill Sedge, but could not bring herself to ask.

'All the same,' Dulcie said, 'I do feel a little uneasy about the whole thing. Supposing we let out that we'd been to Neville's church or that we'd seen Mr Forbes's grave or – oh, so many things!'

'There can be an explanation for anything,' said Viola firmly.

'And we know that truth is stranger than fiction,' she added, smiling down at her letter. 'I'm sure Mrs Williton would be the first to admit that.'

# CHAPTER TWENTY-ONE

Senhor MacBride-Pereira stood at his window with a letter in his hand. It was written on blue deckle-edge paper in a flowing, feminine hand and yet it was about a simple, almost humdrum, matter. Mrs Beltane proposed to raise the rent of his flat, or, as she delicately put it, 'adjust his rental'. He repeated the words over to himself, taking pleasure in the sound of them, which, after a few repetitions, became totally meaningless, like some quaint medieval formula.

She wants more money, he said to himself, perhaps she even *needs* more money; but it was a subject he could not possibly have spoken to her about, though he would have enjoyed the elegant circumlocutions she might have employed. Indeed, he thought ironically, it would have been less painful to both of them had he lived rent-free. The simplest way of achieving this state would obviously be by asking her to marry him, and for a moment he almost considered the idea, only to reject it before it could take any sort of practical form. Marriage was not for him, and he had now become too set in his ways to consider even the marriage of true minds. And she might well find that a little 'tame' (was that the word?), for she was still a handsome woman. She would not be content with the quiet life he liked to lead, and she might mock at the way he liked to sit wearing his kilt in the evenings.

Still standing by the window, he folded the letter and replaced it in its envelope. It would be a simple matter to instruct his bank to increase, no *adjust*, the amount of the banker's order, that flew like a kind of peaceful dove, quarterly and in advance, from his account to hers. Had their relationship been less delicate, he might have run downstairs, with the letter in his hand, telling her that he would of course be glad to pay the extra she demanded. But as it was he had to ponder on the kind of reply he could write, equalling or even surpassing hers in delicacy. He could see that she was in the front garden tending some pot plants, using a new watering can of some white iridescent material – plastic, he supposed – in the form of a swan. Was this perhaps a very slight error of taste, he asked himself thoughtfully, as he watched the water trickling from the bird's beak. Not if he could turn it into poetry, he decided. 'Lines to a Lady with a Watering Can in the Form of a Swan' might be the title; it would be a very minor poem, perhaps even unfinished. Mrs Beltane's Christian name was Doris, which would give it an eighteenth-century touch.

Two figures were strolling along the road, and as they came nearer Senhor MacBride-Pereira saw that one of them was the young girl beloved by Paul Beltane. The other was a middle-aged, good-looking man. Outside the house they stopped and he made some movement towards her, almost as if he had been about to kiss her. Then, evidently remembering that they might be overlooked, he contented himself with taking her hand and raising it to his lips. The girl ran smiling into the house – evidently she had been coming to see Paul – and the man turned and began to walk away in the rather lost manner of somebody in a strange neighbourhood uncertain of where he is going.

The things I see, thought Senhor MacBride-Pereira, moving away from the window and sitting down at his desk to compose a reply to Mrs Beltane's letter.

Aylwin Forbes, meanwhile, after standing undecided in the road for a moment, walked briskly away as if he had made up his mind to take a certain course of action – which, indeed, he had. He would go and see Marjorie and her mother now, while his thoughts were still of Laurel and how pleased she had been to see him again. They had met accidentally in Quince Square – he just back from Italy and she on the way to the suburb where her aunt lived. What a dutiful niece she was, he reflected, not noticing that it was the next-door house she had run into when they parted. It had perhaps been foolish of him to suggest that he came with her on the bus, but there was something peculiarly sweet in being together in such ordinary circumstances. Their conversation had been a little constrained, but that was only to be expected when they had met so seldom and she was shy by nature. It would be a great mistake to rush things, and unthinkable, of course, to *say* anything before the situation with Marjorie was 'clarified'.

After a few minutes' walking, he saw a cruising taxi and hailed it, giving the address of Mrs Williton's house in Deodar Grove. He leaned back, took out his cigarette case, and found to his annoyance that it was empty. He had not thought about smoking when he was on top of the bus with Laurel. The taxi began to slow down and stopped a little too soon, so that he got out by the next-door house, the one with the stone squirrel in the garden.

Aylwin hesitated for a moment, automatically looking for the animal, though it had long ceased to have any meaning for him. He had been thinking that Laurel might have liked it, forgetting for the moment, as men sometimes do, that it had been one of the shared sentimental details of his courtship with Marjorie. But the place on the rockery where it had stood for so long was bare – the squirrel had disappeared. He felt a moment almost of panic and began looking in other parts of the little front garden to see if it had been moved elsewhere. But there was no trace of it. Then he saw that the house had an estate agent's board fixed to the wall, announcing that it had been sold, and he remembered that it had been for sale on his last abortive visit. Had the squirrel been removed by the previous owners, he wondered. He felt he must know.

Hardly realising how ridiculous he might appear, he opened the gate and walked into the garden. The front door of the house was open and some rather highbrow music – Bach, he thought – was coming from one of the rooms. A youngish-looking man in spectacles was standing in the hall, unpacking a crate of books. When he saw Aylwin he moved towards him and they stood staring at each other, both equally embarrassed.

'I'm so sorry,' Aylwin began, 'I think I . . .' He hardly knew what he could say.

'Oh, you're looking for the Fullaloves,' said the young man, with a sudden burst of inspiration. 'I'm afraid they've left here. We moved in last week.'

'Yes, I see,' said Aylwin. The Fullaloves – that had been the unsuitable name of the dried-up elderly couple who used to live there. But did it seem likely that he – Aylwin Forbes – would be looking for them? 'There used to be a stone squirrel in the garden,' he said, making his tone slightly ironical.

'Oh, *that* object!' The young man laughed unkindly. 'It was one of the first things my wife got rid of. She can't bear stone animals of any kind.'

Aylwin murmured, not entirely sympathetically.

'She's a lecturer at the London School of Economics,' the young man went on, hardly explaining her abhorrence of stone animals, Aylwin thought.

'What did she do with it?' he asked.

'Threw it in the dustbin, I think.'

'Oh, I see.' No doubt one of the dustmen had taken it home. Odd to think that it might now be in some other garden, though exactly where was beyond Aylwin's imagination. He thought of 'mean' little houses in Fulham, Hammersmith, or Wandsworth – districts he had sometimes motored through. 'Actually, I'm calling to see the people next door as well,' he explained, backing out of the garden. 'Then I'm afraid you're going to be unlucky again,' said the young man. 'They're away.'

Aylwin looked up at the windows of Mrs Williton's house. They were all tightly shut, the net curtains appearing to be of an even more impenetrable denseness than usual.

'Oh, I see,' he said lamely. 'I must be going, then.'

'Sorry about the squirrel!' the young man called after him.

'Oh, that's all right,' said Aylwin, not knowing what to say. But really the whole episode had upset him. It was obviously an omen of some kind, though it was difficult to guess what it might mean. He continued walking until he came to a pub, into which he went. He ordered a Guinness, feeling that he had need of the qualities it was said to give. While drinking it he decided that Mrs Williton and Marjorie had probably gone to Taviscombe. He would go there the next day and get everything settled once and for all.

He took the morning train from Paddington, travelling first class in a carriage which was already occupied by a clergyman and a woman who looked like his sister. He would have preferred an emptier carriage, and had seen one with only a single lady in it, but just as he was about to enter it he had noticed that the lady was Miss Randall, who had brought him a cup of early-morning tea at the conference last summer. She in her turn, and of course without his knowing, had avoided *him* at an earlier stage in the journey when she had seen him standing at the bookstall. She had not known exactly which train he was getting on, but the thought of a whole journey with Aylwin Forbes talking about 'some problems of an editor', or the equivalent in train small-talk, had been too much for her, especially as the girl at *The Times* Book Club had that morning given her the latest novel by her favourite female author. Thus, there may be mutual avoidance between men and women, the men not always realising that they are not the only ones to be practising the avoidance.

As soon as the train started moving, Aylwin opened the literary weekly he had bought at the bookstall and tried to become absorbed in it, or at least to seem to be absorbed, for he suspected that the clergyman and his sister might well be the kind of people who would try to get into conversation with him. But as he turned the pages he was thinking of Laurel and the charm of her youth and freshness – *à l'ombre des jeunes filles en fleurs* – though of course that sort of thing didn't last for ever. Some women never seemed to have had it.

Miss Mainwaring (Laurel's aunt), Miss Randall, Miss Foy, even Vi Dace – or Viola, as she liked to be called – one could not imagine these women, working on the seedier fringes of the academic world, sparkling with that exciting freshness. True, he had not known any of them at the age of nineteen, so perhaps he wasn't really being fair to them. It was just possible to imagine that Dulcie, who was of course younger than the others, might have had it. Indeed, she still had that trusting, vulnerable look in her eyes which some women never lost, however unsuitably it went with their ageing exteriors.

Aylwin now turned to *The Times* and found himself confronted by an obituary notice of a man well known to him, cut down in his prime, as it were. And of course a contributor, identified only by his initials, had quoted Marlowe's lines from *Dr Faustus*:

Cut is the branch that might have grown full straight,
And burned is Apollo's laurel bough . . .

Perhaps not the happiest of lines if one remembered the whole play, Aylwin thought, wondering if anybody would do the same for him. As he amused himself by thinking of suitable and unsuitable quotations, he was conscious, so sensitive and imaginative was he, of a sweet, almost sickly, smell that immediately took him back to his childhood, to the room in Eagle House banked with wreaths and 'floral tributes', which had been sent for his father's funeral. Then he realized that the smell was in the railway carriage, now, more than thirty years later, and that it seemed to be coming from the luggage rack in the opposite corner. Looking up he saw two shrouded bundles, bunches or sheaves of flowers, judging by the shape. Could it be that the clergyman and his companion were going to a funeral, Aylwin wondered. He was still not anxious to start a conversation with them, so he turned to his reading again and had become absorbed in it when he was aware that the woman was saying something.

'Freda never did have a sense of proportion,' she said, 'and after all it's only for a cousin whom she probably hasn't even seen since the war – I'm sure of that. She and Basil were never very close, anyway.'

'I suppose she thought it was the thing to do,' said the clergyman mildly.

'But the notice in *The Times* distinctly said "cut flowers only".'

'Quite – and you picked something out of the garden, mostly leaves, as far as I remember,' said the clergyman, with a hint of malice.

'That's far more what poor old Basil himself would have wished,' said the woman firmly. 'A few *natural* flowers – whatever there happened to be in the garden, even if it wasn't very much – rather than an expensive sheaf of *wired* flowers from a Kensington florist. He would have hated the idea of *wired* flowers – he *abhorred* cruelty in *all* its forms . . .'

Aylwin, listening quietly, thought again of *The Times* obituaries and wondered if there had been one for cousin Basil.

'Of course, Freda hasn't got a garden, has she?' asked the clergyman.

'She has the *use* of the garden – she could easily have slipped down and got a few flowers. Mrs Wedge would certainly have raised no objection if Freda had explained . . . The whole thing is so . . .' She stopped, at a loss for a word. 'And then asking us to take them to the funeral – so awkward to carry, a big sheaf like that. And when people see the difference in size – so embarrassing – especially when you are taking the service – unfitting, somehow . . .'

'Could you not exchange the cards?' suggested the clergyman. 'That might solve the problem.'

'George! What a dreadful idea! For a clergyman's sister even to *think* of doing a thing like that. Besides, the card might be rather awkward to remove . . .'

'Well, in that case . . . and, as you pointed out, Basil wouldn't have liked the wired flowers.'

Fortunately there had been no need for Aylwin to join in this conversation, and, rather to his relief, the brother and sister left the train at the next stop, taking their sheaves with them. Aylwin also saw Miss Randall hurrying along the platform after them, which gave him a double sense of relief.

The idea of death and funerals, which had so far been the theme of his journey, had depressed him, as if he might find death waiting for him when he arrived at Taviscombe. When the sea came into view there was nobody to exclaim to, no exchange of facetious quips about not being too keen for a dip in *that*, thank you, and his thoughts turned to Arnold's poem, so appropriate to human relationships in general and to his own in particular –

> *Yes! in the sea of life enisled,*
> *With echoing straits between us thrown,*
> *Dotting the shoreless watery wild,*
> *We mortal millions live alone.*

Well, one knew that anyway. The years either brought people nearer together or drove them further apart.

> A God, a God their severance ruled!
> And bade betwixt their shores to be
> The unplumb'd, salt, estranging sea.

But it was less noble than that – his relationship with Marjorie and their drifting apart. Nothing in common but a stone squirrel, he thought derisively, contemplating the rows of beach huts which they were now passing. One of them even had net curtains.

The train drew into Taviscombe. A taxi driver waiting at the station recognised Aylwin and, greeting him as 'Professor', took his bag from him. The small inaccuracy irritated him – these good, simple people, always so pleased to see him and with such exaggerated respect for any kind of book-learning! The last time he had arrived at a country station had been in Italy and he had taken a *carozza*, he thought, with what was surely an unreasonable feeling of irritation. But the contrast was painful. There had been sunshine there and noble architecture, even at the station. Here every building was repellent; there was nothing upon which the eye could dwell with pleasure.

Dulcie, seeing from the window the taxi draw up and Aylwin getting out and giving what seemed to be an over-large tip to the driver, thought, how wonderful if *she* were the person he was coming to see! Impossible that one's heart should not turn over at the unexpected sight of him coming up to the door. Who would come out running, to be gathered to his heart, as it said in the poem so beloved by schoolgirls (and by all women who retained any trace of sentimentality in their make-up)? Not Marjorie, who had gone out for a walk with her mother, not Viola, who was sitting at the dark little table in the writing-room, composing a letter to Bill Sedge. Perhaps he would not be greeted by any woman but his mother, though Neville might well be loitering in the hall in his cassock.

And this was exactly what did happen. Neville had often imagined himself speaking 'strongly' to Aylwin should they come face to face with each other, but he had not thought out the precise words he would use on such an occasion. Something about the sanctity of marriage, the need for give-and-take in every relationship, the shame he was bringing upon his mother and upon himself in his position in the public eye (if it was that), the distress he was causing Mrs Williton and Marjorie. This last was surely the most important aspect of the situation. But here Neville was at a disadvantage, for, having now seen his sister-in-law after some time, he had been struck by her dreariness and found himself wondering how his clever and handsome brother could ever have chosen her as his wife. And Mrs Williton was, if anything, even drearier. Therefore, when the taxi stopped and he saw Aylwin getting out, Neville's first feeling was one of simple pleasure at having another man to keep him company.

'Well, this *is* a surprise!' he said. 'We thought you were in Italy.'

'So I was, but one can't stay there for ever, unfortunately. Work calls one back,' said Aylwin, wondering if it could have done. Then, remembering the unpleasant object of his visit, he said firmly, 'I've come to sort things out here. I thought it was about time I did.'

'Ah, yes,' said Neville gravely, in a clergyman's manner, but that was all he said. 'Mrs Williton and Marjorie have gone out for a walk, I believe.'

Aylwin felt relieved that he would not have to face them just yet. 'And what are *you* doing here?' he asked almost jauntily. 'Leaving your parish like this at the busiest time of the year.'

'Oh, there was some trouble with one of my female parishioners,' said Neville lightly. It seemed so far away now, that business with Miss Spicer, that he hardly even thought of it as 'trouble'.

'Many visitors here?' Aylwin asked.

'No – just two women from London at the moment. Quite pleasant, but we don't see very much of them.'

'Good!'

At the moment both brothers felt that this was just how women should be – not allowing themselves to be much seen. But Aylwin knew that he could not put off his unpleasant task much longer. He had come to see Marjorie and see her he must – probably with her mother in attendance, too.

# CHAPTER TWENTY-TWO

Aylwin was reminded of the conference of the summer before as he unpacked in his room, but this time it was a bottle of whisky he had brought with him – more medicinal, somehow, than gin. Of course he did not need to bring his own and keep it secretly, but he feared his mother's comments. This time, too, there was no photograph of Marjorie and no copy of 'Some problems of an editor' – just a Henry James novel, *The Portrait of a Lady*, which he had been rereading in Italy. He wished sentimentally that he had a snapshot of Laurel to keep it company on his bedside table.

There was a tap on the door and his mother came in.

'It doesn't seem right, somehow, you and Marjorie not being together,' she said. 'I was just saying to Nev, I'm sure Mrs Williton would turn out if you wanted the other bed – it's the twin beds, you know.'

Oh, the dreadful cosiness of family life, Aylwin thought 'I should hardly feel like asking her,' he said rather coldly, 'and I'm sure it's the last thing Marjorie would want. I suppose they've already – er – retired for the night?'

'Yes. They had their Ovaltine – they needed it too, when I told them you'd come. You should've seen their faces! I can't think why you didn't burst in on them – give them a surprise. A bit of a joke that would've been.' Mrs Forbes laughed – callously, it seemed to Aylwin.

'Their sense of humour might not have been equal to it,' he said. 'I plan to see them tomorrow. Things are usually easier in the morning,' he added, hoping that they would be.

'What time will you have breakfast? Half past eight?' asked his mother.

Aylwin hesitated. He had imagined himself taking coffee and croissants in his room at about nine o'clock. He should have remembered that breakfast at Eagle House had always meant tackling a plate of bacon and eggs and drinking strong tea, downstairs and fully dressed. Besides, if he suggested breakfasting in his room his mother would immediately jump to the conclusion that he was ill and suggest some homely remedy or even call the doctor.

'We've got some people come for bed and breakfast,' said Mrs Forbes craftily. 'It's easier to make all the toast at once and do the cooking – saves fuel. And they tell us to save fuel, don't they.'

'*Who* tells us?' asked Aylwin irritably. 'You must be thinking of the war, Mother. Now that it's a question of one's own fuel bills one can surely do as one likes – and if you're in any financial difficulties, you know you've only got to say so.'

'You're a good lad,' said Mrs Forbes affectionately. 'You'll be down to breakfast about half past eight, then?'

'Not if Marjorie and Mrs Williton are going to be there. I couldn't face them so early and at the breakfast table.'

'I'll put them in the dining-room – don't you worry. They may not want to see you either, first thing!'

243

So it was that Dulcie and Viola, going to their table in the window next morning, were surprised to see Mrs Williton and Marjorie at another table in the room. There were also two couples who had stayed overnight for bed and breakfast, so that the dining-room seemed quite full.

A sort of early-morning murmur of conversation was going on – almost like the conversation at dinner that first evening at The Anchorage, but there was a different quality about it, as morning is different from evening. Perhaps there was more hope in it, with the promise of the new day, but Marjorie and her mother had an air of grim purpose about them and barely responded to Dulcie's and Viola's greetings. It was a fine morning, yes, finer than yesterday, but they did not seem disposed to go further than that.

After breakfast Dulcie decided to go into the lounge and look for a book to read. The bookcase was by one of the two doors leading into the room, and there was an old screen covered with Victorian scraps, behind which Dulcie was hidden as she crouched down, her fingers moving over the shelves among the Marie Corellis, Hall Caines and Annie S. Swans. She was aware that somebody had come into the room through the other door, but took no notice until she heard Aylwin's voice saying, 'Well, I suppose this is as good a place as any other.'

Dulcie sat rigid, as if frozen or turned to stone, *Kelly's Directory of Somerset* for 1905 clasped to her breast. Escape was impossible now, for she saw that Mrs Williton and Marjorie were in the room. If she had been going to move she should have done so immediately and spontaneously: now she would have to stay where she was. Whatever had induced them to choose this public room for a discussion of their private affairs, she wondered, as she settled herself into a rather less cramped position and began to turn the pages of *Kelly*. It would be interesting to see who had owned the Eagle House Private Hotel in those days, she thought, but it was too dark in her corner to be able to read the small print properly, and in any case impossible to shut her ears to the conversation going on around her.

To begin with there was not much conversation at all – or at least none that a gentlewoman might feel ashamed of overhearing. 'Quite chilly this morning, isn't it,' said Mrs Williton.

'Oh, then we'll put the electric fire on,' said Aylwin.

'One bar will be quite enough,' said Mrs Williton firmly.

'You mean we shall generate the extra heat by our discussion,' said Aylwin – much too frivolously, Dulcie felt.

'What an odd smell,' said Marjorie. 'I suppose it's the dust burning on the fire. When they aren't used much they do get dusty.'

'It was a shock to us to see you here,' said Mrs Williton, coming a little nearer to the point. 'I brought Marjorie for a breath of sea air, like you suggested. I didn't think anything upsetting like this was going to happen.'

Aylwin's frivolous tone had really been assumed to conceal the fact that he was feeling a little nervous, annoying though it was to have to admit it. He fixed his eyes on the little jewelled poodle, pinned to the lapel of his mother-in-law's grey tweed suit. She was also wearing ear-clips in the shape of bluebirds carrying something – what could it be? – in their beaks. Or perhaps they were doves bearing olive branches? Odd, her love of trinkets, he thought. She was in so many ways not that kind of person. Even the word 'trinket', with its gay and slightly silly associations, seemed inappropriate to her. It suited Marjorie much better, but at her he dared not look.

She did not appear to be in the least upset. Perhaps love for somebody totally unsuitable dies more completely, when it does die, than any other kind of love. Aylwin himself could not recapture the smallest vestige of his feelings for her – even the stone squirrel seemed ridiculous and embarrassing when associated with Marjorie. He was an impetuous romantic – that was the trouble, Aylwin thought, liking this picture of himself, and here he was being true to form, thinking of marrying a girl half his age!

His thoughts were brought back to reality with a jolt by Mrs Williton asking him point-blank what he proposed to 'do' about Marjorie.

'*Do?*' he echoed. 'What is there – could there be – that I could – as it were – *do?*'

'You could put your marriage to rights.'

'But what about Marjorie herself? Will she – speak her mind?'

'I don't know what to say,' murmured Marjorie listlessly. 'I haven't made a success of being your wife – we just aren't suited to each other.'

'Don't blame yourself, dear,' said Mrs Williton grimly.

There was a pause. Then Aylwin, who had been pacing about the room, came to a standstill in front of the sofa where the two women were sitting. 'I may as well tell you,' he said firmly, 'that I intend to provide you with evidence for divorce as soon as possible.'

'Ah, *Tuscany*!' hissed Mrs Williton.

'Not at all,' said Aylwin. 'I spent most of my time there looking at churches and art galleries.'

Marjorie let out a nervous giggle, and Dulcie was very much afraid that she might too. It was a dreadful position to find oneself in – that of eavesdropper – and yet she could not help feeling that if anyone had to overhear what was going on it was best that it should be herself, with her genuine interest in Aylwin Forbes – just as a bona fide research worker may be granted access to private letters or diaries considered too shocking to be gloated over by the general public.

'I'm as anxious as you are to get this unhappy business straightened out,' Aylwin went on.

'I suppose you want to get married again yourself,' said Mrs Williton sharply, 'that's what it is. Some Italian señorita, no doubt.'

'She would be a signorina, if she existed,' said Aylwin, smiling faintly, unable to resist correcting his mother-in-law.

'So she's not Italian?'

'No – and the whole affair is at present of too nebulous a nature to be even – one might say – *dreamed* of. I have not – I *dare* not, indeed – you must understand this – say more. It would be most imprudent, to say the least of it.' Aylwin resumed his pacing and stood over by the window, his eyes fixed on a distant height just visible through the private hotels and boarding-houses opposite.

Why was Aylwin talking in this odd pseudo-Henry-Jamesian way, Dulcie wondered. Was it an affectation, the outcome of his sojourn in Italy, or did it indicate real uncertainty of mind? And who was this unknown, vaguely hinted-at, 'other woman'? Not Italian – that was something, but it didn't get one very far. Perhaps this time it was a sensible person of his own age or a little younger, with similar academic and literary interests – somebody he had met at the conference somebody like herself, or, she thought suddenly, like Viola. It would certainly be ironical if, after all this time, he should decide to turn to Viola. But no, it must be somebody unknown to them and there was a curious kind of relief in acknowledging this – like finding only Pontings' catalogue lying on the mat instead of the more interesting but trouble-bringing letter.

Mrs Williton, too, thought Aylwin's way of talking odd, but she attributed it to his having been drinking, probably since early morning.

'Well, if that's the case . . .' she began, rather at a loss, for divorce was against her principles, and yet she would have liked to retort that Marjorie herself had found somebody else, if only to keep her end up.

'I'm going back to London this morning,' he said, 'so there will be no need for you to cut your holiday short. You realise, of course, that we mustn't have any communication about this business – you have heard of collusion and that sort of thing, I imagine.'

Mrs Williton's answer was inaudible to Dulcie, but she heard Aylwin go over to the door – luckily not the one she was crouching by – and walk out, closing it behind him. She would have liked to stand up and reveal her presence, if only to ease her cramped position, but she was suddenly aware that Marjorie Forbes was weeping and her mother apparently com-forting her, mainly by abuse of Aylwin. Very cautiously, Dulcie stood up and saw that they were sitting on a sofa, quite unaware of her. She guessed that they would soon go out, probably in search of the much-needed solace of a cup of tea. Now would have been the time for Neville to enter the room with a word of comfort and hope. But he did not come, and, sorry though Dulcie was for poor Marjorie, she did not feel equal to the role of comforter herself. Besides, it might have seemed presumptuous, and what could she have said? As it was, she crept quietly and unobserved out of the door, saddened and a little surprised at Marjorie's tears. The astonishing thing was that the whole scene had taken less than a quarter of an hour. Passing the writing-room, she saw that Viola was engrossed in a letter, so she did not disturb her but began walking down the road towards the sea, not quite sure where she was going or what she was going to do when she got anywhere, but feeling the need for solitude.

The sun had come out in a rather watery sky and people were strolling on the promenade or sitting in the shelters reading newspapers, talking, or just sitting with that air of hopeless resignation that people on holiday so often seem to have. Dulcie felt that there would be something comforting about the sea; its cold grey detachment (she also remembered Matthew Arnold's lines, as Aylwin had) might bring consolation after the upsetting scene she had just overheard. I too know what it is to be rejected, she said to herself, and wondered if it might forge some kind of bond between herself and Marjorie. But then she realised that Marjorie was in a superior position, for she had at least acquired a husband and been married to him for some years, whereas she herself had only got as far as a fiancé. So there could really be no bond, when the rejections had been on such different planes, and then there was that china donkey, Dulcie remembered. Could she really have any kind of bond with somebody who had thought it sweet?

She walked on rather briskly until she had left the crowds behind her and met only solitary figures. She was not surprised to see that one of them was Aylwin, standing by the sea wall, looking down at the flat stones from which the tide was now receding.

But if Dulcie had expected to see Aylwin she was by no means as sure of what she ought to do. For, in spite of Viola's reassurances, might he not think it extremely odd, suspicious almost, that she should be in Taviscombe at this moment and staying at Eagle House? Trying to make up her mind quickly, she decided that she must either greet him as if it were the most natural thing in the world, or walk straight past him, leaving him alone with his grief, if, indeed, it was grief.

Fortunately the decision was taken out of her hands, for just as she came up to him he turned away from his contemplation of the stones and Dulcie, finding herself face-to-face with him, was forced to say 'Good morning.'

'Why, it's Miss Mainwaring – Laurel's aunt – isn't it?' he said in a surprised tone.

'Yes, it is,' Dulcie agreed, for of course she was Miss Mainwaring and Laurel's aunt. But she felt curiously depressed by this description of herself and by the fact that he seemed to have forgotten her Christian name.

Aylwin, for his part, was thinking what a very odd coincidence that Laurel's aunt should be staying in Taviscombe when Laurel was so much in his thoughts. Then he suddenly remembered what his brother had told him last night – about the 'two women from London' staying at Eagle House – could they be Miss Mainwaring – Dulcie – and Viola Dace? Oh, please not Viola, he almost prayed, under the same roof as Marjorie, under the same *roof*, he repeated, as if the actual physical structure of the roof somehow made it worse – that would be *too* much!

Dulcie, plucking up her courage, found herself saying in a kind of burst, 'Viola and I are staying at Eagle House – I expect you heard.' She realised that she had not seen him in full daylight before, and that it was as suitable a setting for his good looks as a lecture platform or library.

'Yes, my brother told me. It was a pleasant surprise,' he added rather formally.

'It's very nice here – the sea and everything,' said Dulcie, feeling very foolish.

'Yes, I suppose I'm so used to it that I don't notice.' He glanced indifferently towards the horizon. 'I was turned out of my room – the woman was making my bed. '

'Yes, after breakfast is an awkward time in a hotel,' Dulcie said. 'One has no right to exist between the hours of half past nine and twelve. So much work is going on that it makes one feel guilty.'

'I suppose women – nice women – feel guilty. Men are only irritated,' said Aylwin. He paused for a moment and then went on, 'Seeing you here reminds me of Laurel, of course. I've grown so fond of her these last weeks. And I believe – I even dare to *hope* – that she cares a little for me.'

'*Laurel* – care for *you*?' burst out Dulcie in amazement. 'But you're old enough to be her father! She's only nineteen, you know.'

'It's true, I am some twenty years older than she is,' he began.

'Some *twenty*! Thirty would be nearer the mark!' Dulcie interrupted him indignantly. 'She thinks of you as an old man – I'm sure of it.'

When the words were out, she was sorry that she had been so cruel, but was she not only being 'cruel to be kind', as the saying went? Or was there some other reason for her indignation at the idea of Laurel and Aylwin together?

But Aylwin's natural male conceit soon reasserted itself, and he smiled in such a way that Dulcie felt she was being naive and unworldly.

'I hope you haven't said anything to Laurel about caring for her,' she went on, unnerved by his silence. 'Because you've no right to while you're still married. If you were free, it might be different, though I'm sure her parents wouldn't approve.' And yet her sister Charlotte might well think it rather romantic; she could not imagine her brother-in-law having any opinion in the matter.

'You could hardly describe me as an old man,' Aylwin went on, ignoring Dulcie's last remarks. 'I think you might say I was in the prime of life.' He smiled, trying to turn the whole thing into a joke.

'Oh, yes, I might say so,' Dulcie agreed. 'But Laurel is much too young for you. '

There was silence between them, perhaps an awkward silence, but fortunately a few drops of rain began to fall.

'Haven't you got a coat or anything with you?' Aylwin said.

'No, I came out without one. I didn't think it would rain.'

'Why didst thou promise such a beauteous day,
And make me travel forth without my cloak,'

he quoted in a mocking tone. 'You should always carry a mac-intosh in Taviscombe. Didn't you know that?'

'Your mother told us it was a very dry place. I can sit in this shelter.' Dulcie began to move towards it, wondering if the rather disgruntled-looking occupants would move up to make room for her. They looked as if nothing could displace them.

'You'd better have my coat.'

'No, thank you, that would embarrass me,' said Dulcie, thinking it rather odd that he should have remembered his macintosh after what must surely have been a rather upsetting scene with his wife and mother-in-law. But perhaps his early upbringing in Taviscombe had made it automatic.

'Well,' he said, as they lingered on the threshold of the shelter, 'if you're really determined to stay here, I'll leave you. No doubt we shall meet in London.'

'Oh, I dare say . . . will you be seeing Laurel?'

'I hope so. I must know how she feels – how she *would* feel if by any chance . . .' he said uncertainly.

'Oh, why do you always want such unsuitable wives!' Dulcie burst out impatiently.

'You make me sound like a polygynous African chief – I've only had one wife so far,' he said lightly.

'It's time you made a *sensible* marriage,' said Dulcie boldly. 'You should choose quite a different kind of wife – somebody who can appreciate your work and help you with it – an older woman, perhaps.'

'That doesn't sound very attractive, if I may say so.'

'No, probably not,' Dulcie admitted, for it really did sound as if she meant Viola or somebody like that. And of course, in a sense, she did. He might even think that she was putting herself forward as a possible candidate. She went suddenly hot with embarrassment at the idea of it. She was by no means at her best this morning, though if it had been a romantic novel, she thought, he would have been struck by how handsome she looked when she was angry, the sea breeze having whipped some colour into her normally pale cheeks. Certainly he was looking at her more intently than before, but perhaps only because he was surprised at her outburst.

'I had no idea you felt so strongly about my work,' he said ironically.

'I'm sorry,' she said meekly. 'It's none of my business – except that I'm Laurel's aunt. Perhaps I've said too much.'

'Oh, that's all right. It's better when people say what they really think.'

'Is it? How could we ever carry on with our everyday life if we did that?'

The people in the shelter seemed to draw nearer to each other. Aylwin smiled and looked at his watch.

'Your train – you mustn't miss it,' said Dulcie, looking out to sea. 'Goodbye.'

Aylwin hurried away. What a surprising conversation with that nice Miss Mainwaring – Dulcie – he thought. Perhaps there were hidden depths there. He realised that he was almost afraid of her and glanced back quickly over his shoulder to see if she were following. But Dulcie was sitting humbly in the shelter, wondering what could have made her talk to Aylwin Forbes like that.

# CHAPTER TWENTY-THREE

Leaving Taviscombe was, for Dulcie, an almost painful experience, only to be endured because of the certainty that she would go there again, and because Aylwin had already returned to London. And yet it was also a relief to leave the scene of so much drama and emotion.

Dulcie sat in the train with Viola, drained of all feeling, reading a woman's magazine of the type she usually despised. 'God gave us Memories', she read, 'that we might have Roses in December'. It was the end-piece of a page, enclosed in a flowery border, but, like so many 'beautiful' sayings, it wasn't strictly true. Dulcie thought how often roses bloomed on the blackened suburban trees on Christmas Eve, and she was sure that many such bloomed in Mrs Williton's garden in Deodar Grove. But she, and Marjorie too, no doubt, would treasure the saying. They were staying a day or two longer in Taviscombe. The weather had improved, and it was thought that the sea air might do them good. It might also help them to forget that last distressing interview with Aylwin, though this had not been mentioned. Dulcie's thoughts had often turned to her own conversation with him by the sea, but her memories were shameful ones. How ever could she have said what she did – what must he have thought of her! Most likely he thought nothing at all, which was at once comforting and depressing.

Neville had been hanging about the hall when Dulcie and Viola left. Dulcie had said – rather too brightly, she realised – 'I must visit your church some time' and just for a second a shadow had crossed his face, as if he were remembering that he must soon return to his London parish to face Miss Spicer and his parishioners: perhaps the thought of Dulcie – another unattached woman being added to all this was too much for him. But he soon rallied, and said that he hoped to see her there.

'Now then, Nev,' Mrs Forbes had said meaningly, and nobody had quite known what to answer.

Luckily the taxi had arrived at that moment and Dulcie's last sight had been of Mrs Forbes plucking a feather from the tail of the moulting eagle and waving it at them.

'I was wondering whether I might take a job when I get back to London,' said Viola rather self-consciously. 'Bill tells me they're wanting a new staff supervisor at the head office.'

'Wouldn't you find it too much of a change from the kind of work you're used to?' said Dulcie.

'Oh, that academic stuff – where does it get one,' said Viola impatiently. 'One only meets people like Aylwin Forbes, and what use are they?'

'None whatever,' said Dulcie sadly. 'What kind of work would you be doing?'

'Oh, engaging staff to work in the various shops – travelling round a bit, I gather.'

'But do you think *he* would like it?' asked Dulcie seriously. 'After all, it isn't like shared academic work. A man who moves in that kind of world might not like you to see how he made his living or meet the kind of people he has to mix with.'

'The same might be said of the academic world,' said Viola. 'One can share in any kind of work. That's where Marjorie Forbes has failed – not being able to share Aylwin's interests.'

'Well, she hardly could if the interests were other women,' said Dulcie, suddenly frivolous. 'Those are the kind of interests wives really *can't* be expected to share. Anyway, poor Marjorie probably tried – to begin with, at any rate. Don't you think it's also a man's fault for choosing an unsuitable wife?'

A steward came round, announcing that the first luncheon was now being served, and Dulcie and Viola got up to go to the restaurant car.

The small tables were already occupied, and they were shown to a table for four, where a woman was already sitting.

'Why, it's Miss Randall!' said Dulcie. 'I don't suppose you remember me, but my friend and I were at the conference last summer. I very much enjoyed your lecture on "Some problems of indexing".'

'Thank you,' said Miss Randall, with simple dignity. 'It's so seldom that one meets anyone who appreciates one's work, or who even knows that there can be problems of indexing.'

'Soup, ladies?' said a waiter rather threateningly, standing over them with three plates balanced in his hands.

'Yes, please,' said Dulcie, not wishing to give him the trouble of an extra journey; but she need not have been so considerate, for both Viola and Miss Randall demanded tomato juice, which she would really have preferred herself.

'I've been down in the West Country at a funeral,' said Miss Randall, carefully seasoning her tomato juice.

'How upsetting for you,' murmured Dulcie.

'Well, it wasn't really so very upsetting,' said Miss Randall, her voice ringing out through the restaurant car. 'It was only a cousin, and poor Basil and I never got on very well as children; but as one gets older one feels the pull of family ties, however distant. There was another cousin there, a clergyman who took the service, with his sister – I never liked them much either.' She laughed heartily. 'But we all got together over the funeral baked meats. You know, a glass or two of really good sherry works wonders on these occasions. Oh – and whom do you think I saw at Paddington when I was waiting for the train?'

Dulcie somehow guessed who it would be, but did not say.

'Dr Forbes! Aylwin Forbes, you know,' Miss Randall brought out triumphantly. 'I expect you remember him fainting at the lecture. "Some problems of an editor".' She chuckled reminiscently. 'I'm afraid I deliberately avoided him. I wasn't feeling in the mood for *his* kind of talk.'

What could be more delightful than Aylwin's kind of talk, *whatever* the subject, Dulcie thought, dismayed at her immediate reaction to Miss Randall's words. Was she then in love with him, or merely infatuated, like poor Miss Spicer with Neville?

'We saw him at Taviscombe,' said Viola. 'As a matter of fact we were staying at his mother's hotel.'

'I believe she's quite a "character", as they say,' said Miss Randall. 'Married a son of the local gentry, who was disowned by his family. Quite a suitable background for A. F., one feels.'

'Yes, it seems right that he should have an unusual background,' said Dulcie. 'He's such a rare person.'

'A rare person?' echoed Miss Randall. 'A rather good-looking man who has made a mess of his marriage, by all accounts – I shouldn't have thought that was rare at all.'

Dulcie was silent, mainly because she did not know how to explain Aylwin's rareness, but also because she was embarrassed by the penetrating quality of Miss Randall's voice.

They began to talk of more ordinary things, and finally parted in the corridor.

'No doubt we shall meet in London,' Miss Randall boomed. 'Perhaps at the B. M. or the Public Record Office, if we can get past the queues waiting with their magnifying glasses to examine the Casement diaries,' she chuckled.

'What a relief it will be not to have to do that dreary sort of work,' said Viola.

'I thought you liked helping Aylwin with his index,' said Dulcie reproachfully. 'But if you're going to marry Bill Sedge . . .' she went on, doubt colouring her tone.

'Marriage isn't necessarily the answer to all one's problems,' said Viola evasively, from which Dulcie concluded that he had not yet proposed to her.

'No, one sees that it isn't always the answer,' she agreed. 'But women like to settle down, mostly. Affairs and liaisons get to be rather dreary for ordinary people approaching middle age. Of course there are exceptions,' she added hastily. 'If one were the mistress of some great man, perhaps . . .'

'You mean a poet or a king or a politician?' said Viola sardonically.

'Well, poets seem not to be great nowadays in the same way that they used to be,' said Dulcie vaguely, 'and there are so few kings left. As for politicians, with the Welfare State one feels that even the home life of our Conservative leaders is above reproach. So perhaps it isn't so easy nowadays . . . I wonder if Miss Lord will have thought of getting anything in for supper? I expect she will have been giving the house a good clean this morning.'

Miss Lord was waiting for them in the hall when the taxi drew up at the door.

'East or West, Home is Best,' she announced cheerfully. 'Well, Miss Mainwaring, you don't look as if the sea air has done you much good, but Miss Dace has got quite a colour. And these flowers came for you, Miss Dace.' She thrust a cellophane-wrapped sheaf of carnations into Viola's arms. 'The short dark gentleman brought them – he said you'd know whom they were from.'

Viola took the flowers and hurried upstairs with them. Dulcie wondered if she minded Miss Lord describing her future husband as 'the short dark gentleman'. Then it occurred to her that perhaps she would not. When one loved somebody, everything about him – imperfections, vices even – became rare and special.

'Bill wants me to have dinner with him,' said Viola, coming down with a note in her haud.

'Oh, but you'll be too tired after the train journey,' Dulcie exclaimed without thinking.

Viola gave her a pitying look. 'I don't find a train journey all that exhausting,' she said. 'I must go up and change.'

'Miss Dace will be dining out?' said Miss Lord rather grandly.

'Yes. I hope you hadn't gone to too much trouble to get something for us,' said Dulcie, immediately feeling guilty.

'Oh, not really,' said Miss Lord, in the off-hand tone that in many people is a sure indication of umbrage having been taken, 'but I did think you'd both be ready for something after your long journey, so I did take just a *little* trouble to have things nice. But there you are,' she added with a little laugh, 'we never know what's going to happen, do we.'

'But Miss Lord, *I* shall be here, and I'm certainly ready for your delicious supper,' said Dulcie, wondering if Miss Lord would have taken so much trouble if she had been alone. 'I'm hungry enough to eat for two.'

'I don't know about delicious,' said Miss Lord, slightly mollified. 'It's fillets of plaice in a mushroom sauce.'

'It certainly *sounds* delicious. '

'You see, the sauce is really that concentrated soup you just pour it on,' Miss Lord explained. 'I saw it on TV.'

'How fascinating.' So she had not spent hours making a *roux* and carefully blending in various subtle ingredients, Dulcie thought. That was certainly a relief. 'Miss Dace will be sorry to have missed it, but she had this sudden invitation to go out to dinner.'

'With that short dark gentleman,' declared Miss Lord flatly.

'Yes, with Mr Sedge.'

'Jewish, isn't he?'

'I don't know. I suppose he may be – partly, at any rate. He came from Vienna before the war.'

'I suppose he'll eat with his hat on,' said Miss Lord. 'That's what they do, Miss Mainwaring. I've seen them in the kosher restaurant near where I live – eating with their hats on. A little skull cap doesn't look so bad, quite distinguished, really, but a black trilby's another thing. I wonder how Miss Dace'll like *that*.'

Dulcie sat down at the kitchen table, exhausted.

'And wearing their hats in church, too,' Miss Lord continued. 'In the synagogue, that is.'

'Yes, I believe they do. Isn't that Miss Dace going out now? I should like my supper quite soon, please, Miss Lord.'

'And a glass of sherry, too, Miss Mainwaring. That's what I'm going to get you. You look quite washed out.'

'Thank you,' said Dulcie ironically, letting Miss Lord bustle round her. 'And won't you have one yourself? You must be needing one as much as I do.'

'Well, I wouldn't say need, Miss Mainwaring, but it's one of those little extra luxuries that it's nice to have sometimes.'

Please don't tell me that you can't afford it, said Dulcie to herself; but when Miss Lord came back with two glasses of sherry she was on the subject of Dulcie again.

'It's you that ought to be going out,' she said, 'being wined and dined, as they say. Oh, Miss Mainwaring, I can't think what went wrong between you and Mr Clive. I didn't like to say too much at the time, but he was such a nice young gentleman. It was a great blow to me when the engagement was broken off, I can tell you.'

'Oh, these things happen,' said Dulcie casually. 'I suppose we weren't really suited to each other, and it's better to find out before it's too late.'

'Yes, a broken marriage would be a dreadful thing,' said Miss Lord in a hushed tone. 'But I did hope, that evening in the winter when he came to dinner, that perhaps it might be all on again.'

'No, there's no chance of that ever happening,' said Dulcie, wishing Miss Lord would go.

'I wonder why men do these things,' said Miss Lord, peering

intently at Dulcie. 'If I may say so, Miss Mainwaring, you'd make a very good wife. Of course,' she went on quickly, 'you're not *glamorous*.'

'No,' said Dulcie.

'Do you think –' Miss Lord began hesitantly. 'Oh, Miss Mainwaring, you won't mind if I speak frankly?'

'Of course not,' said Dulcie, wondering what could be coming. Some hint about personal 'daintiness', doubly embarrassing from a social inferior? She nerved herself to face the worst, but when it did come it wasn't really so bad – just something she had always known about herself.

'You could make so much *more* of yourself, Miss Mainwaring,' said Miss Lord almost on a despairing note, 'if only you would.'

'What should I do?' Dulcie smiled.

'Well, you could have your hair restyled by one of those Italian hairdressers – in the bouffant style, they call it – it would add fullness to your face, make your head look bigger.'

'Do I want my head to look bigger?' Dulcie fingered her fine, smooth hair. 'Would it be an advantage? Anyway, I don't think my hair would go like that.'

'You could have a perm – to give it body,' said Miss Lord eagerly. 'They use rollers to set it, you know. And you could use more eye make-up. It would make your eyes look bigger.'

Dulcie laughed. 'Goodness! Head bigger and eyes bigger – then what?'

'Then *you'd* be the one to get the bunches of carnations,' said Miss Lord triumphantly. 'Well, I must be getting you your supper. You didn't mind me talking like this, did you? But oh, Miss Mainwaring, I should so like to see you get married.'

'I think getting married depends on more than that,' said Dulcie. 'It comes from within, an attitude of mind, somehow.'

'Yes, but a man's got to notice you, hasn't he – that's the first step.'

'Yes, I know.' Men *have* noticed me, in a sense, thought Dulcie, remembering Maurice and Aylwin and Neville Forbes, but nothing has come of it. Miss Lord meant 'notice' in a different way, obviously.

'You read too much, that's your trouble,' said Miss Lord, seeing Dulcie settling down at the table with a book. 'They don't like it.'

'No, I don't think they do,' said Dulcie, but absently now, as the world of the book began to seem the real one.

When she had finished eating, she sat reading for a while longer, then washed up, unpacked her suitcase, and prepared to have a bath and go to bed. She brushed her hair out and tried to make it look 'bouffant', and decided, peering into the glass, that perhaps her eyes *were* rather on the small side. She was still sitting at her dressing-table, but thinking now about the richness of Aylwin's background in Taviscombe, when she heard Viola's key in the front door.

'Dulcie!' she called. 'Do come down!'

'But I'm going to bed, or nearly,' Dulcie called back. 'I'm in my dressing-gown.'

'Oh, don't bother about that,' said Viola impatiently. 'Bill and I have some news for you.'

They're engaged, Dulcie thought, disliking herself for the slight sinking feeling she experienced. And it will be all *jolly*, and I shan't really know what to say, especially in my dressing-gown.

'Good evening,' she said rather formally to Bill Sedge, who

was standing in the drawing-room with Viola. 'Do excuse me for appearing like this –' 'appearing' was the word, she felt – 'but you know how it is,' she concluded lamely, for how could he know?

'You look *charming*,' said Bill Sedge. 'Only an English-woman can *really* wear blue,' he added, making it seem to Dulcie a doubtful compliment from a Viennese. 'Nylon, isn't it?' he said knowledgeably.

'Yes, you're supposed to be able to wash it, though as it's quilted, I rather wonder . . .'

'But you can, I assure you. These nylon housecoats have been one of our most successful lines.'

'Ah, yes, I suppose you would know these things,' said Dulcie, a little embarrassed.

'Oh, Bill, tell her our news,' broke in Viola impatiently.

'Yes, do – but I think I can guess,' said Dulcie, whipping herself into eagerness.

'Viola has done me the honour of accepting me as her hus-band,' said Bill Sedge, bowing towards his fiancée.

'Oh, how lovely! I'm so glad. I'm sure you'll both be very happy. This calls for a celebration, doesn't it. We must have a drink,' said Dulcie. But *what?* she thought helplessly. She her-self, having had her bath and being ready for bed, had been looking forward to a cup of Ovaltine, but that was out of the question now. Was there enough sherry for three, she won-dered, trying to remember the look of the decanter.

'If you will allow me . . .' Bill Sedge had, characteristically, produced an interesting-looking bottle, apparently from nowhere. 'I have brought a bottle with me. I thought you might not have champagne,' he added apologetically.

'You might not have champagne'! Dulcie laughed to

herself. How right he had been! But did many women living on their own keep a bottle or two of champagne in the house? There might be some who did, rare creatures, hardly of this world.

'I'll get some glasses,' said Viola.

Really, she looks almost beautiful, thought Dulcie, with her rather gaunt features softened by love. And the whole thing is so incongruous, unsuitable, almost. If we hadn't gone to Neville Forbes's church that evening, we shouldn't have seen Bill Sedge arranging the knitwear in the window . . .

The sight of a foaming champagne bottle can produce laughter and gaiety even in a suburban drawing-room, perhaps there more than anywhere

'And next it will be your turn, Miss Mainwaring,' said Bill Sedge, gallantly raising his glass to her. 'Romance is in the air. Even in West Hampstead,' he added, surprisingly.

'West Hampstead?' Dulcie echoed. 'Yes, I suppose there as much as anywhere else.'

'It is fine news about your auntie – one likes to see an older lady getting married – that is good,' he declared.

'You mean Aunt Hermione? Getting married?' said Dulcie in amazement. 'But who?'

'That I don't know – the name of the fortunate man.'

'I don't know about fortunate,' said Dulcie.

'But surely! Any man is fortunate to marry the woman of his choice. Miss Mainwaring, your glass is empty – that will never do!'

Dulcie allowed her glass to be refilled. On this surprising evening, even the idea of anyone marrying Aunt Hermione seemed not too incongruous. But who *was* the fortunate man?

# CHAPTER TWENTY-FOUR

Although it was now early summer there was little change in the house as Dulcie approached it. The variegated laurels did not alter with the time of year, and neither Bertram nor Hermione had thought to mark the season with suitable plants as their neighbours had done. Even Dulcie's entrance reminded her of the visit she had paid before Christmas, for her Aunt Hermione, as then, came to the door in her hat and apologised for being in the middle of a telephone call.

This time her loud clear tones were addressed to the London Electricity Board, and the conversation seemed to be about power plugs and something called a 'ring circuit', which Dulcie found rather mystifying.

Bertram was sitting in the drawing-room, playing with a Corinthian bagatelle board. The metallic clash of the little balls absorbed all his attention, so that he hardly looked up when Dulcie came in.

'Six fifty!' he called out. 'That's pretty good for Hermione and the Vicar, don't you think? I've just played a game for each of us – I only got three hundred and ten for myself, but I can do much better than that. I'm going to the Abbey, you know, at Corpus Christi. Much better to start off in the summer, I felt.'

'And Aunt Hermione is to marry the Vicar?' asked Dulcie, a little bewildered. 'The one whose sister died?'

'Yes – he has turned to Hermione at last, or rather she has indicated the direction he should take. I suppose women always do that, really,' said Bertram. 'Now, Dulcie, my dear, shall I play a game for you?'

'If you like,' said Dulcie, humouring him.

'Bertram, do put that ridiculous toy away,' said Hermione, coming into the room. 'You won't be able to have it at the Abbey, you know.'

'All the more reason for playing with it now – and I must do one for Dulcie.'

'Congratulations, Aunt Hermione,' said Dulcie, kissing her on the cheek. 'This is wonderful news – and what a pretty ring you're wearing.'

'Thank you, dear. Yes, I insisted on an engagement ring,' said Hermione, stretching out her hand the better to display the gold ring set with three diamonds. 'People *will* gossip, you know, and I've been doing so much popping in and out of the vicarage lately. Would you believe it, there was no power there at all – not a single power point in any of the rooms! I was shocked, I can tell you. Now –' she took off her hat and prepared to settle down – 'Mrs Sedge will have tea ready in a minute.'

'Oh, *dear* . . .' The last little silver ball rolled into place. 'Only a hundred and five for *you*, Dulcie. I don't think I've ever made such a low score as that,' said Bertram smugly. 'Still, it's only a game, you know. You mustn't be upset by the low score.'

Dulcie smiled. 'I'll try not to be. And what's going to happen to Mrs Sedge?'

'She has been lucky enough to find a very good post,' said Hermione, 'which will suit her very well, I think.'

'Yes, and I like to think that *I* was largely responsible for that,' said Bertram. 'She is to be cook at the house of the Principal of the Teachers' Training College, where I used to be.'

'It should be just the thing for her,' said Dulcie.

'She will have a comfortable bed-sitting-room – with television of course,' said Hermione.

'A pity she isn't going to cook for the students,' said Bertram. 'She does boiled baby to perfection, though only on a small scale.'

Mrs Sedge, who must surely have been listening outside the door, came into the room at that moment with the tea. It was not often that she condescended to leave her basement, but she must have decided that Dulcie's visit was worth the ascent.

'Good afternoon, Miss Mainwaring,' she said. 'My brother has told me the good news. It is good, yes?'

'News – *you*, Dulcie?' said Hermione. 'Have you been keeping something from us?'

'No – I mean, it isn't me the news is about,' said Dulcie. 'My friend, Viola Dace, is going to marry Mrs Sedge's brother.'

'Your friend to marry Mrs Sedge's brother?' repeated Bertram, in a puzzled tone. 'But how can that be? Do they know each other?'

'Now, Bertram, don't be silly,' said Hermione sharply. 'Obviously they must know each other. Thank you, Mrs Sedge, I think we can manage now. Please congratulate your brother from me on his good fortune. Now Dulcie,' she went on, when Mrs Sedge appeared to be safely out of earshot, 'what is this nonsense? How can your friend be going to marry Mrs Sedge's brother?'

Dulcie explained how it had come about.

'Well,' said Hermione, when she had finished, 'one can only hope that they'll be happy. It all sounds *most* unsuitable.'

'But love isn't always suitable,' said Dulcie, a little impatiently. 'Viola is a difficult sort of person, and not all that young. Isn't it better that she should take this chance of happiness even if it *does* seem to be a rather incongruous match in some ways?'

'Well, as long as he can give her a comfortable home,' said Hermione complacently, no doubt thinking of the power points about to be installed at the vicarage.

'But we should be talking about you,' said Dulcie more warmly. 'How sensible of the vicar to realise what a good wife you would make,' she began, and then wondered if it had perhaps been more romantic than that.

'It was after Maisie went back to Nottingham,' said Hermione, smiling. 'She had been a *tower* of strength, as you may remember, but when that tower was taken away . . .'

'Removed to Nottingham,' interposed Bertram.

'I gave him a week or two – poor man, he soon got into a fine old muddle! Then one day I thought I'd take him by surprise, so I popped round one morning and what do you think he was doing? Trying to wash his surplices! He was worried because they didn't seem as white as they ought to be.'

Here was a new line for the washing-powder manufacturers who advertised on television, Dulcie thought. She must ask Miss Lord whether they had yet got round to the worried clergyman, shamed by the whiteness of a visiting preacher's surplice. It would not be practical to do the famous 'window test' in a church or cathedral.

'So what did you do?' Dulcie asked, unable to imagine her aunt actually washing them herself.

'I advised him to send them to the laundry. He couldn't remember what his sister Gladys – the one who died, you know – had done about it. Well, after that, one thing led to another, in the way things do.'

Dulcie listened to her aunt's voice going on and on, and thought how trivial the beginnings of love often seemed to be. The marriage between her aunt and the vicar – older people with interests in common – was at once satisfactory and depressing, just the kind of 'suitable' marriage she had advised Aylwin Forbes to make and which he obviously never would.

When she got home there was a letter lying in the hall. She recognised Maurice's handwriting on the envelope. He suggested that they should meet for lunch one day. 'I do feel', he wrote, 'that we should remain friends, and it could be such a pleasant relationship – you've no idea how I sometimes long to have somebody to tell my troubles to, and if she were a charming and sympathetic woman, so much the better!'

Dulcie stood for a moment with the letter in her hand, remembering other letters in that extravagant writing, and then rejected the idea of herself in this role. She wrote back rather vaguely, saying that she was too busy at the moment but would get in touch with him some time.

So that was another tie broken, and in a day or two Viola was leaving to spend the few weeks before her marriage at her parents' house in Sydenham.

'It does seem rather conventional,' Viola said apologetically, 'but you know what men are. Bill would expect it. We shall just have a quiet wedding at the registrar's office.'

'And what they call a small family luncheon afterwards?'

'Yes, just family, really.'

'I hope it won't be cooked by Mrs Sedge,' Dulcie couldn't resist saying. 'It would have been nice if you could have been married at Neville Forbes's church, or even at Father Benger's, but I suppose it wouldn't be legal in the flower-decorated upper room near Harrods. Anyway, I hope everything goes well.'

'We are to live in Neasden,' said Viola. 'You must come and see us.'

'I'd love to, ' said Dulcie, wondering if she ever would go. 'Will you still do indexes and odd bits of research in your spare time? No, obviously not. But just think – if it hadn't been for that conference last summer, you'd never have met me and, through me, Bill Sedge.'

'No, I suppose I shouldn't,' Viola agreed. 'Strange, isn't it, the turns life takes – all that misery over Aylwin Forbes – how one wastes one's emotions!'

Are they wasted, Dulcie wondered. She asked herself the same question the next day, when she and Miss Lord were tidying out Viola's room. For there in the wastepaper basket, not even decently torn up, was a signed off-print of one of Aylwin Forbes's articles, just cast out with all the other rubbish. Dulcie retrieved it telling herself that it should at least gather dust respectably in her own bookshelves.

'Untidy, wasn't she, Miss Dace,' said Miss Lord in an elegiac tone, as she gathered some torn-up papers out of the fireplace. 'And it looks as if she's put down a hot cup or something on this little table – it's made quite a nasty mark. I'd like to see what *her* home is like, Miss Mainwaring, I don't mind telling you.'

'I expect all the tables will have marks from hot things put down on them,' said Dulcie absently. 'Though people do sometimes change when they marry. Perhaps Mr Sedge . . .'

'Oh, he'll be house-proud all right,' said Miss Lord vigorously. 'I know the type.' She went downstairs muttering something about respect for other people's property.

Dulcie was expecting Laurel to come to tea, and went into the kitchen to make a cake, as if Laurel were still a child for whom treats must be prepared. But when she saw her coming along the road she realised how much she had changed in less than a year in London. Now she wore high heels and a tight narrow skirt; her hair no longer hung loose on her shoulders but was swathed round her head into a sort of beehive shape, which seemed to be the latest fashion. She looked like a young girl of the very early 'twenties, before short hair was thought of.

'You'll never guess who I had lunch with today,' said Laurel.

Dulcie could guess, but allowed herself to be mystified.

'Dr Forbes!'

How odd it sounded, to hear Aylwin described like that, Dulcie thought.

'How nice of him to ask you,' she said. 'Where did you go?'

'To a club – the ladies' annex, he said it was. I suppose it would be – a lot of elderly men – some clergymen, even – having lunch with girls. It was rather funny, really.'

'Goodness!' said Dulcie, wondering if it had been the Athenaeum. 'I hope the food was good?'

'It was all right, but I'm not used to eating much for lunch.

And we had a lot of wine. I felt I was getting rather red in the face,' she added disarmingly.

'And what did you talk about?'

'Oh, this and that,' said Laurel, irritatingly cool. 'Has Miss Dace gone yet?'

'Yes, she's getting married next week, you know,' said Dulcie, annoyed at the change of subject.

'She rather fancied Dr Forbes, didn't she? That evening when he came to dinner. You could tell somehow – one always can . . .'

'Can one?' said Dulcie, rather alarmed; but then she realised that one's aunt, whatever her age, would probably be regarded as too old to have any such feelings.

'A good thing she found somebody else,' said Laurel. 'I think he found her rather a bore.'

Dulcie was silent, disconcerted by Laurel's frankness. She felt she ought to change the subject, and yet she wanted to go on talking about Aylwin. She could also sense that Laurel had something more to say about the lunch. Could it be that Aylwin had hinted at his love for her, or even declared his feelings more strongly? If so, it had been very wrong of him, especially after their conversation at Taviscombe. Had it meant nothing to him, because it had taken place in a holiday resort, looking down at the sea – the kind of setting in which promises – romantic ones, at least – were made only to be broken?

'He told me . . . Oh, I hardly know how to say this, it was so incredible!' Laurel burst out. 'He told me he loved me and hoped to marry me one day! It was when we were having coffee in a sort of lounge with leather armchairs and little tables – talk about the time and the place and the loved one

274

all together! What a place for a proposal!' She laughed, looking very pretty in her merriment.

'He wanted to *marry* you?' questioned Dulcie sternly. 'But my dear Laurel, he has a wife already – you know that perfectly well. And so does he,' she added lamely, for it seemed as if he had temporarily forgotten; perhaps it was the kind of thing men did forget at such times.

'Oh, I know. But she *has* behaved shockingly to him – even you must admit that.'

'She left him, certainly,' Dulcie agreed. 'But I imagine she had some provocation. He must have – well, *driven* her to it – by his behaviour.' Libertine, she thought, remembering the lady at the jumble sale in aid of the organ fund.

'Yes, but he did ask her to go back to him – at least, he said he did. But now that she's gone off with this man – you must admit *he* never went as far as that. I was really quite sorry for him.'

'But *what* man?' asked Dulcie, when she had recovered from the shock of the news she had just heard. 'I didn't know anything about this. Not the organist, surely?'

'No – a man she met in the train coming back from Taviscombe – in the dining car, I think. Apparently her mother didn't feel like having lunch and Mrs Forbes went by herself. Quite romantic, really,' said Laurel, in a detached tone. 'It only happened about a week ago. I should have thought Dr Forbes – Aylwin – might have waited a bit longer before looking round for another wife.'

'Perhaps his mind was a little unhinged by shock and grief,' said Dulcie unconvincingly. 'Though I do know,' she added hastily, 'that he *is* very fond of you. He must have been so much in need of comfort, and felt that you could give it. I don't think we should ever be too hard on people at times like this – one just never knows . . .'

'Yes, I realise that, and of course I'm sorry for him though he didn't seem to be particularly *grieving*, if you know what I mean. But the idea of me marrying him! Why, he's older than Daddy!'

'Yes, I suppose he is. Still, older men often make better husbands than younger ones,' said Dulcie, almost, in her selflessness, urging Laurel to reconsider Aylwin's proposal.

'But I could never marry him,' said Laurel firmly, 'and I told him so.'

'Was he very upset?'

'I suppose so, in a way. It was hard to tell, when we were in such a public place. I felt rather a fool. You know,' – she giggled – 'I couldn't help wondering if all the other old men having lunch with girls were asking them to marry them.'

'Oh, I shouldn't think so,' said Dulcie, rather shocked. 'Poor Aylwin,' she went on, still unable to adjust herself to the situation. 'Fancy Marjorie doing a thing like that – who would ever have thought it! And poor Mrs Williton, what a shock it must have been to her.'

'I never met his wife,' said Laurel, 'though I did see his mother-in-law once. A little woman in a pink felt hat – funny, isn't it, how you remember people.'

'And are you seeing much of Paul?' asked Dulcie, in a brighter tone.

'Oh yes, off and on,' said Laurel casually. 'He's rather sweet really. Marian and I had a party and he did the flowers.'

They went on to talk of various things, Dulcie giving only a small part of her attention to the conversation. She was wondering if she should perhaps write to Aylwin. But what could she say? Did one write to people when things like this happened? It might be more appropriate to write to Mrs Williton; and yet, sorry though Dulcie felt for her, she decided she could hardly find the necessary words to grieve with her over her daughter's fall.

And yet, she felt, perhaps because of the conversation by the sea at Taviscombe, there was some kind of bond between Aylwin and herself, and after Laurel had gone she sat down to compose a letter. It was a vague kind of letter, referring to 'this sad news' and 'your trouble', almost as if he were bereaved. Obviously, she thought, as she opened the gate to take it to the post, it wouldn't do at all.

The evening air was sweet with the scent of wallflowers and laburnums, and it seemed sad to think of Mrs Williton, such a true suburban dweller, sitting alone in her house facing the common. Perhaps a visit might bring her some comfort? Dulcie saw herself approaching the house. 'I was so sorry to her about Marjorie,' she would say. Or, better, 'I thought you might be in need of company now that you're on your own . . .'

'You look sad, Miss Mainwaring,' said Mrs Beltane, who was taking Felix for his evening walk. 'Has something upset you?'

'I've just heard some rather bad news,' said Dulcie, too much taken by surprise to weigh the accuracy of her words. 'I've been writing a letter to a friend – I mean, the friend to whom it's happened.'

'Father Benger brings wonderful comfort to the bereaved,' said Mrs Beltane, her eyes shining. 'I know people who have lost their loved ones – yes, and animals, too – who have been so much helped by him.'

'Yes, I'm sure,' said Dulcie, looking down and meeting the fierce beady-eyed stare of Felix.

'Why don't you come along with me on Sunday, Miss Mainwaring? I'm sure you'd find the service *most* comforting, and Father Benger would have a special word with you afterwards.'

'Thank you,' said Dulcie sincerely, 'it's very kind of you to suggest it, but there's another church I ought to go to.' She patted Felix, and then went on her way to the post box.

But when she reached it she saw that the last evening collection had gone, and as she stood uncertainly with the letter in her hand she knew what she had known all the time – that she could not possibly send it. So she went slowly home and tore it up.

# CHAPTER TWENTY-FIVE

The unexpected news about Marjorie Forbes had made Dulcie realise how completely out of touch she was with the worlds of Aylwin and Neville and of Taviscombe. She did not even know whether Neville had returned to his church to brave the hazards of Miss Spicer and her love. It was difficult to know how best to start her inquiries, until she remembered that she had told Neville that she would visit his church some time and that he had seemed to accept this as inevitable. And if he were not there, that nice friendly housekeeper would be sure to know the latest news of him.

As she sat waiting for the evening service to begin, Dulcie felt that she merged almost too well with the congregation. But this was in some ways an advantage, for she was able to look around her for signs of Miss Spicer and the housekeeper and anything else that might indicate whether the clergyman who ate cold brussels sprouts in the middle of the night was still taking the services. There were several women who looked something like Miss Spicer, though as Dulcie had seen her only once, and then very briefly and in tears, a definite identification was impossible. She came to the conclusion that all churches must have in their congregations several Miss Spicers, though it was to be hoped that not all of them would fall in love with the vicar.

As the time for the service approached, a kind of hush fell on the congregation. The housekeeper entered, smiling at people around her and almost bowing, as if she were the leader of an orchestra, the last person to enter before the maestro himself. When she saw Dulcie, she gave her a broad wink.

The service began, and now Dulcie realised the full beauty of Neville Forbes in church – not so splendid, certainly, as he would have been in vestments for a High Mass, but the light and sympathetic atmosphere of an evening service lent a peculiar grace and dignity to his appearance. At Taviscombe he had seemed slightly ridiculous, wandering about the hotel in his cassock, and only for that brief moment among the tombstones in the cemetery had Dulcie glimpsed how he might really look in his proper setting.

Neville did not seem to be a particularly good preacher, though Dulcie did not set herself up as a judge of sermons. What he said was simple and obvious, almost too much so. At one point it seemed to her that his glance rested on her. She wondered how many other women had felt the same.

After the service was over, the housekeeper was quick to come over to Dulcie and ask if she would join them for a cup of tea in the hall.

'Father Forbes is back, dear,' she said, almost digging her in the ribs. 'What did I tell you!'

Dulcie was not sure, nor could she decide whether she

ought to reveal that she had already met him. She decided to let things 'take their course', whatever that might be.

In the hall the loud music, the dancing and the cups of tea seemed to invite the exchange of confidences, if only because they would be unlikely to be overheard.

'My dear,' the housekeeper began characteristically, 'such goings-on since you were here last!'

'Not more trouble, I hope,' said Dulcie.

'Well, I suppose you might call it that in a way. To begin with, Father Forbes came back unexpectedly when the other man was still here – just as if nothing had happened. I'd just made a cauliflower *au gratin* and there wasn't really enough for two. Oh, I know it's a trivial detail' – she laid her hand on Dulcie's arm for a moment – 'but those are the things that make up life, aren't they – Father Forbes back and no supper for him. I was upset, I can tell you.'

'Was he?' Dulcie asked.

'Oh, he's good – said he'd just have bread and cheese, and there wasn't even all that much cheese.'

'Didn't the other clergyman feel he should have given up his cauliflower *au gratin*?' asked Dulcie simply.

'He didn't know! That was the point. I'd kept them apart. Father Smith was in the dining-room, and I gave Father Forbes a tray in the study. Oh, the time I had! Sugar, dear?' She thrust the pink plastic apostle spoon towards Dulcie.

'So what happened in the end?'

'Well, Father Smith went, of course. But he was a bit put out. I think the two of them had words of some kind in the study, but of course' – she lowered her eyes virtuously – 'exactly what was said I don't know.'

'And what's happened to Miss er – Spicer?'

'Oh, very good news.'

'Is she married, then?' For that seemed the only thing that could really be good news.

'No, dear. She and her mother have bought a house in Eastbourne.'

'That does sound splendid,' said Dulcie. 'Eastbourne. I believe the air is very good and there are sure to be lots of churches.'

'Yes. Old Mrs Spicer has taken on a new lease of life. We shall all be popping down to Eastbourne for our holidays. '

'I hope you won't forsake Taviscombe, Miss Mainwaring,' said Neville's pleasant voice. 'How nice to see you here. And how is Miss Dace?'

'Oh, she's getting married soon.'

'Married?' said the housekeeper eagerly. 'The friend who came with you that other evening?'

'Other evening?' asked Neville. 'Then you've been here before?'

'You never told me you knew Father Forbes,' said the housekeeper accusingly.

'I didn't know him *then*,' said Dulcie, covered with confusion, hardly able to remember whether she did or not. 'We actually met at Taviscombe.'

'Oh, I see.' The housekeeper nodded, apparently satisfied.

'She knows my brother,' Neville explained.

'Yes,' said Dulcie firmly. 'We met at a conference last summer.' That, at least, was true.

'Fancy your friend getting married,' said the housekeeper rather cryptically. 'Are you living on your own now, then?'

'Yes. I've got quite a big house that used to belong to my parents – too big for me, really.'

'Are you thinking of moving?'

'I don't know. I hadn't really thought about it. I find one gets rather into a rut,' said Dulcie apologetically.

'A nice unfurnished flat is what you want,' said the house-keeper. 'With a bit of garden.'

'Yes, I should like to have a garden,' said Dulcie. She had a dreadful feeling that something was about to be arranged for her against her will.

'There is such a flat vacant near here,' said Neville. 'It might suit you very well. The lady who used to live there with her mother is moving to Eastbourne.'

Miss Spicer's flat – oh, the horror of it! Dulcie thought. And perhaps the same story happening all over again – herself seen by another prying stranger, running into the church in tears. And yet nothing was ever quite the same, and would Neville have suggested it if he had thought that there was any possibility that it could be? But men were so naive and insensitive; he would see it only as a practical proposition for her, not realising that she knew Miss Spicer's story.

Afterwards, when she had said she must go, he walked out of the hall with her.

Dulcie wanted to ask him about Marjorie Forbes, but did not know how to begin.

'I hope your brother is well?' she said tentatively. 'I haven't seen him lately.'

'Oh, there's been trouble there,' said Neville. 'Marjorie, his wife . . .'

'Yes, I did hear that,' said Dulcie.

'It was all very distressing; and most unexpected, but you know what women are.' He sighed rather absentmindedly, and once again Dulcie felt as she had with Bill Sedge, that she was somehow a woman manquée, who could not be expected to know what women were. She could not decide what answer to make, so said nothing.

'Poor Mrs Williton – I tried to do what I could, which was little enough. She – Marjorie – was quite determined to do this thing. Father Tulliver – her parish priest – and I both tried to dissuade her. But there you are –' He sighed again – 'She wouldn't listen to us.'

'I wonder if she'll regret it,' said Dulcie rather smugly. 'Was your brother very upset?'

'Surprisingly so, all things considered. I suppose it was the last thing he expected.'

'And your mother?' said Dulcie, feeling slightly ridiculous.

'Oh, Mother took it all in her stride. She's a strange woman, with her own ideas. Things of that kind often happened in Taviscombe, she said.'

Dulcie could imagine her saying it.

'And now I suppose' – Neville sighed for the third time – 'my brother will divorce Marjorie and make another unsuitable marriage.'

Dulcie, startled at his frankness, did not know what to say. Obviously he was right. Not Laurel, of course, but there were so many other young girls.

'Really he has been rather troublesome lately,' said Neville, using the words Aylwin had used of him. 'Are you thinking seriously of taking Miss Spicer's flat?' he went on. 'Because if you are I could put in a word for you. The landlord is one of my churchwardens and is anxious to get a congenial tenant, I know. It would be very pleasant to have you living in the parish.'

Dulcie looked up at him quickly, but his face revealed

284

nothing. 'I don't think I should be much of an asset,' she said. 'I've never done any parish work or even been to church very much.'

'Oh, we'd soon have you in the thick of things,' said Neville, with rather alarming heartiness. And Dulcie could see how it would be. Apart from the occasional kind word and fair distribution of favours he would be impersonal and aloof – as a celibate priest must be. And might she not find herself falling in love with him – unlikely though it seemed at the moment? All that church work, with so little reward, might well become an intolerable burden – a thankless task, indeed.

'I must think it over,' she said. 'I hadn't really any idea of moving.'

'A change does everyone good,' said Neville.

'Well, yes, but there are changes and changes,' said Dulcie. 'Goodbye!'

'Goodbye, and I expect we shall meet again quite soon. I can somehow *see* you in that flat!'

Dulcie made her way to the bus stop, feeling at once elated and depressed. Elated at the idea that life could change so completely, but depressed because she too saw herself in the flat, becoming another Miss Spicer. Yet, after all, would it be so very different from her present situation? – unrequited love for Aylwin or Neville might amount to much the same thing, a kind of choice of brothers. But at least she need not *see* Aylwin – Neville would be always on view.

As the bus slowed down in Ladbroke Grove, Dulcie was struck by the face of a man walking on the pavement – a familiar face, she would have said, and yet she could think of nobody she knew who lived in those parts. Then it came to her – the man was one of her beggars, a particularly ragged one for these days, who shook with a kind of ague and offered matches for sale in Oxford Street. She had often given him money, though she had not seen him lately. Now he walked briskly in the evening sunshine, wearing a good suit and smoking a cigarette, not shaking at all.

Surely this was an omen of some sort? But of what sort she hardly knew. Letting herself into the house, she realised that she was alone. Viola had gone, and Laurel too; she had rejected Maurice's offer of friendship, and even the comfort of Father Benger and his church. It only remained now for her to turn away from the life that Neville Forbes had seemed to offer her.

But she still had her work. She was in the middle of making an index for a complicated anthropological book, and this would occupy her for some weeks. And now that she really was alone she might well consider letting rooms to students – perhaps Africans, who would fill the house with gay laughter and cook yams on their gas-rings. Then there was a summer holiday to be planned, perhaps in Dorset with her sister and brother-in-law at their cottage, or at another learned conference, if there was one.

This last thought must have brought Aylwin Forbes even more vividly into her mind, so that when the telephone rang she was not surprised to hear his voice.

'Miss Mainwaring – Dulcie. It's Aylwin – Aylwin Forbes. I was wondering if you could help me with a piece of work.'

'An index?' Dulcie managed to bring out.

'Well, not exactly.' He sounded so vague that Dulcie said rather sharply. 'Surely an index either is or isn't?'

'Perhaps I could come over and discuss it with you.'

'Why, certainly – that might be best. Come to tea this afternoon.'

To buy any of our books and to find out more
about Virago Press and Virago Modern Classics,
our authors and titles, visit our websites

**www.virago.co.uk**
**www.littlebrown.co.uk**

and follow us on Twitter

**@ViragoBooks**

To order any Virago titles p & p free in the UK,
please contact our mail order supplier on:

**+ 44 (0)1832 737525**

Customers not based in the UK should contact
the same number for appropriate postage
and packing costs.

Better to get it over quickly, whatever it was. It would be nice to work for him, more satisfying than living in Miss Spicer's flat and getting involved with Neville's church. Perhaps, in his loneliness, he was 'turning' to her, or whatever had been the expression Viola had used when talking about him at the conference to describe what he had not done to her. She began to wonder what if anything, she could say about Marjorie.

Leaning forward in the taxi – for he had still not worked out how to get to Dulcie's suburb by public transport – Aylwin wondered how he was going to convince her of this curious change in his feelings, when such a short time ago he had foolishly confided in her his love for Laurel. Obviously the pretext of having some work that she might do for him was the best way of arranging to see her, though surely she would not have refused a word of comfort to a lonely and deserted man, he thought, seeing himself now as this character, which was not unlike the lonely old man whom Laurel was to have solaced.

As for his apparent change of heart, he had suddenly remembered the end of *Mansfield Park*, and how Edmund fell out of love with Mary Crawford and came to care for Fanny. Dulcie must surely know the novel well, and would understand how such things can happen. What a surprise it would be, not least to his family and to Dulcie herself, who had so often urged him to make a 'suitable' marriage, if, when he was free, this very marriage should come about! Yet here he was being true to type after all. For what might seem to the rest of the world an eminently 'suitable' marriage to a woman no longer very young, who could help him with his work, now seemed to him the most unsuitable that could be imagined, simply because it had never occurred to him that he could love such a person. It was all most delightfully incongruous. Just the sort of thing Aylwin Forbes would do.

Who will run down to greet him and be gathered to his heart, Dulcie asked herself, as she had in Taviscombe, the last time she had watched Aylwin arriving in a taxi. Obviously only she could do it, but in her shyness she opened the door cautiously, wondering why he had brought a bunch of flowers when she had so many in the garden.

Senhor MacBride-Pereira, watching in his window, had heard the taxi, but was not quick enough to see who got out. He took a mauve sugared almond out of a bag and sucked it thoughtfully, wondering what, if anything, he had missed.

To buy any of our books and to find out more
about Virago Press and Virago Modern Classics,
our authors and titles, visit our websites

**www.virago.co.uk**
**www.littlebrown.co.uk**

and follow us on Twitter

**@ViragoBooks**

To order any Virago titles p & p free in the UK,
please contact our mail order supplier on:

**+ 44 (0)1832 737525**

Customers not based in the UK should contact
the same number for appropriate postage
and packing costs.